FRIDAY BROWN

VIKKI WAKEFIELD

FRIDAY BROWN

HOT KEY BOOKS

First published in Australia in 2012 by The Text Publishing Company

Text copyright © Vikki Wakefield 2012
Cover illustration copyright © Justin Santora 2013

A CIP catalogue record for this book is available from the British Library.

ISBN: 978-1-4714-0135-0

1

Typeset by Palimpsest Book Production Limited, Falkirk, Stirlingshire
This book is typeset in Sabon 10.5/15.5 pt

Printed and bound by Clays Ltd, St Ives Plc

Hot Key Books supports the Forest Stewardship Council (FSC),
the leading international forest certification organisation, and is committed
to printing only on Greenpeace-approved FSC-certified paper.

www.hotkeybooks.com

For Mia, my girl, my heart.

Then

My life has been told to me through campfire tales—stories that spill over when the fire has burned low and silence must be filled. They're like old coats hauled from the back of the cupboard. Dusted off, aired out, good as new. My mother, Vivienne, doled them out as reward or consolation, depending on her mood. And so I came to know myself— through the telling and retelling. They became as much a part of me as blood or bone. On the night of my eleventh birthday, Vivienne told me that I was cursed. It was her gift, she said. When she was gone the Brown women's curse would pass to me and, if I ever knew which way death would come, I should run hard in the other direction.

I listened to her with wide eyes, bitten nails and a delicious detachment, like watching a horror film and knowing it couldn't reach through the screen. I could leave her stories in the dark, remember them when I felt like it and forget them when I didn't. When you're eleven, you don't think of before or after. Only that moment and maybe tomorrow.

That night.

Vivienne was drunk. We were sleeping rough under a blanket of stars after leaving a hostel in our usual way: beds unmade, bills unpaid, through a back door. Vivienne had outstayed her welcome again, had taken something that wasn't hers to take. In the morning we would leave our dusty campsite and hitch a ride to another four-syllable town. I knew the routine well.

It was cold. A mallee stump smouldered and hissed and I watched her through a veil of smoke and shooting sparks.

She was chain-smoking. Drinking from a bottle of vodka as she spoke. Stops and starts, like punctuation, she puffed and swigged.

'Corrie-anne Brown,' she slurred. 'Nineteen-oh-four. It was a Saturday. Corrie-anne Brown marched through the centre of town, a woman on a mission. Some said she looked like she carried the weight of the world on her shoulders that day. But no one stopped her or asked where she was going. She walked into the river, leaving her baby son abandoned in his cradle for two days. When they pulled her out of the river she was wearing every single item of clothing she owned—four skirts, seven blouses, three pairs of stockings and one Sunday hat.'

'Why?' I asked.

'So she wouldn't float, silly.'

'Did she die? Why would she leave her baby? Did he die?'

'Of course she died. She weighed more than a small elephant. And the baby was fine. Now be quiet and listen.'

'I'm listening,' I said.

'In nineteen-twenty-six, Marieke Brown went with her husband and three children to a country fair. She was bobbing for apples, going for the record, and there were people all around cheering as she went under for the ninth time in a minute.' Puff. Swig. Exhale. 'After two minutes somebody thought to pull her out,' she went on. 'That record-breaking apple, only the size of a plum, was stuck in her throat. It was a Saturday.'

I remember finishing a bag of liquorice and feeling sick.

'Alicia Brown, nineteen-forty-two. She married Marieke's eldest son. Alicia was a Red Cross nurse in the Second World War. She couldn't pass a bundle of fur by the roadside without stopping to check for a pulse. One day she pulled over to drag a dead cat out of the middle of the road and she was clipped by another car. She landed face first in a ditch and drowned in a few centimetres of mud.'

'Which day?' I was dog-tired and all I wanted to do was close my eyes, but when Vivienne was on a roll, you had to play along.

'What do you think?'

'Was it a Saturday?'

'Now you're catching on.' She tipped the dregs of the vodka onto the hot coals and stared at the eerie blue flame. 'Belle Brown, nineteen-fifty-six. Saturday night, of course. Belle was going dancing with a nice boy from a good family. She ran a hot bath and stepped in . . .'

'She drowned in the bath?'

'No. Before she could sit down, the phone rang. Belle got out of the bath, went to the kitchen, picked up the receiver and slipped on the wet floor. She hit her head, the cord wrapped around her throat and she choked to death.'

'That's not drowning.'

'But there's always water. Don't you see?'

'Belle didn't have kids, then,' I said, yawning. 'So who was next?'

'Now we're getting to the good stuff. Belle had a younger brother. My father. He was only ten when his sister died and he never forgot about the Brown women's curse. He vowed never to marry—but he fell in love.'

'Who with?'

'Here's the amazing thing. She was an athlete, a swimmer. Arielle Dubois. She'd crossed the English Channel three times before they even met, and once after. If there was ever a woman who could beat the curse, she was the one.'

'My grandmother? How did she die?' I imagined a tall woman with gills and a pattern of shimmering, blue-green scales instead of skin. I still think of her like that.

'Well, they married late and Arielle Dubois stayed Arielle Dubois. She never took the Brown name. When my father became a judge they moved to a big house with no water, only what came out of the taps. But Arielle was miserable. She was dying inside. Like a mermaid out of water, she was shrivelling up.'

I could picture my grandmother so clearly: she was leaning, reaching towards the sea like a carved maiden on the bow of a ship. 'Did she run away?'

'No,' Vivienne said. 'He knew he was losing her, so my father dug up the backyard and put in a swimming pool.'

I drew in my breath. 'Did that make her happy?'

'She was in heaven. Arielle swam laps every day, even when she was pregnant with me. My first memories are of two worlds: a blue one that held my mother under it, and mine with my father, the house, a porch shaped like a hexagon, and a yellow sunhat. My father would pace while she swam the length of the pool and he watched me like a hawk. But every time she'd emerge, sleek as a seal, and he could breathe again.'

Vivienne didn't speak for a while. She stood up, wandered away into the dark and stared at the sky. She lit another cigarette and smoked it, alone.

I waited quietly, as I knew I should. This was a new story and I wasn't sure how it would finish. I waited so long, my eyes closed, and when she spoke again she sounded like she was still far away.

'When I was five, there was a heatwave. The ground was baked hard and the pool had to be topped up every day. After many weeks, when it finally did rain, it poured for days, with thunder and lightning. Arielle had to stay inside. She sat by the window and stared out at the pool.' Vivienne sat down opposite me with her knees to her chest. 'On that first clear day—Saturday—Arielle peeled off her pyjamas and left them on the floor. She ran outside and dived in. Overnight, the pool had spilled over and the earth had swollen. A huge crack had appeared in the side of the concrete pool and all the water had drained away.'

Just then a piece of wood popped in the fire. Vivienne and I jumped. That's the noise I hear when I imagine my grandmother's spine snapping as she hit the bottom—that wood popping. *Crack*.

'What did he do? Your father?'

'I'll tell you what he did. He filled that pool up with concrete. Filled it right to the top using a hand-mixer. It took him over a year. I sat on the back step every day, watching my mother's world disappear.'

'How do you break a curse?' I asked.

I wondered why, if water was dangerous, she was so drawn to it. Every creek, lake or ocean we passed as we travelled, she'd shuck off her clothes and swim, even in winter. I wondered why she held me under every chance she got and counted a few seconds more each time, until I could hold my breath for a full three minutes.

Vivienne wedged her tongue between the gap in her teeth, something she did when she was thinking. 'The way I see it, you have two options. Run, run like hell,' she said. 'Or dive in.' She stood and leaned so close to the fire, I thought she might fall. As an afterthought, she said, 'That's why I called you Friday.'

She swayed like a strong wind had caught her, fell sideways onto her canvas swag, and passed out.

It was a story that left me feeling bereft. But in the end I was an eleven-year-old girl with a belly full of baked beans and liquorice; sleep won, and the next day the sun came up like it always did and we moved on like we always had.

When death finally caught up with my mother, it was no stealth attack—she knew it was coming. It started as a lump in her breast. The lump got bigger and she got smaller and smaller until there was nothing of her left. It seemed the Brown curse had missed its mark and plain old cancer had got there first.

Watching someone you love die is like driving through fog. You know you're headed somewhere but you can't see your hand in front of your face; you're so focused on steering without crashing that you never say the things you want to say. I'll tell you what else you don't do—you don't laugh, you don't dance, you don't play loud music. You don't put on what she called 'your teenager face' and take food from her plate. You don't borrow her clothes any more because all you can think when you're wearing them is that she won't. Wear them. Again. And the most important thing you don't do is ask her all the questions you have racked up like flashcards—cards that you want to flip over and have her fire off answers so you can write them on the back for future reference.

Before you go. How do you get mascara off a white T-shirt?

Will I ever be a C-cup?

I knew she would probably have laughed at that, but I couldn't risk it going the other way.

How do you know when it's love?

Who am I, without you?

Touch was impossible. Anger ruined everything and our last conversations were thick with it. We kept inching forwards, through the fog, and we made the whole journey that way. Before we knew it, we were there. The lights came on, the fog cleared—and she was gone.

The night she died, I overheard a conversation between Vivienne's nurse and the doctor who came to sign her out.

'Cause of death? What gave out first?' the nurse said.

The doctor shook his head. 'It's unusual to happen so quickly, but her lungs were full of fluid. Out of the blue, just like that. She drowned.'

PART 1

THE CITY

Who you are from moment to moment is just a story.
Chuck Palahniuk, *Invisible Monsters*

Chapter One

I left in the night.

The clock downstairs chimed the witching hour—*gong, gong*—and I used the sound to smother the grate of the zipper on my backpack. I laced up my boots and slipped on my fleece-lined jacket. I took only what was mine: my swag, my clothes and the photograph, because without it I had nowhere to go.

That photo was my one planned move—after that, life was a lucky dip. The edges were fuzzy and worn thin. One corner was peeling away. The faded image of the man with his arm slung across Vivienne's shoulder was familiar, not because he was somebody I'd met, but because I'd looked at it a thousand times, trying to picture myself as a hybrid version of the two of them. I looked like Vivienne. She would have been a couple of years older than I was then. Like me, she let her dark hair grow down to her waist and rarely wore make-up; unlike me she was tall and thin as a reed. We had the same grey eyes. But it was a bitter truth when I realised that I wasn't beautiful like her, that a milli-metre here or there could be the difference between people staring or being indifferent.

That night, I left a room I'd dreamed about since I was

little. A doll's room, with white furniture and lace curtains. Innocent things. A bed and bookcase and desk that seemed like one creation, flowing from one to the other. You could run a finger along the surfaces and end up right back where you started.

I left the things Grandfather had given me in a sad pile on the desk—a watch that looked too big on my wrist, a laptop computer, a string of pearls, a set of keys.

Every step was deafening. My breathing was too loud, my jeans scraped as I walked. The corner of my jacket caught on the newel post at the top of the stairs. I flailed in space before my hand found the rail with a *smack*.

I waited for a long minute. From there I could get back to my room—any further downstairs and I risked discovery, and lockdown. I checked behind me, along the dark hallway. Nothing.

The house had wings. I'd never seen anything like it. The east wing, where Grandfather slept, was to my right. The west wing, all my own, to the left. There were seven doors off the west wing and I'd only ever stepped through two of them. The house was too still—it didn't sigh or shift its weight the way old houses should. It seemed to be holding its breath.

The staircase was a gauntlet of eyes: ancient portraits of men wearing flowing gowns and dusty white wigs. There was only one painting of a young woman. She had the glassy gaze of a reluctant sitter, pearls choking her throat, her nails polished and smooth. It was Vivienne, but from another time. Before. The Vivienne I knew had nails that were bitten and she wore junk jewellery with marbled stones that were like tiny worlds. She never wore pearls. And she could never sit still that long.

At the bottom of the stairs was a room that used to be a sitting room. A lamp was switched on, an unblinking eye, watching. There was the bed where Vivienne had lain for three months while her spirit soared on a morphine cloud, a dent still in the mattress, a groove where her hip bones had dug in, the precious hollow in the pillow.

I couldn't pass it without looking—but there was nothing for me any more.

I stepped through the entrance hall on the balls of my feet. Into the dining room with its boardroom table, tinkling chandelier and an everlasting decanter of whisky. It seemed never to empty, though Grandfather filled his glass over and over.

For forty-two nights, he and I had sat at each end of the table, as divided as continents, pushing food around our plates. We went days without speaking. Vivienne had taken me back to her father's house so that she could die and I could have a future, but I wanted to be gone because, without her, none of it was bearable. Everything tidy and polished and civilised—even our grief.

I passed through the endless galley kitchen and slipped out through the back door.

The night air was cold and still. I hoisted my backpack and buttoned my jacket. Grandfather's cat wound between my legs and beseeched me with lime-coloured eyes. I ran my hand along its rippling spine. The feel of it—so *alive*— made my eyes ache.

I took my hand away and the cat wailed and slashed the air with its tail.

'Shhh!' I hissed and stomped my foot. The gravel crunched underneath.

I looked back at the house.

In another life it could be a country house from an Enid Blyton book—all rambling garden and dappled sunlight and hidden treasure. Fond cousins and lashings of lemonade with the odd mystery and midnight feast. It was a house made for happy endings, but there I was, standing in the dark with a yowling cat, everything I owned crammed into a backpack.

I was the sum of two people, one dead, the other unknown. I'd lived in a hundred small towns and I'd never known another person for my whole life, except Vivienne. Every memory before this was sweet and real. But now she'd got it wrong—this wasn't my future. Her legacy should be more than a string of pearls and a grandfather I didn't know. Vivienne taught me that life was short, and if it wasn't sweet you were in the wrong place with the wrong people.

Time to go, Friday Brown, she'd say, and so the next chapter would begin. Sometimes it would be a whisper in the dark and I would feel her broken heart beating against my back; other times, a casual aside in conversation, as if it had just occurred to her that she had somewhere else to be. We craved new beginnings.

Suddenly the sensor lights flicked on and I was drowning in brightness. I blinked and raised my arm over my eyes. An upstairs window flew up. For a second I saw my mother there, framed in a halo of light, but it was just him, Grandfather, with his old man's hair gone static and wild. He frowned, fists braced against the sill.

14

I had the sensation of time winding in a loop.

He stared at me.

I stared at him.

I knew I'd be away before he even got to the landing, but still I felt trapped in his glare.

He lobbed something at me. A bundle, the size of a half-brick, that fell short and tumbled to my feet. He nodded at it and regarded me carefully as if what I did next would give him some measure of me.

I picked it up, felt its weight in my palm, caught the scent of new ink. A wad of fifties, bound in rubber bands. Hundreds of them, probably more than ten thousand dollars. I thought of Vivienne—turned away from here with nothing, my lifetime ago—and I made my choice. It was a choice based on stupid pride and dumb loyalty, and it would change everything.

I threw the bundle onto the porch, turned my back and started walking.

I had a purse with my own money. Enough to start over. If there was one thing I knew—one thing I could do without a map, with my eyes closed and my hands tied behind my back—it was starting over. Except this time I had to do it on my own.

The sensor lights flicked off.

Clouds of breath, numbness in my fingers and toes. A pale slice of moon threw a sickly light, just enough to see by. When I reached the front gates, I looked back.

He was gone. The windows were dark and shuttered.

Grandfather was letting me go.

Chapter Two

Hitchhiking was dangerous.

Vivienne had rules about it and, like the one she made about not calling her Mum, they were absolute. Never hitch alone. Never get into a car with a man on his own. Never get in with a man who makes his dog ride in the tray or has a crucifix hanging from the rear-view mirror. She reckoned people who dangled a crucifix needed absolution for something more than everyday sin. And never, ever, stay with a person who doesn't ask your name.

An old man in a blue ute picked me up on the freeway. I'd been walking for about an hour, blinking like a possum in the headlights. Huddled into myself from the cold.

The cab was stifling. Empty cans rolled on the floor. The man had lizard skin and fists like boxing gloves.

'Shouldn't be out here. It's the middle of the night. I've got a granddaughter about your age,' he said. Then, 'What's your name?'

I told him I was Liliane Brown but they called me Friday. I couldn't remember who 'they' were anymore. I told him my mother was dead and I was going to live with my father. That I was seventeen. I asked him to drop me in the city so I could catch a train to my father's house.

I pulled the photograph out of my backpack. *Prof. Green, Uni, 1994* was scrawled on the back in Vivienne's handwriting. The man clutched a book to his chest, the word *Henry* just visible between his fingers. These were my only clues. He could have been nobody important, but it was his smallness, his dancer-grace that made me think there was more to him. Over time, Vivienne had discarded or lost the few old photos she'd had. Some were left behind; some were burned in fits of despair. But she kept that one.

I showed the old man the photo with its furred creases and he saw a resemblance, even though there was none. I said I was going to finish school and then go to university. That my father loved and missed me very much but my mother wouldn't let me see him.

Not much of it was truth.

He clucked his tongue and I heard the pop and suck of false teeth. 'I'll drop you at the station,' he said, and reached across my legs with his scaly arm.

I couldn't help it, I shrank back.

He looked at me with pity and flipped open the glove box. A jumble of stuff fell out but he left it on the floor. He fumbled about and dropped a plastic-wrapped square onto my lap. A sandwich. Corned beef and pickle and something limp and green.

I hadn't cried for forty-two days. Not since the nurse had unhooked Vivienne, the day they took the last of her away and a half-empty saline bag dripped onto the floor. I hadn't cried since that night when I slept in her T-shirt so I could smell her, but all that was left was the scorching scent of bleach and Betadine.

But that sandwich did it. The crusts were off and the cling wrap had hospital corners. I blubbered the whole way.

The old man dropped me right out the front of the train station. He watched me as I walked into the station and didn't pull away until I waved.

It seemed the city had no curfew. I expected everything to be dead that early in the morning but there were people everywhere. Not just night-people. A woman pushing a covered pram shoved past me. Three guys with sullen faces squatted, smoking, by the doors. One flicked his butt at my feet and waggled his tongue. I looked away. Tall buildings leaned in and squeezed the air out; the dark there was more sinister than any dark I'd ever felt, even with a million pinpricks of light from windows and doorways. Give me the absolute dark of the outback at midnight, where you can sense what's coming. The city felt alien and unsafe.

I found a bench inside the station and curled up on my side with my backpack for a pillow. A rain moth the size of a sparrow crawled out of a drain and headed towards the light, antennae twitching. I watched it for a while. I closed my eyes and when I opened them again, it was gone. My eyelids were so heavy. Trains came and went as sleep dragged me under.

I dozed. I cupped my hands over my ears to shut out the commotion, but most of the white noise was inside my head. Something fluttered near my ear and I slapped it away. I felt the dry brush of wings against my neck, but my hand closed over air. I grabbed again and felt something warm. Skin.

I snapped upright and my neck was cricked, my
and stiff.

A boy was crouched next to me, stone-still, his hand
outstretched. Part feral child, part old man. Clear blue eyes
and matted hair like silvery fairy floss.

'Hey, what are you doing?' I croaked.

He scuttled sideways like a sand crab. He could have
been twelve or forty and he was strange-looking, other-
worldly. Then he smiled and I saw that he was younger
than I was because he didn't quite fit into his teeth.

'What are you smiling at? I haven't got anything. Look.'
I wrenched open my pack and pawed through my things.
'See, nothing. I haven't got anything for you!' I yelled. 'Go
away.'

He sidled closer and whipped out a packet of cigarettes.
He shook one out and it fell to the ground. Nonchalantly,
he picked it up and jammed it between his lips. He sat next
to me with his back against the wall and smoked the whole
thing without using his hands.

'What do you want?' I asked.

He shrugged.

I pretended to be busy rummaging through my bag. Early
commuters were lining up along the platform. A train
whooshed in and out. The platform was left nearly empty.

Still he sat there. He pulled his hoodie over his face,
folded his arms, crossed his ankles. Appeared to fall asleep.

I could smell bacon or something greasy and good. I needed
food. My stomach whined and the boy shifted. I jammed my
backpack on, hoisted my swag and thought about what to
do next.

ut thinking, I fished out a twenty-dollar note.

Everything happened at once.

The boy, not sleeping, darted in front of me, quick as a rat. I yanked my hand away and spun around. He was fast and fluid like a practised thief, except that he was past me and the twenty was still in my hand.

'Hah,' I gloated.

He was gone, empty-handed.

He bolted for the platform and I could see what had got him moving. The young mother, turned away from her baby in its pram, holding her phone up to the light. The pram, rolling away, down towards the track. A pink fist waving. A woollen sock dangling from a tiny foot.

I went after him but my legs were stiff, my boots heavy. The boy got there as the pram tipped over the edge. He hesitated for a moment, then leaped onto the track.

'Your baby!' I screamed at the woman.

She was registering the vanished pram, the coming train, the gurgling screams from below. Her comprehension was slow and painful. The train screeched and slowed, but not enough, not in time.

I reached the edge of the platform and looked over the edge. The pram came back up, as if plucked by the hand of God. I grabbed the handle and heaved the pram onto the platform.

The mother snatched the baby up and crushed it to her chest. It was red-faced and screaming, but whole. Alive. The train lurched two, three times, hissed and stopped.

People came from everywhere. A security guard questioned the mother.

'He's still down there!' I yelled at him.

'Who?' he asked.

'The boy. The one who saved the baby! Move the train!'

The mother turned her white, shocked face to me. 'I didn't see a boy. Only you.' Her voice was calm and she nuzzled her child as if memorising his smell. 'I saw you pull him up.'

I wanted to slap her.

'He's still under it. Move the train!' I paced along the edge of the platform, shouting, arms raised. Fistfuls of hair. 'Pleeaaase. Just move the train!'

After some discussion, the driver stepped onto the platform. He pointed at me. 'I saw her pull it up. That's it. There's nobody down there.'

I paced some more.

The guard looked at me with suspicion. After long minutes, the driver moved the train.

I stared down at the rails. Nothing. No blood or pieces. No proof of a wild boy with silver hair. I wasn't convinced until the guard jumped down onto the track and looked under the carriage. Still nothing.

I collapsed onto the bench and tried to breathe. Half the crowd was calling me a hero, the other half was saying I must be crazy, on drugs. A guy held his mobile phone in front of my face and took my picture.

The mother was escorted to an office, still clutching her baby close. The guard asked me to stay to answer some questions for a report.

'It's a miracle,' said a batty old woman in pyjama bottoms. Her eyes were murky with age, but she was the only person who looked me in the eye.

I stared after the mother and baby. A group of people huddled around them, trying to touch the miracle baby.

This was not my miracle, it was theirs. I just witnessed it. Moments like that, I thought maybe there was a God, a fickle puppet-master who decided it was time to remind us that life isn't just an echo of the Big Bang—that we're here, with beating hearts.

The guy with the mobile phone snapped another picture. I jerked my hand up to cover my face and the phone clattered to the ground.

'Hey!' he yelled.

The crowd turned to stare.

I grabbed my things, sprinted out of the train station and onto the street. A taxi driver swerved and swore. Pale fingers of morning light poked between the buildings, and the bacon smell made my stomach groan.

Life is full of wrong turns and dead ends and pathways that peter out. They all count, even the wrong turns; they all add more to who you become. Nobody wants to be a one-way street. There are signposts if you cared to look, Vivienne always said. Something will always tell you which way to go. It could be a wet finger held up to the breeze, a scrap of paper caught underfoot, a too-bright star that calls you west.

I thought maybe I'd missed it.

I spun around. I looked up. It could be as simple as a feeling, or a sound. It could be something that would reveal itself in its own time and I'd just have to wait.

Or it could be a boy nobody saw.

Chapter Three

The boy found me.

I was sitting in a café down a crooked street. I'd eaten a full breakfast special and ordered another. I was slurping a bottomless coffee and waiting for my order, except the food had gone down and I was full. Around me the city was awake and crawling. Buildings rose into low cloud and when I looked up, I felt dizzy. Too many people in too little space. All I wanted was to escape the crush, feel dust between my toes and taste clean air.

The boy slid into the chair opposite. He grabbed a packet of sugar and poured it into his mouth. He stuck out his tongue and tried to look at it, cross-eyed, as the crystals dissolved.

'How?' I asked him.

He tapped his nose with a grimy finger. He grinned and mimicked a magician's flourish with spread hands. *Where did he go?* Wonder-eyed, he looked around. Dusted off his hands, gave a seated bow and leaned back with his ankles crossed.

'You saved that baby,' I said. 'I thought you were dead.'

He shook his head.

I wondered if he was deaf. But he didn't speak at all,

didn't look at my lips when I spoke, didn't even open his mouth except to pour more sugar in. He seemed to mime everything, like a scruffy, life-sized Pierrot. When the plate came, he flashed a wistful look at it. Turned away. Even feigned disinterest was pure performance.

'You have it. I'm full,' I told him.

He nodded graciously like he was doing me a favour, discarded the fork and folded the food into rolls. He fed them in like his tongue was a conveyor belt, stuffed it all in, no chewing.

I watched him the whole time.

Some days, when we were on the road, Vivienne and I would go for days without real food. One season, when we were picking fruit, I ate nothing but oranges and mandarins for a week. Another time it was tinned tuna and toast with sugared tomatoes for dessert. I remembered hunger like that, the kind that gnawed at my gut and woke me when I was sleeping.

'What's your name?'

He pressed his hand to his throat, pinched there, and a sigh escaped. He waggled his Adam's apple. A faint sound came away, but I got what he said by the shape of his mouth.

Silence.

'That figures,' I told him.

He pointed at me. You?

'Lili. Liliane. But mostly I get called Friday. Why can't you speak?'

He brushed the question away like it was stupid, or he didn't want to talk about it, or maybe the story was just too long and too painful to tell. He pulled out a twenty-dollar note and slipped it under the pepper shaker.

'No,' I told him. 'I've got it.' I gave him my twenty.

He took it for a moment, then handed it back, shaking his head. His expression was regretful, but he insisted, shoving it at me and letting it go.

I grabbed the note and went to take it up to the counter.

He snatched it back and stuffed it in my front pocket. He stabbed his note with his finger. The impact folded back one corner and I could see it was blank underneath.

'Is that a fake?' I said, too loudly.

He put his finger to his lips and grabbed my elbow. Steered me upright and moved to leave.

'We can't. What if we get caught?'

Come on, he mouthed. *Now*.

We walked away casually and broke into a sprint when we reached the corner. He was laughing or wheezing, I didn't know which. I followed him to a park in the middle of the city that was more like a few acres of lawn where they had forgotten to put a building. A bronze statue of a horse and rider reared into the sky and a fountain dribbled pale, green water.

Silence wedged himself between the horse's rear hooves and opened a battered leather wallet. He flipped through the compartments and turned up nothing. He tipped it upside down and shook it.

I sat next to him. 'You can have this.' I held out my twenty. 'Do you need to get home? Where do you live?'

He grinned and held his arms out wide to encompass the whole city.

'Seriously. Everyone has a home, don't they?' Except me.

He took the twenty, made a nick in one side of it with his tooth, and tore it neatly into two unequal pieces. My eyes bulged and he smiled, tapped his nose again. He put the smaller piece into his pocket and crooked his finger. *Come.*

Silence sauntered into a bank like he was a secret millionaire. We waited in the queue until we were called up by a weary-looking woman who eyeballed Silence with affection and suspicion.

'Another mute?' she said and held out her hand.

'That's not very nice,' I told her.

Silence handed over the larger piece of his torn note and the woman gave him a slick new one, snapping it between her fingers. Silence kissed her ringed hand and she blew him one back.

'I don't even want to know what kind of racket you have going, mister,' she said and winked. 'Mutes. Mutilated notes,' she said to me. 'We exchange them if you have more than a half.'

I turned red.

'So, what do you do with the smaller piece?' I asked Silence when we were outside.

Using hand movements, he showed that he stuck two smaller pieces together.

'Does that always work?'

He cocked his head and shrugged. *Sometimes.* He pulled out his phone and texted one-handed while the other rubbed his forelock fringe into a matted mess. A minute later he received a reply that made him bounce on the balls of his feet.

Gotta go, he mimed. *Have to meet someone.*

'Okay. Well, thanks for the survival lesson. I'll see you.'

He hesitated and for a second seemed to change his mind. Then he stuffed the new twenty-dollar note into my hip pocket and left me there on the footpath.

He walked away.

I didn't want to be alone. Not there. Not even in broad daylight. I didn't know anything about the city, just that it smelled and my feet hurt and the people didn't make eye contact. The air was too thick and stuck in my throat. The noise was constant and I couldn't think about what I was going to say before it came out of my mouth. Everything was garbled and strange.

Even if my father were there, somewhere, there was no reason why he'd even suspect I existed. Vivienne was gone and with her any sure thing I'd ever had.

'Hey!'

He stopped. Raised one silvery eyebrow. The morning sun caught in the fine mat of his hair and it floated around his head like dandelion fluff.

'I have money. I can give you money.' I rummaged in my bag until my hand closed over my purse. I held it out like a prayer. 'Here, take whatever you need,' I babbled.

He stared at the purse and shook his head.

'Take me with you,' I said, and shoved two fifties towards him. I blurted out something that had been wound in my gut like a rabbit-trap. In that moment it snapped closed and became real. 'I don't have anywhere else to go.'

Chapter Four

Silence moved through the pedestrian traffic like quick-silver. It was hard to keep up, lugging my backpack and swag. I slogged against the flow, rebounding off people's shoulders and handbags like a giant pinball. Just when I thought I'd lost him, he would reappear on a street corner, waiting.

'Hang on,' I puffed and repositioned my backpack so the straps didn't dig in.

Silence checked his phone again and his mouth moved. *Hurry*, he mouthed at me. He pointed to himself and drew a finger across his throat.

We jogged for at least five or six city blocks, weaving in and out of traffic. Silence jaywalked most of the time. Taxi drivers beeped at him, but other cars stopped as if he was a policeman directing traffic. Some smiled and waved us past and Silence bowed his thanks.

Outside the centre of the city, buildings were smaller, the people less harried. We cut through an underground car park and came up in a quiet lane where seedpods burst under my feet. I wondered if that was how roller-skating felt. We worked our way through winding streets and alleys into a residential area where rows of old terraced houses were strung along like paper chains. Some looked abandoned and unloved, with gappy picket fences like a mouthful of rotten teeth. Climbing vines shrouded the fences and spread over the footpath. There were windows so thick with grime, you couldn't see through them. Some houses had been renovated and restored: porches swept clean, Audis parked outside, topiaries in pots by the doors.

My feet burned in my tight boots.

'How much further? Where are we going?' Even with the cool breeze I was sweating and out of breath.

Silence grabbed my hand and pulled me into another laneway. The smell of something recently dead made me gag.

It was unnaturally quiet.

'Is this where you live?'

Silence pursed his lips. *Shhh*. Crooked his finger again. *Follow me*. He pressed on a panel in a timber-slatted fence and it swung open like a trapdoor.

The garden beyond was a jungle of tangled, shoulder-high weeds, except for a narrow path trodden through the middle. I stepped over a patch of singed grass, perfectly round like a crop circle, where a fire must have started but not caught. A massive fig tree leaned over a rickety fence; its roots had punched through a concrete path.

He led me past a shallow, stagnant pond covered with a layer of green scum. The air around us vibrated with the hum and click of insects. A black and eel-like thing uncoiled and slid under the surface; something else skittered away through the tall grass, leaving a trail of waving stalks.

'Nice place you have here,' I joked to cover my unease.

Silence frowned and pressed a finger to his lips. *Shhh*.

We exited the jungle under a drooping verandah at the rear of a terraced house. Yellowed newspaper was taped to the windows. The door was padlocked shut. Silence crept along an uneven stone path and tapped on a darkened window that I figured must lead to a basement or cellar. He waited. When nothing happened, he reached up and knocked gently on a ground-floor window. *Taptap . . . taptaptap . . . tap*. Nothing. Again, the same sequence. *Taptap . . . taptaptap . . . tap*.

'Maybe there's no one home,' I whispered.

Silence slumped. He slid down the wall and wrapped his arms around his knees.

I looked up at the window and a white face appeared. I gasped and took a step backwards. 'There's someone in there.'

Silence scrambled to his feet and waved at the face. He pulled me over to the basement window. A snap, a click, and the window shuddered open, leaving just enough space to crawl through. Silence went first, dragging my backpack with him. He gestured for me to follow.

I hesitated for a moment. I stared into that gaping hole, then looked back at the sunlit garden. I had a fear of dark, enclosed spaces that bordered on claustrophobia. My heart was beating too fast. Another sinuous movement, a hissing noise in the sun-striped grass and I grabbed Silence's hand and let him pull me into the cellar.

He reached through the window and hauled my swag after him.

Inside, the air was damp and cold. There was nothing but an old fridge and crates of empty bottles and cans.

Swift and sure-footed, Silence moved towards a steep staircase over the other side of the room, my backpack slung over his shoulder.

I stayed perched on the sill to let my eyes adjust to the dim light.

The girl who let us in sat on the bottom step of the staircase. She looked about sixteen. Everything about her was faded: her short yellow hair, washed-out blue eyes, denim jacket. She was so thin and pale she seemed almost transparent.

She chewed viciously on a fingernail and glared at us.

'You're in trouble,' she taunted Silence, without taking her eyes off me. 'You've had two lockouts and you're sixty down on your contributions.'

Silence flipped her the finger, then curled it into a 'come hither' for me.

The girl snapped, 'And now you bring her here. You're so screwed.' She ran up the steps, through a doorway that leaked weak light into the cellar.

Silence shrugged, but the gesture seemed forced. He started up the stairs, treading carefully over missing steps.

I jumped down from the ledge and followed him, dragging my swag behind me.

The hallway was almost as dark as the cellar and my boots caught on threadbare carpet that reeked of dust and mould. The walls were papered with newspaper clippings and handwritten notes that looked like shopping lists. More mouldering newspapers were stacked in towers all

31

along one side, leaving only a narrow space to walk through.

Silence led me into a kitchen that had nothing but a sink, a single row of chipped cupboards and an old door balanced on top of two crates. A guy who looked like he belonged to the same era as the house stood by the makeshift table. I thought he must have been about seventeen, eighteen maybe. He wore a shirt with puffy sleeves, bib 'n' brace trousers and a bowler hat.

He glanced at me without surprise, boredom even, and went back to peeling an apple in one continuous corkscrew twist.

Silence pointed. *Joe*, he said.

'Joe?'

'Joe,' the guy confirmed.

'Hi,' I said and stuffed my hands into my pockets.

Another girl came into the kitchen. She moved quickly and lightly for a big girl and her mouth was a tight red slash. She wore all black, her hair was shaved stubble, and she had piercings in her ears and lips.

'Carrie,' Joe supplied.

'Where have you been?' Carrie asked Silence.

Silence gestured at her, then turned to me. He curled his index fingers and poked them from the sides of his mouth like vampire fangs. He wheezed a laugh.

Carrie lifted her arms like batwings and hissed at him. Sure enough, her eyeteeth had been filed to sharp points. The effect was unsettling. She helped herself to a cigarette from the packet in Joe's shirt pocket, sat on a crate and surveyed me warily.

32

'Where'd you find her?' she said. 'Does Arden know you brought her here?'

'She just got here,' Joe said. 'Where did he find you?'

'At the train station,' I mumbled.

Carrie nodded. 'That's where he found Darcy, too.'

'Who's Darcy?' I asked.

The faded girl slunk into the kitchen. 'Does Arden know she's here yet?'

'Darcy thinks Silence is hers. That's why she doesn't like you,' Carrie said bluntly.

Silence blushed.

Darcy turned away. 'You are such a bitch, Carrie.'

Joe bounced his apple-peel twist up and down like a yoyo. He looked up. 'Arden's upstairs. Go on. Get it over with,' he told Silence.

Everything they said was whispered or mumbled. Joe's upward glance was echoed by the others and I imagined there was a sleeping giant, or worse, up there.

'Hey, Joe. Shouldn't you be out *working*?' Carrie said and snapped the peel twist.

'Hey, Carrie. Shouldn't you be out burning effigies or something?' Joe fired back.

'Nah, I'm the brains of the outfit.'

'Well, take your erudite self and . . .'

Carrie laughed. 'Er-u-dite.' She played with the word. 'What's that, some kind of rock? Did he just call mc a rock?' she asked nobody in particular.

Come on. Silence grabbed me by the hand.

'Better knock,' Carrie warned.

'I don't want to get you into trouble,' I said.

Again, that resigned shrug.

Silence led me up another staircase flanked by more walls papered with clippings. Decades of stories stuck down for reasons I couldn't begin to understand. The steps were shallow, uneven, and Silence skipped two at a time. It was warmer up there and darker still. The air swam with dust.

Silence stopped outside a closed door. He knocked once.

'What?' growled a voice.

Silence turned the knob and the door swung open. He took a step back and I moved with him. My fingernails bit into my palms and I held my breath.

In the gloom, I could make out two figures lying entwined on a mattress on the floor. There were dozens of photos, or postcards, of old buildings stuck to the wall in the shape of a question mark.

The figure on top rose and crouched on all fours above the person underneath. A face turned to glare at us.

It was a she. Long-limbed with pale eyes. Her head looked too large for her body and her naked back was moon-white and inscribed with ink. Ribs pressed sharp as blades against her skin. A predator poised over its prey.

The girl released her grip on the person beneath her and stood in one fluid motion. She seemed unfazed by her nakedness.

I realised that her head looked too big because she had dreadlocks that hung like hanks of rope to her waist.

The girl wrapped a sheet around her body. Her gaze flicked past Silence, to me.

'This had better be good,' she drawled. 'Another one of your strays?'

Silence cowered.

'I asked to come,' I squeaked.

The girl pulled a cigarette from a pack on the floor and lit it. She sauntered over and leaned against the doorframe.

Her face was feline and beautiful. She looked foreign, exotic. And tall, probably close to five ten. Her skin looked like it had never seen the sun.

'You're small,' she said and reached past Silence to stroke my face.

Her touch was ice-cold.

'And pretty. But you should cut your hair. Don't you think, Malik?'

The guy on the mattress turned on his side and propped his head on his hand. He grunted. His hair was shaved close to his head, his bare chest smooth and muscular. Around his neck hung a gold chain that he dragged between his teeth, then flicked out with his tongue.

The intimacy of the moment was too much for me. I felt a blush crawl up my throat and flood my cheeks.

'We could use another small one, don't you think?' she said to nobody in particular. 'What's her name?'

'Li . . .' I started.

'Don't tell me your real name. What does Silence call you?'

Silence relaxed visibly. He pulled out a small, spiral-bound notebook from his back pocket. He scribbled something and showed it to her.

'Friday,' she said, and laughed. 'Original. I'm Arden. Do you have people? Did you run away, do you have family looking for you? You look young, what are you? Fourteen?'

'Seventeen,' I said. 'There's nobody. My mother died.' It was the second time I had said it aloud and it hurt just the same. Died. Nobody. Dead. Nothing.

'I'm sorry.' Arden cupped my shoulder with her hand. Her silver eyes bled compassion and something else.

My whole being responded like a divining rod. I leaned into her. She looked like a shadow, but she felt solid and real. Charisma radiated from her in waves.

For some reason I wanted to tell her, right then: *I am afraid. I'm afraid of everything. I'm afraid of the dark, of closed-in spaces, of being alone and of getting too close. I'm afraid that I'll never again have the life I've always known, my feet in the dust and my heart full. I'm afraid of being alive; I'm afraid to die.*

The spell was broken by a hacking cough from the bed. Malik reached into a black, rectangular metal box on the floor. He placed something under his tongue and tipped his head back as he swallowed.

Silence dug in his pocket and pulled out the two fifties I had given him. He offered the notes to Arden and she tucked them into the space between the sheet and her skin.

'Well. You have been busy. Now you're forty up.' Arden let the sheet drop and sashayed over to Malik, trailing the sheet behind her. 'Show Friday around. Tell the others. We'll have an induction tonight.'

She waved her hand—a dismissive flick—and Malik pulled her back down onto the mattress. Her dreadlocks coiled over her shoulder.

The tattoo on her back was harsh against her skin. It read:

No

more

tears

now.

I

will

think

upon

revenge.

A wicked-sharp knife was tattooed beneath the script.

'Mary, Queen of Scots,' Arden said when she noticed my stare.

'Are you Scottish?' I asked.

'Am I Scottish?' She looked at Malik and snorted. 'No.' Her gaze slid back to me. 'I am vengeful.' She laughed hard and pressed her hand against her stomach. 'You should see your face.'

Silence moved towards the stairs.

I followed him and reached behind to shut the door.

At the same time, Arden ducked beneath the sheet and Malik arched his back, as if he was being drawn upward by an invisible thread.

My hand on the doorknob, I was torn between repulsion and fascination. The moment lasted a few seconds, but it was a drawn-out, painful reminder of Vivienne and the nights her door was closed to me.

'Leave it open,' Arden said.

Chapter Five

We judge others by their appearance: their eyes, their expression, their clothes or hair.

I learned also to judge a person by their shoes.

I could only put it down to the many nights I spent dozing under pool tables in front bars while Vivienne used her considerable intellect to pull beers so she could scrape together enough money for us to live.

My earliest memories were about shoes. Vivienne wouldn't leave me alone in a motel room and we never stayed in a town long enough to learn who to trust. She'd tuck me under the pool table with a blanket and a packet of chips; I'd doze to the sound of balls ricocheting off the cushion and the clink of pint glasses on teeth. I learned to reset the jukebox when a song played four times in a row and a drunk patron grew maudlin. I watched feet shuffle around the table: leather boots were working men; scuffed flats meant waitress-on-a-break; when stiletto heels got wobbly they went outside with leather boots; thongs were well-worn drunks who slipped me fruit-cups under the table; bare brown feet with splayed toes were indigenous locals. Sometimes, there would be a stranger in wedge heels or sandals, or black courts you could see your face in, which meant the Jehovahs were doing country service. There wasn't much I couldn't figure out without ever seeing a person's face.

Downstairs, only Darcy was still in the kitchen. She sat cross-legged on a crate, plucking at the laces on her sneakers. They had been white—now they were covered with puff-paint graffiti and black marker pen symbols.

'Are you in or out?' she asked bluntly.

Silence put his thumb up.

'In, I guess,' I said.

'Oh goody, an induction,' she said.

'What happens at an induction?' I asked. My stomach was doing flip-flops.

Carrie breezed back into the kitchen. 'You pledge your allegiance and we sacrifice a virgin. Oh, that'd be you, Darce,' she said wide-eyed.

I couldn't help it. I laughed. All the emotion that had been boiling and festering since I'd left Grandfather's house overflowed. I made my first enemy without even trying.

Darcy fired a poisonous look and stormed out.

'Don't worry about her. She pulls faces at blind people. See you guys tonight.' Carrie heaved a bag over her shoulder and left.

Silence wrote in his notebook.

Do you have a sleeping bag?

'I have the swag,' I said.

He nodded and led me to a bedroom with scarred floor-boards and a sagging ceiling. There were three mattresses. Two showed signs of occupation: pillows, unzipped sleeping bags and jumbled clothes. A make-up bag, an open book and a one-eyed teddy bear. The spare mattress, leaning up against a wall, was bare and stained.

'Who sleeps here?'

Carrie and Bree, he wrote.

'How many of you are there?'

Eight. Nine with you.

'Are you all renting?'

He shook his head. *Squatting.*

'How long have you all been here?'

Silence held up six fingers.

'Six months?'

I tipped the mattress onto the floor and a cloud of dust exploded in our faces.

Silence sneezed. Upstairs a floorboard creaked and he looked up, holding his breath.

Come on.

'Where are we going?'

Work.

I went to pick up my backpack but Silence gestured for me to leave it. I stuffed the photo into my jeans pocket and followed.

We left the way we came, through the cellar window. Outside, the sun was warm and the air was still, expectant. We scrambled through the trapdoor fence, into the alleyway. I noted the street name—Jacaranda Lane—and paid attention to landmarks as we made our way back into the city. Individual corner shops and houses gave way to office blocks and furniture stores. Then came the multistorey towers, malls and tramlines.

Breathing felt like inhaling soup.

Silence walked with his head down, shoulders hunched, as if he was heading into a gale-force wind.

So, he picked up strays. I was officially a stray. A street kid. I'd heard about them, read about them. Maybe living on the street was a kind of freedom. Or was it a sentence? It felt like freedom to me then.

Wc passed under a bridge and walked along a path next to a slow-moving brown river. I kept well away from it. Cyclists whizzed past. I felt lighter without my backpack, or maybe it was more than that. There was a weight gone, a physical burden. It was nice to be *led*.

Silence seemed to be looking for something, or someone. He veered off through a brick arch and into a park. Not just any old park—there the trees were massive and ancient. They blocked out the buildings and I could barely see the sky. Beyond the canopy, pieces of blue like a broken puzzle and the sound of bickering birds. It was like finding the Secret Garden in the middle of a desert.

Silence stripped a handful of birch seeds and crushed them in his hand. He threw them up into the sky and they coasted on the breeze like a swarm of insects.

'Where are we going?'

He pointed to a glasshouse.

'What's in there?'

He cupped his hands together and made a movement like a fish.

'We're going fishing?'

He snorted and shot off, weaving through trees and shrubs, taking paths that looked like they weren't often taken.

When I got to the glasshouse, he was already there,

sitting on the edge of a circular bricked pond. The water was dark green and murky. Silence bent over and dipped the tip of his nose into the water. I watched him as hundreds of tiny fish swarmed beneath his reflection, nibbling at him. His teeth flashed white, he laughed, his breath dimpled the surface and they darted away.

'I like it here,' I said.

He jumped, like he'd forgotten I was there.

Me too.

Then his mind came back from a faraway place. His mouth was tight and he walked out of the glasshouse, his hands deep in his pockets. That resolute walk, like he was late for an appointment.

I ran to catch up. We passed a small lake. Turtles bobbed at the edges and a one-legged heron perched on a rock. There was a kiosk and tables with red and white striped umbrellas. Thirty or so Japanese tourists vied for a place in the queue, long-lens cameras swinging from their shoulders.

Silence moved into the line.

I waited at one of the tables and pulled out the photo. I stared at the man with his arm around Vivienne's shoulder. It reminded me that I was there for a reason—to find him. If he wanted to be found. If he didn't, it would be another dead end and a new beginning for me.

Part of me wanted to go back to the last place I was happy—before Vivienne got sick—a little town up north. A friendly street, a sun-soaked place where nobody stared at my bare feet and tangled hair. I went to the local high school and started Year Twelve, even though technically I hadn't finished Year Eleven before we left the last town.

Silence was having a conversation with one of the tourists, moving his hands in a language of his own. He pulled his hood away from his hair and mussed the front.

A woman laughed. She touched his hair. She nodded and bowed and said, 'Yes, yes! You have photo? Yes?'

Silence seemed embarrassed. *No, no.*

The woman pointed at him and some of the others smiled and raised their cameras. She put her arm around his shoulder.

I saw how still he was. Lines of concentration on his forehead.

He moved away from her.

No, no, he waved his hand. Abruptly, Silence left the line.

I knew that look already. That casual swagger. I stood and put the photo back in my pocket.

The Japanese tourist who had found Silence so engaging was at the front of the queue. She was digging in her bag. I knew her hand would come up empty.

Silence kept moving towards me.

I met him halfway.

As he fumbled and tried to shove the purse down the front of his jeans, I grabbed it and hid it behind my back. I moved smoothly into the line.

The woman wailed and spat rapid-fire Japanese. She turned and pointed at Silence.

He was frozen, probably torn between saving himself and waiting for me. That moment of hesitation was his downfall; a tour-bus driver in khaki shorts grabbed him by the shoulder and pinned him there. Silence wriggled and twisted but the driver had him by his hoodie.

'Is this yours?' I stooped and pretended to pick up the purse. 'You must have dropped it.'

The woman put her arm down. She took the purse and bowed, red-faced.

The driver let Silence go.

Silence milked it. He tugged his hoodie back into place and scowled.

'Sorry, mate,' the driver said. 'Lots of purse snatchings lately.'

I stood, incredulous, as the Japanese woman pressed a ten-dollar note into my palm. She peeled off another and handed it to Silence. He bowed. She bowed back. The two of them looked like a couple of bobbing birds.

I grabbed Silence's hand and pulled him away. We sat on a flight of cold stone steps overlooking a water fountain.

Silence's ears were pink and he wouldn't look at me.

'That was stupid,' I said. 'How many times a day do you do that?'

He held up three fingers, then flicked up a fourth.

'And is that what you call *work*?'

Yes.

'Is that what the others call *work*, too?'

Some.

'It's theft, is what it is. What if you took that poor woman's passport and she couldn't go home? What happens if you steal a man's wallet and his kids can't eat?'

Silence let his shoulders drop. He looked down at his feet.

'Aren't you scared of getting caught?' My voice was shrill. 'Why do you do this?'

He shrugged again. He pulled out his notebook and wrote: *I need to make $200 a week.*

'For what? To live?'

To stay.

Silence jerked to his feet and beckoned me to follow. We traipsed along a sawdust pathway between rows of shedding plane trees, through an archway draped with vines, and into a clearing. He pushed his way through a cluster of bamboo stalks and stooped to prise open a green box that looked like an old water meter. The lid flipped open and he stood there, shamefaced.

There was a graveyard of wallets and purses scattered in the bottom of the pit.

I sucked in my breath, then let it out with a whistle. 'You're pretty good at this,' I said. 'You're the Artful friggin' Dodger, reincarnated.'

Silence frowned. I think he knew it wasn't meant to be a compliment.

'If you need money, I'll give you what I have. You can't keep doing this. How old are you, anyway?'

He gave me three bunches of fives.

'You'll have to find another way to make a living. First this, then you'll graduate to home invasions and muggings.'

Silence looked mortified. He put the lid back on the box and dusted off his hands.

'How do we get out of here? I'm hungry.' I changed the subject because all those lost things made me feel unbearably sad.

Silence took me to a takeaway shop in a dirty street full of bars with blacked-out windows. Sandwich boards advertised happy hours and silhouettes of female bodies promised good times. We ate greasy kebabs on a park bench and watched men come and go through the curtained doorways.

'Do you know where I can find the university?' I asked. 'There's somebody I need to check out.'

Silence nodded. He pointed to his watch and showed me that it was nearly six. He wiped his chin and stood up.

'Do we need to go? Back to the house?' I said. There was a seesawing sensation in my belly.

Induction. The word sounded like it described the process of sucking dry, like dragging the dregs of a milkshake through a straw. Some words just don't match their meaning at all.

'Okay. I'm ready,' I lied and bit my lip.

You could say one thing, and mean something else.

Chapter Six

Rats. Another thing that gave me the pinprick terrors. We passed through the trapdoor. On both sides, lumpy bodies scurried along the fence line between the houses. The fig tree was alive with dark, writhing shapes and high-pitched squeaks.

Silence picked up an apple core and buzzed it at the fence. A few seconds of stillness, then the rats resumed their dusk raid as if we weren't even there. My teeth ground and I squeezed his hand as we made our way along the flattened path through the weeds.

Darcy let us in. She stood back and watched me without expression as I lost my balance and landed hard on the concrete floor. When Silence offered his hand she sighed and flounced up the stairs.

'She hates me,' I said as I wiped off my backside.

Silence snapped his hand open and shut—*yap yap yap*—which I took to mean that Darcy hated everybody.

I was the centre of my mother's world for sixteen years. It was a strange feeling, that someone I barely knew could dish out dislike based on a badly timed giggle. It made me wonder whether my opinion of myself was wrong. Vivienne protested too much sometimes. She told me she loved me enough for two, that fathers were overrated. She kept me close, even closer when she was out of love. Was I in fact deserving of dislike? How could I measure my own character with only one reference?

I resolved to be nicer to Darcy with the see-through skin.

Silence led me into the kitchen. Crates were lined up around the table but there was nobody there. Coke sat flat in plastic cups, swimming with cigarette butts. Cold chips—just the overcooked and greenish ones—were lying on a sheet of butcher's paper. It seemed as if there had been a meeting, abandoned.

Silence scraped together a handful of chips and shoved them into his mouth.

'Where is everybody?' I asked.

He pointed up.

'What's up there?'

Attic, Silence whispered. The word seemed to stick in his throat. He cleared it. The effort made him cough and even that sounded like someone had turned his volume down. After a minute of breathless hacking and hoicking into the sink, his face was pale. He collapsed onto the floor, his chest an over-inflated balloon. I heard his lungs crackle.

I patted him on the back. 'Should I get someone? Tell me what to do.' *Don't die, don't die on me, kid.* I wanted to run for help but my feet felt like they were fused to the floor.

'He needs his inhaler,' an Aboriginal girl said from the doorway. 'I'll get it.' She disappeared up the staircase. When she came back, she held a small, blue canister to Silence's lips and cupped the back of his neck.

He inhaled the mist. Within seconds, his breathing steadied and he leaned back against the wall and closed his eyes.

'I'm Bree,' the girl said. She had short, curly black hair, a dimpled white smile that took up most of her face. Bottomless eyes. She grabbed my hand and squeezed it. 'Relax, will you? He'll be fine in a few minutes. It happens all the time. Asthma.'

Her accent was warm and familiar, her voice gravelly. Her words rolled over each other like marbles in a cup.

'Do you need more?' she asked Silence.

He pushed her hands away.

'Dust sets him off,' she said to me. 'Are you ready? Come on, everyone's upstairs.'

I thought about what Carrie said. *Pledge. Allegiance. Sacrifice. Virgin.* Well, maybe not the virgin part, but the other things sounded serious and binding. And what I needed then was not to be bound, not by anything, especially people.

'Arden said you were small,' Bree said and started up the stairs.

Silence followed. He looked back at me standing by the sink and raised his eyebrows.

I shook my head. 'I should go.'

'It's dark,' Bree said and kept walking. 'Come on. I brought rum. Carrie's got vodka and pretzels.'

Silence clapped.

Pretzels. Pretzels were harmless enough.

The attic space was cavernous, echoing. We entered through a square in the ceiling after climbing a rickety ladder that groaned and flexed under our weight. The windows were blacked out and a sloping roof touched the top of my head in places. The light from two candles drew looming shadows on the walls.

They sat on the floor in a semicircle.

Arden wore a trench coat that spread like a dark pool around her. Cigarette smoke drifted in a halo around her face. She handed the butt to Malik and he crushed it on the sole of his boot.

'Here she is,' Arden smiled.

Joe added to a chain of pretzels by biting the corner off one and linking it to the next.

Carrie gave me a fang-toothed smile and slapped the empty space next to her. She offered me a bottle of vodka and lemon, but I shook my head.

Silence sucked another blast from his inhaler.

'Sit,' Arden said. 'Are you okay?' she asked Silence.

'He got wheezy,' Bree said. She opened a twist-top bottle with her teeth, chugged and swallowed. 'He's better now.'

Darcy shuffled to close the space between her and Carrie.

Carrie jabbed Darcy with her elbow.

I sat next to a young boy with long hair the colour of rain-soaked wheat and shifty eyes that rolled and flicked from side to side. His fingers were bitten and raw, swollen around the nails, like burst sausages. He looked about nine or ten.

'AiAi,' Arden said and reached across to tousle his hair. *Aye-aye*. 'He's the baby of the family. Who else have you met? Joe? Carrie? Darcy, our little ray of sunshine?'

Carrie snorted. She was so big she couldn't cross her legs properly and her chin touched her chest.

Joe and I nodded to each other. He offered the bag of pretzels.

'We don't need her,' Darcy said. 'The group's getting too big. We'll get found if we get too big. If they find me they'll take me back.'

Arden looked over at Darcy.

The girl shrank.

Arden turned her laser stare to me. 'So, tell us about you. Where are you from? And what have you done?'

'I haven't done anything,' I stammered. 'I'm from the country . . .'

'Everybody's done something, country girl.' She lit another cigarette and lazily pulled a flick knife out of her boot. She flipped it open and sliced a ragged tip from her fingernail. 'I know it. We all know it.' She waited. The tip of the knife was pointed in my direction.

Dread made my arms tingle. 'I ran away,' was all I gave her.

Her laughter was short. 'We're all running,' she sighed. 'There's something you need to understand about us. We're not a gang. We're family.'

Family. The word struck like a gong.

'There are rules we follow so that we can stay together,' she continued. 'Some of us are listed as missing persons and that means there are people looking for us. Who's looking for you? Are you missing?'

'Nobody.' I wasn't missed.

'Well, you're lucky. If you want to stay, you need to keep our secrets. Can you keep other people's secrets, Friday?' Her eyes glittered.

'Yes.'

'AiAi here has a junkie for a mother. He's had so many broken bones he rattles when he walks. He's got one leg shorter than the other and he's missing more teeth than he's got left. Did Silence tell you why he can't speak?'

'No.'

'His father stood on his throat. In boots. For a long time. And Carrie pretends she's a vampire dyke to keep the . . .'

'Stop,' Carrie said in a hoarse voice. 'She gets the picture. We're all really fucked up.'

'Speak for yourself,' Darcy said.

'Yeah? Hey, Darce, tell us how you earn your keep,' Carrie hissed.

'I earn more than you do . . .'

'Dysfunction is the new black,' Joe smirked.

Arden held up her hand and their bickering stopped. 'Here's the deal. We all contribute two hundred dollars a week to the family budget. We don't care how you get it. Nobody will judge you. That money is looked after by me,' she pointed to Malik, 'and him. You feed yourself during the day and we meet back here every night at six for dinner. We watch each other's backs. We are invisible. We're quiet and we don't get caught.'

'I got caught,' AiAi said.

Arden smacked him on the top of his head and his mouth snapped shut.

'What happens with the money?' I asked.

Arden frowned. 'Expenses. If you need a doctor, stuff like that. It's for our future.'

AiAi said, 'Tell her about the place, Arden.'

Arden ignored him. 'So, can you keep our secrets, Friday?'

Silence grabbed my hand and squeezed it.

Carrie's eyes were dark with something unsaid and Darcy stared at a crack in the floorboards.

Bree closed one eye and looked into her empty bottle. She turned it as if it was a kaleidoscope.

Only Joe nodded and smiled encouragement.

'I can't stay long,' I said. 'I need to find my father.' It felt like a lie as it left my lips.

Arden pounced. 'I thought you said nobody was looking for you.'

'He's not looking. *I'm* looking. He doesn't know I exist.'

'Then why do you want to find him? Look, we have a good life here. Nobody tells us what to do or when to do it. It's perfect.'

It sounded perfect. So why did I feel like somebody had walked through my web, like all the strands of my life were just floating in the breeze? It seemed wiser to hole up in a hotel until my money was gone or until I found a new beginning, whichever happened first. I could at least sleep in a real bed and live by my own rules.

Silence timed his beseeching look perfectly.

My resolve slipped. 'Maybe I could just stay for a while. If that's okay with everyone, I mean. I have enough money for a couple of weeks.' I looked around. 'Just until I can sort out something else.'

Arden glanced at Malik.

Darcy got up and flounced off.

Malik shrugged as if he didn't care but his eyes were blinking like a camera shutter on high speed. I sensed violence curled up inside him, waiting for a nudge. I couldn't erase the image of him lying with Arden on the bed. He made me squirm, even though he was perfect, aesthetically—built like a fireman on a calendar. His expression was indifferent but he was wound tight.

More rapid, reptilian blinks. He twisted one of Arden's dreadlocks around his finger and brushed the end over his chin stubble. He looked straight through me.

Chapter Seven

When Arden dismissed us all like children at nine o'clock, I discovered that Darcy had made up my bed with a blanket and pillow. My backpack was lying next to the mattress and a corner of the blanket had been turned down. This unexpected kindness left me confused but grateful. I climbed in and waited for my body heat to build up, but the cold kept getting colder and my toes went numb inside my socks.

Nights were the worst. Insomnia came when Vivienne left—just as I felt the descent into sleep a switch would trip in my brain and my eyes would spring open. My body had turned traitor. The harder I chased sleep, the further it drifted away.

I'd been lying awake for hours. I shivered in bouts and remembered vaguely that it was the body's way of increasing blood flow and temperature. It wasn't working. My jaw was clenched so tight I was waiting for a tooth to crack.

Outside, a branch scraped against the window, caught by the wind, and the headlights of passing cars projected shapes and shadows onto the walls like a scratchy silent movie. When it was quiet, I could hear the rhythmic breaths of Carrie and Bree.

I couldn't count the number of different beds I'd slept in. Mostly they were motel mattresses, warped and flattened by too many bodies. Often they were doubles and Vivienne and I shared. We'd drifted from town to town for sixteen years before she finally took me back with her to Grandfather's house. The way she'd spoken about him, like he was a ghost of the past, I'd assumed he was dead. That first night, I couldn't sleep. I wasn't acquainted with luxury. The sheets were new and slippy and everything glowed white in the dark, like I was drifting in a cloud.

I sneaked into Vivienne's room.

She was still awake, lying on her back and staring at the ceiling.

'Can't sleep? Me neither,' she said and made room for me beside her. 'Damn ghosts.'

I could feel her bones through her skin. She stroked my hair because she had none of her own, and I prayed. I prayed to rewind back to the last time she was whole, really alive, jigging to her favourite song while her beer slopped all over the dance floor and men turned to watch. Sometimes I got tired of moving on and all I wanted to do was stay— if I found a new friend, or settled into a school where the teachers found some promise in me, or fell in love with a town that made us feel like we'd lived there forever. But leaving was worth it every time—to see Vivienne emerge from her blue funk or whatever it was that brought out misery in her. Beginnings were always exciting.

'He can give you things I never could,' she whispered. 'I'm so tired. I can't run any more.'

'Tell me why you left.' I could feel the familiar

frustration of unanswered questions warring with my need to protect her.

'It's complicated,' she said. Then, as usual, whenever I asked the wrong question at the wrong time, she steered me off in another direction. 'Everything you need for the rest of your life is right in here.' She pressed her finger into my chest. 'When I'm gone, never forget who you are.'

'Who's that, then?'

'Friday Brown, you are a twentieth-generation direct descendant of Owain Glyndwr, a man revered in Wales during the fourteenth century. He was the Welsh equivalent of King Arthur. Or William Wallace.'

I'd heard this one before. So many times. 'William Wallace?' I asked to keep her talking. But that night I had no desire to play along.

'Braveheart,' she said. 'The guy with the blue face. He turned back a whole army. He led a revolution.'

'Well, shit,' I replied. 'A dude with a blue face would frighten the crap out of anyone.'

'Don't swear.' She swatted my shoulder. 'Owain Glyndwr was the last true Prince of Wales, before the English claimed the title. Shakespeare wrote about him in *Henry IV* two centuries later. They say he was as brave as Hector, as magical as Merlin, elusive as the Scarlet Pimpernel.'

'The Scarlet Pimpernel sounds like a skin eruption.'

She sighed. 'Owain Glyndwr was a hero to his *people*.'

'Oh.'

'Is that all you have to say? Oh? Friday Brown, you are descended from kings.'

'That's like saying a flu capsule is pure heroin.'

'I didn't raise you to be a cynic,' she huffed and withdrew her arm.

'You used to tell me there was magic everywhere. There's no magic here. I don't want to stay.'

'So, now you're a sceptic, too,' she said. Her tone was heavy with exhaustion. Or perhaps it was disappointment. 'I didn't say magic was always a good thing. Others will give it another name, like serendipity, or irony. Bad juju, good luck, premonition, omens. It's all magic to me. When there are things we can't explain, we give them a name. I call it magic. It happens.'

'Shit happens. That's the original bumper sticker. I'm starting to think it's all in the interpretation.'

'What do you mean?'

'Shit happens to us all the time. It's only after it's happened that you say it was a sign. Did you see *this* coming?'

She knew what I meant by 'this'. This thing that was killing her.

'This is normal,' she said, almost to herself. 'You growing away from me.'

'There's nothing normal about what's happening to us,' I cried.

She stroked my hair again. 'It would kill me if you stopped believing in me.'

We both fell silent at that.

'You're growing up,' she said firmly. 'It takes time to believe again. It took me sixteen years, but I hope it takes you less. That's where you'll find your peace.'

'What are you talking about?'

'We've had our differences, my father and me, but we've

forgiven each other. There are things you need to know.'

'Like what? How to make *good choices*?' I said bitterly.

She shook her head. 'You can't always make good choices. Sometimes you have to settle for making a choice you can live with.'

'Can't we just go back? Let's go up north. I liked it there.'

She shook her head. 'I've come full circle. He's not such a bad old guy and you'll be able to finish school. He'll look after you.'

'I don't need looking after.'

'It's too *soon*,' she said fiercely. 'You have to be brave now. This is the last new beginning for me.'

Which sounded to me like it was an ending. Which it was.

Three months with Vivienne, forty-two days without her. That's how I defined my time in that house. I didn't want to remember any of it.

The ceiling of the squat seemed to press down. I burrowed further under the blanket and pinned the edges underneath my arms and legs. I felt a burning in my sinuses and a lump in my throat that meant tears were coming, so I pinched the bridge of my nose to stop them.

'Damn ghosts,' I whispered to the dark.

Another car drove by. For a few seconds, the news-papered walls lit up.

My eyes were playing tricks.

A slow-moving shadow crept down the hallway: the shape of a head, shoulders, a pointed chin. The shadow froze until the car had passed.

My body went rigid. I kept my head so still. My eyes

ached from staring sideways at that shadow and, after long minutes, it started moving in my direction. The dark shape sidled through the doorway. It crouched low and leaned over me.

I felt the soft weight of a blanket pressing down. Scratchy fibres scraped my cheek. The shadow moved away and I heard the wheeze of laboured breath.

'Silence, what are you doing?' Bree hissed. 'Go back to bed.'

The shadow gave a salute.

Bree sighed and rolled over.

Creeping warmth made my toes tingle and my eyes close. When my heart stopped pounding, I fell into ruptured sleep.

A toilet flushed. Somebody coughed. Shards of morning stabbed between the gaps in the newspaper; the exposed pipes that ran like veins through the creaky old house shuddered. Footsteps overhead and the cobweb-strung globe above swayed. I needed to pee, desperately, but I knew once I released the heat from the blankets it would be impossible to get it back.

Carrie's and Bree's beds were empty.

I hadn't heard them get up which meant I'd slept harder than I liked. I curled myself into a ball on my side and waited.

'Wake up, sleepyhead.'

I jumped and sat up.

Arden lounged in the doorway dressed in a long, black T-shirt. Her legs were white and endless, with the hard-edged muscle of a dancer, or a gymnast. Lines that begged to be drawn, if I could draw, and I couldn't. Her dreads were tied in a clumped knot that sat like a sewer-rat on her shoulder. I noticed that her breasts were full, but high, even without a bra—like Vivienne's had been. I would keep registering these similarities but I didn't know what to make of them; they brought pain, but at the same time comfort.

'Sleep well?' Arden drawled.

'Yes, thanks,' I lied.

She was hiding something behind her back.

'Was there something you didn't understand about being invisible?'

At that moment the creeping light burst into a wall of sunshine. Arden moved to stand in it. A newspaper exploded in my face, the pages separating, fluttering down around me.

I cowered and put my hands up.

'There mustn't be much happening in the world today.' Arden said. She rummaged through the paper and spread a page out over my legs. 'Look who's made headlines.'

I crossed my legs and smoothed the paper.

TEENAGER SAVES BABY, screamed the front page. There was a picture of me pulling the pram onto the edge of the platform, one of those Big Brother images that looked grainy and indistinct. Below it, a close-up of my face with my hand up, fingers spread, like I was trying to ward off the paparazzi.

A mystery girl's quick thinking averted tragedy yesterday morning when seven-month-old Reilly Cooper's pram rolled . . .

'But I didn't . . .' I started.

'You'll have to leave. You're putting us all in danger.'

'But it was Si . . .' I stopped. If Arden was making me leave, what would she do to Silence?

Arden gathered the scattered pages to her chest, had a second thought, then threw the crumpled mess back on the floor. 'No hard feelings, hey. It's for the best.'

She sounded like someone much older.

As if she realised it, she laughed at herself. Her expression turned serious. 'You don't fit in, really. You don't seem . . . damaged enough.'

I slid out from under the blankets and pushed the newspaper pages away from the mattress. I pulled my backpack close and looked inside for some clean clothes.

Arden stood over me, frowning. 'There is another way, I suppose.'

My stuff seemed loose, like there were things missing, or out of place. 'What do you mean?' I pushed the clothes aside and felt for my purse. It wasn't there. 'My purse is gone,' I mumbled.

'It must be there somewhere,' Arden said, irritated. 'We could cut your hair.'

'Why? What for?' I sounded breathless. 'It's gone.' My money was gone.

'So nobody will recognise you. Then you could stay.'

'It was here last night.' *Darcy*, I thought.

'Did you hear me? You could stay. Let me cut your hair. You'll be unrecognisable.' Her eyes were shattered glass.

'It's okay. I'm leaving.'

'Where are you going?'

'I thought you wanted me to go?'

'I do, but Silence won't be happy.'

'He doesn't even know me.'

'I think you remind him of his sister. She looked a bit like you.' She bent down, grabbed a hank of my hair and inspected the ends. 'When was the last time you cut this?'

'Not since I was about ten.' *When was the last time you cut yours?* I thought, looking at her snarled dreadlocks. I backed away from her and she held on a moment too long until the roots pulled. 'What happened to her? Silence's sister?'

'Who said anything happened to her?'

'You used the past tense.'

'I didn't. Oh, come on. Let me cut it.' Arden cut the air with two fingers, *snip snip*. She knelt behind me and ran her fingers through my hair, combing the tangles. 'Stop covering up that pretty face.'

After a minute, I relaxed against her. It felt good, like I was five years old again. I closed my eyes and she could have been Vivienne, winding sections into a fishtail braid. I sank deep into the pleasure and pain of pull and release.

Arden's fingers moved to my scalp and started to massage hard, hypnotic circles.

'Do you like that?'

I nodded. 'I need to get dressed,' I said but didn't move. I couldn't.

Her hands moved to my shoulders and she dug her thumbs into the tight muscles.

I groaned.

Arden caught and held her breath. She worked one cool hand from my shoulder, down, between the fabric and skin, until she scooped and cradled one of my breasts.

I froze.

She held me there until her hand grew warm.

And I let her.

I'm not sure who moved first.

She let me go, stood up, looked down at her near-nakedness and shrugged. 'See you downstairs.'

I was shaking. I took my time and turfed all of my stuff out onto the mattress—two pairs of jeans, a few T-shirts, thongs, underwear, my jacket and a thin jumper. I wanted to put them all on.

My purse was definitely gone. The thought made me feel sick. Finally, I got dressed and went downstairs.

Only Carrie, Darcy, Arden and AiAi were there. AiAi was wolfing bread, his hand dipping into a brown paper bag to break chunks from a crusty loaf. Darcy was quiet and shifty, sitting on a crate, nursing a mug.

I gave her my best accusing stare but she wouldn't look at me.

Carrie was stirring crazy circles in her mug with a teaspoon.

'Where's Silence?' I asked.

Carrie looked up. 'Gone out,' she said.

Arden slurped the last of her drink and handed her mug to Carrie. She hadn't bothered to put on more clothes, despite the chill of the house. *Snip, snip*, went her fingers. She behaved as if nothing had happened and I was relieved.

I looked at Carrie's and Darcy's short hair.

Bree wandered in, yawning.

I checked out her cropped curls and wondered. It crossed my mind that I'd been manipulated in some way, but I was embarrassed and confused.

'What's going on?' Bree said.

Arden hauled a crate into the middle of the room and slapped it.

I thought it was a test. A girl rite of passage that must be endured. It was hair. Only hair. Dying cells oozing through pores, that's all it was.

Arden was waiting, daring me.

Carrie ran her hand over her own stubbled head, almost like she wasn't aware she was doing it.

Bree took a chunk of bread out of AiAi's hand and said, 'Gotta go. See you all tonight.' Her eyes darted to me, then away. She left in a hurry.

I sat on the crate and gathered my heavy hair into a ponytail with both hands. I handed it to Arden.

Arden started to cut. But not with scissors. With her knife.

The dragging, sawing sensation was awful. My scalp burned.

Arden hacked through the hair just below her hand and let go.

A raggedy, concave bob swung around my face, just past my chin. The feeling of lightness was nice. Just an even-up and I could have lived with it. I didn't know why I hadn't done it sooner, except that Vivienne had kept hers long and I'd just never even thought about doing something different.

'Hey, thanks. It feels good,' I said, touching the blunt ends. 'Maybe just go around the edges again . . .'

Arden lifted a piece and cut again, this time only a couple of centimetres from my scalp.

I turned around and said, 'I like it. You can stop cutting.'

She twisted my shoulders to the front and said, 'You still look like you.'

I made a swollen lump on my lip with my teeth. Apart

from violence, there was no exit. I made my mind empty, filled it back up with the resignation that I could summon whenever I remembered that the worst had already happened. Nothing else would ever hurt as much again.

It was only hair.

Darcy left and came back with the round hand-mirror that sat over the bathroom basin. She held it in front of me so I could watch.

Arden continued cutting.

When she had finished, there were uneven tufts and zigzag edges, but my new haircut was short and wispy. Without all that weight, it stood straight up; without all that hair, my eyes were enormous.

Darcy angled the mirror so I could see the back.

The nape of my neck was cold, bare, and so white. Childlike.

I ran my hands over the skin and brushed away the amputated ends. I could see Darcy's reflection behind me but I couldn't read her expression.

'I think she looks pretty,' AiAi said through a mouthful of bread.

'I think she looks like one of Carrie's dyke friends,' said Darcy.

Carrie yelled, 'For fuck's sake, go find your happy place, Darce.' She slammed her cup into the sink and stomped up the stairs.

Arden's mouth was thin as a paper cut. 'Clean up this mess,' she spat.

I scooped up handfuls of hair. It was already drying, dying, no longer a part of me.

Maybe I wasn't supposed to look pretty. Maybe none of us were.

I swept up the rest of the hair, stuffed it into a plastic shopping bag and took it outside.

Bree was smoking, leaning up against the wall of the house. She had her iPod headphones in, her eyes closed. Her mouth moved silently to music I couldn't hear.

I touched her arm.

She jumped and plucked out her headphones. 'Wow,' she said. 'You look different.'

'Not like me,' I said.

'No. You still look like you. Just lighter.' She smiled. Her dimples were deep, like someone had pressed their thumbs into her face. A quick flash and they were gone. 'I've gotta go somewhere. Come if you want.'

I got the feeling she'd been waiting for me. I leaned the bag up against the side of the house and left it there.

'Did Arden cut your hair, too?' I asked her. 'And the others?'

'No.' She tucked her iPod into the waistband of her jeans. Her mouth twisted. 'The boys already had short hair.'

Chapter Eight

'Two hundred bucks a week is a lot,' I said.

Bree led the way through a maze of alleys between double-storey townhouses. She walked quickly and smoked. Four cigarettes already and we'd only been walking for fifteen minutes. The air was razor-sharp and stung my throat like a strong mint.

'Yeah, it is. But it's actually not that hard. Joe helps out at the markets. He sorts through fruit and vegetables and gets rid of all the rotten stuff. Sweeps the floor. The greengrocers just sling him some cash here and there. It all adds up.'

'What about benefits?'

'We're not supposed to get money from the government, otherwise it's too easy to track us down. We don't exist, remember? It's better that way.'

'Better for who?' I asked but she didn't answer. 'So what do you do?'

Bree looked uncomfortable. 'You're limping,' she said, changing the subject. She stared down at my feet.

'I don't like wearing shoes. These are too tight. Come on, it can't be that bad. I know what Silence does.'

She laughed. 'You've seen him in action? Quick little

bugger, isn't he? He's nearly been caught a few times. I reckon his ear's half hanging off by now.'

I nodded. 'What about Darcy?'

'Darce? Umm. Guys like her.' She said it in a rush, as if the admission had a bad taste. 'If you know what I mean.'

I knew what she meant. The thought of it made me feel empty.

'Don't feel bad,' Bree said. 'She brags that she only has to work one day a week. She's a cold one. Crappy child-hood and all that.'

'So what about the others?'

'Arden looks out for the rest of us. Makes sure we brush our teeth.' Again, that flashing smile.

'Like Wendy Darling.'

Bree shook her head.

'Peter Pan. The Lost Boys.'

Still blank.

'Never mind.'

'Malik deals,' she went on. 'He works the clubs. That's why he's always asleep in the daytime. And AiAi is pretty good at selling stuff to tourists.'

'Stuff? Like what?'

'Once he got forty bucks for a potato that looked like Mary McKillop.'

We laughed. Blunt ends of hair were making my neck itch. I brushed my hand through what was left and a few stray, long pieces caught in my fingers. I yanked them out.

'It's not so bad,' Bree said. 'You have a good-shaped head.' She offered me a cigarette.

'No, thanks. Where are we going?'

She shrugged and headed off down the path by the river.

I kept my distance and stuck to the far side of the path. The river was brown and sluggish and it reminded me of Willy Wonka's chocolate river. A few tourists pedalled madly in paddleboats, shrieking, skirting the spray from a fountain.

'I had some money, but it's gone,' I confessed because the worry wouldn't leave me.

'Gone? Gone how?'

'I'm not sure. It was in my backpack last night and this morning it wasn't there.' I tried to keep accusation from my tone.

'Someone nicked it, you mean?' She frowned. 'Darcy, you think? Wouldn't surprise me.'

'I'd hate to be wrong.'

'Yeah. But you probably wouldn't be. How much are we talking?'

She flicked her butt into the water. It landed at the river's edge, suspended in phosphorescent ripples of scum. A duck sailed in to check it out, followed by the rest of the fleet.

'A few hundred.'

'Shit.'

'Yeah. Shit.' I spat the word out.

'Don't make a big deal about it to Arden,' she said. 'She looks after us. But if you're new, like you are, she makes you earn it. Your place here. Do you get what I'm saying? You have to prove you won't screw anyone over.'

'She was going to make me leave this morning.'

'I know, she blows hot and cold. But we're all she has.'

'Where's her family?' I asked.

'She ran off when she was fifteen. She's been on the street

for two years. Reckons she's never going back. Anyway, I shouldn't be talking about her business.'

I guess I was trying to understand why anyone would choose to live on the street when they had a home and a family somewhere.

'We're the same age,' I said. 'She seems older.' I thought of Arden's hand and my skin prickled. 'That squat is pretty bad,' I blurted to change the subject. 'And I've . . .'

'Why are you here?' Bree interrupted. 'Don't you have a nice white family who treats you good? 'Cause, to me, you look like you're just trying on a bit of rough. Like you're having some big adventure. What the fuck do you know about us?'

'I'm sorry,' I said. I meant it.

'Cooee you in your too-tight shoes,' she said, but not unkindly. 'The squat's a palace. It's better than nothing. Better than getting pissed on while you're sleeping in a doorway.'

She was right. I just didn't understand it. Vivienne and I clashed often, and I didn't always get why she felt the need for perpetual motion, but I would never have left her. Not while she was living. Surely the family you had was better than no family at all.

Bree stopped by a man reclining on a concrete slope beneath a bridge. He appeared to be asleep, or dead. She leaned over and touched him gently on the leg.

This was the image I saw when I thought about homeless people. Pods of them, basking, lazy seals on a beach. Daytime sleepers wrapped in newspaper like giant parcels of fish and chips. Hands gripping brown paper bags, their belongings stuffed in shopping trolleys. Or no belongings at all.

'Hey, Tom,' she said to him. 'Seen the others?'

The man sat up, blinking. He held out his hand and she passed him a cigarette.

'Nup. Park, probably. Giss a few extra, Bree.'

She gave him a couple more. 'Which park?'

'The big 'un in the middle.'

She thanked him and kept walking, long strides, with me trotting after her.

'So where do you come from? In the country, I mean?' Bree asked.

'You know—all over. Small towns. We moved around a lot, me and my mum.' I stopped. I pretended to tie my bootlace because my eyes were stinging.

When I looked up, she was waiting.

'No, I don't know. I've only ever lived here.' She spread her arms, held out her hands like cups. Behind her, the blueish silhouette of buildings shrouded in smog, made miniature by distance and held in her palms. 'What was it like?'

I remembered every one of those towns.

I told her about the best and the worst. The slow and sleepy places where weekdays rolled past like weekends and Mondays didn't matter. Battered shacks perched on cliffs overlooking the endless, rumpled sea. Afternoons spent waiting on the docks, swinging my legs off a pier until boats rolled in with crates full of oysters and crayfish still gasping. Pulling fishhooks out of my feet because I never wore shoes, playing with other kids whose names I never knew. Those were the unforgettable summers. There were outback towns where you couldn't see the roads for red dust, grids of streets with wandering dogs and children who ran wild and swam naked in creeks. I remembered climbing ancient trees that had a heartbeat if you pressed your ear to them. *Boomboom-boomboom.* Dreamy nights sleeping by the campfire and waking up covered in fine ash, as if I'd slept through a nuclear holocaust. We were wanderers, always with our faces to the sun.

And there were towns where Vivienne and I learned fast about survival on the fly, where travellers and workers would flit in and flit out, leaving their money at the bar. It was possible to reinvent yourself in every new place and leave your sins behind. And in every town Vivienne left a sin behind—usually a man who wasn't hers, often unpaid rent. Once we had all our money stolen from our motel room and another time we were turfed out of a truck in the middle of nowhere, in the middle of the night. We walked the highway in pitch darkness until another truckie picked us up and set us down somewhere new. If I could have plotted our route on a map it would have looked like a child's mad scribble on a wall.

Bree listened, a faraway expression on her face. 'I've never even climbed a tree,' she said.

'We moved around a lot,' I said again. 'We were free.' I sat on a bench and unlaced my boots. Recollection hurt so much; I could barely remember my unbroken self.

'What are you doing?'

'We're going to climb a tree,' I answered.

'I don't do heights,' she said.

'It's easy.' My feet were white and pinched. I rubbed them and flexed my toes like a dancer.

I chose a drooping willow that arced across the river. Its bark was serrated and tore at the soles of my feet, but Bree was watching, so I scooted up, up, until the branches levelled out. I saw abandoned birds' nests hidden in the canopy, a deflated balloon on a string, trapped, carved initials and declarations of love etched in the bark. There was no view up there, only a sea of hazy green. And the churning river below.

I faltered. My foot slipped.

I felt it then, the fear of that unpredictable river. Like a dog you've known all your life that suddenly bares its teeth and you see that it was always wild, never tame; how easily it could turn.

I froze. That had never happened to me before.

I didn't want to be dangling over that water. I knew then that Vivienne's legacies weren't all good, that this one was starting to eat away at me from the inside.

'Come down. You're freaking me out,' Bree called. 'You'll fall and land on your head.'

I've never fallen, I thought. 'Come up,' I called back, but my voice was small.

'I'm going,' she said. And went.

I edged down slowly. When I dropped onto the footpath she was out of sight. I felt awkward, as if I'd been caught dancing by myself.

I shouldn't have showed off. What bloody use was it there, in the city, to be able to climb a tree? I ran my hand over my bare neck and I felt like crying again.

A few weeks before she died, Vivienne woke me with

her stare. I felt its burn as I dozed in the chair next to her bed. That sudden scrutiny, her stuttering breath, it made me realise that this was it. She was going. And instead of holding her outstretched hand and taking her as far as I could, I backed away.

She felt it. And she didn't blame me, not really.

Beautiful girl, her eyes told me, though they were sunken and yellow.

She had become a shadow that slept all the time. The morphine was a steady drip and it kept her from talking. When she did she made no sense. I can't remember the last thing she said to me. Or the last thing I said to her.

I put my boots back on and thought about trying to find Silence. My stomach whined and I realised I hadn't eaten since the night before. A man walked past with a chocolate doughnut and a steaming coffee. He took three quick bites and tossed the last of the doughnut, minus icing, to the ducks. I nearly dived for it but it rolled into the river and the ducks got there first.

I walked. I didn't know where I was going—but I was used to that. I found a few green, unripe apples that hung over a fence and stuffed them into my pockets. I ate one slowly, pulling a face as the sour juice ran down my chin.

I knew I was getting to the heart of the city as traffic slowed and grew congested. There was a rhythmic beat to the footsteps, the tooting horns, the clanging trams. It seemed like everyone was travelling in one direction and I was moving in the other, in slow motion, like a badly shot music video, mouthing words to a song I didn't know.

I ended up near the entrance to the train station where

Silence had found me. There was a portable newsagent stand and dozens of copies of my face in black and white. I was front-page news, except I didn't look like that any more.

I stopped and stared.

The old guy shoved a newspaper at me and held out his hand for change. He didn't look twice at my face, or the picture.

I shook my head and he lost interest. That was how easily you could disappear.

I wandered for hours.

After a few laps of what seemed to be the hub of the city, I started to find my bearings. I followed a gaggle of people from a tour bus into a skyscraper with a viewing deck on the forty-third floor. Up there, I could see the river snaking its way through a stripe of vegetation that connected a series of parks. I worked out the direction Bree and I had come from that morning. Below, people looked like a line of ants ferrying food back to the nest.

With a dozen or more lenses zooming past my nose, I spotted that strangely vacant square of green where I had sat with Silence on my first day in the city. It was a world inside a snow dome, but without the snow.

I was drawn to it. That was where I'd go.

When I reached the park, I headed straight for the statue. I felt the ridges of the horse's hooves and the strain of its tendons. Its rider was standing in the saddle, a sword raised above his head in triumph. Over what, I didn't know. The base was covered with gobs of old gum, cracks stuffed with rubbish, bricks defaced with tags and graffiti.

'How'd you find me?' Bree said.

She was watching me from the other side of the statue.

'I didn't. You found me,' I said.

'Whatever,' she said.

'Are you alone?' I asked.

'Course not.' Bree gestured to a group of Aboriginal men and women sitting in a circle on the grass. They were darker-skinned than Bree, dressed in traditional costume, their faces and arms painted with streaks of grey. 'They're doing a performance for the festival.'

'Can I watch?' I walked closer to the group and Bree followed, reluctantly. 'What do you do?'

She shook her head. 'I help out but I don't . . . you know. I just don't.'

'Why not?'

'It's not my thing,' she said and kicked the ground.

'Oh.'

One of the men pulled a didgeridoo onto his lap. He ran his hands over it, like he was checking for breaks, then lifted the end to his lips. His cheeks ballooned and a long, deep sound vibrated.

It was just a test note, but I shivered.

'I love that sound,' I said. 'It goes through my bones and leaves through my feet.'

Bree laughed. 'You're weird, you know that?'

I blushed.

'That's my mum, over there. My uncle plays the didge.' She said it fiercely.

She had a family. A close one, judging by the easy banter I heard.

'So why do you sleep at the squat?'

She sighed. 'I'd have to share a bedroom with two younger brothers. It's shit.'

'But you share a room with me and Carrie.'

'That's different.'

'You're lucky,' I told her. 'To have your mum, I mean.'

'What happened to yours?'

I pointed at the sky. Not because I believed in heaven, but because it was effective shorthand for dead and gone.

'Sorry.'

'Me too.'

There was an awkward pause. Another blast from the didgeridoo.

'They're getting started.' I waited for her to invite me to stay.

'Yeah. You'd better go,' she said. 'Don't get lost. It's a big city.'

Chapter Nine

The days went like this: we woke with chattering teeth and stumbled about in the dark as winter ended and spring began; the first person up boiled an ancient kettle that looked like a penguin, using stolen electricity from a series of concealed extension cords leading to the basement next door; ten chipped mugs were lined up, instant coffees were poured and distributed like handouts in a soup kitchen. Low, inane chatter, like polite conversation at a funeral. Some days Carrie's and Darcy's niggling sped up the exodus and one by one we'd slink out through the cellar window, through the trapdoor.

There was a laundry roster: an off-white linen bag sat clumped by a back door that didn't open. To keep costs down, clothes had to be worn three times before washing. Arden gave the rostered kids a stack of dollar coins and they heaved the bag into a three-wheeled shopping trolley that veered left. It took two of us to steer the trolley to the laundromat, three blocks away. Everyone liked laundry duty. It meant fifty bucks off your weekly contribution because it was down time. It was nice to sit and daydream in the humid room, to inhale the scent of washing powder and damp air, time to not think about anything, to just listen to the rhythmic hum of clothes flopping and tumbling in the dryer.

Nobody volunteered for dinner or shopping. Only Carrie made an effort in the ramshackle kitchen. She tried to serve up healthy meals but the best she could produce was pasta with a packet of grated cheese mixed through, topped with Worcestershire sauce. It smelled good but anaesthetised my tongue for two days. Usually it was chips and bread, occasionally overheated pumpkin soup with clots of curdled cream. Our diet made me nostalgic for tuna on toast and fresh-picked mandarins.

In the first week I was given a reprieve by Silence. He slipped me two hundred dollars and shook his head when I tried to give it back. He knew that my purse was gone and sent his poisonous looks Darcy's way whenever she was around. I hadn't figured out a way to earn money, a way that wasn't illegal or immoral, or both.

I had a soft spot for AiAi, who scampered about like an untrained pet, and Joe, who kept to himself but who occasionally let fly with his barbed wisdom. Carrie could always be counted on for laughs.

Bree was often absent as she divided her time between her two families. Of them all, she was the easiest to be around.

Arden was a stickler for routine and quick with her slaps. AiAi copped it regularly for not brushing his teeth and Darcy was adept at sensing one coming. I noticed her duck whenever something nasty came out of her mouth, even if Arden wasn't around. Often there was so much talk flying back and forth that I would tune out. I learned to listen for the quiet.

Mostly, I watched Arden. I wanted her confidence. Apart from her occasional violent outbursts, I wanted to be like her, so at ease in her skin. I felt I could absorb her energy simply by being near her, spinning in her orbit. Every morning, I woke, convinced I would move on; every evening I found myself back in that kitchen, a small part of Arden's universe.

On my ninth morning in the city, I got up early. Bree and Carrie were still sleeping. I went downstairs, expecting an empty kitchen, but Arden and AiAi were there.

Arden was teaching him to tie his shoelaces.

'Bunny ears. Look. Over, under, bunny ears, over, under, pull it tight. Do it again.'

AiAi tried, but his bow fell apart.

'Do it again. Hold the first bit down with your ring finger, then do the loops, otherwise it comes loose.'

AiAi sighed and his shoulders slumped.

Arden went through the motions again, counting each move aloud.

I was struck by her patience, her tenderness, as she guided AiAi's fingers in a ritual that was familiar but too distant for me to remember it clearly. Where was I when Vivienne held my small hands like that?

AiAi tied his first bow, unaided. It was lopsided and loose, but it stayed together.

Arden tied it off in a double knot. 'See? Now, stop bugging me to do up your laces every morning. Or else get Velcro shoes.'

She spotted me in the doorway and smiled. When she did that, it was unexpected, and beautiful.

'You.' She pointed at me. 'Me. We got a date later.'

'What?' I stammered.

'I need you to do something for me.'

'Why me?'

'You're small,' she said in her cryptic way. 'And Bree said you climb trees.'

'Okay,' I agreed, as if I'd made a choice.

I went up to the bathroom to brush my teeth. On my way back down, Silence was standing on the stairs, reading the walls. He did that a lot. By now I'd realised that it was him, pasting the clippings to the walls, and that it was more than something he did to pass time.

He'd started a whole new section, working his way through a pile of newspapers tied together with an old stocking. He ran his finger beneath the words as he read.

'Can you show me where the uni is today?' I asked him.

He nodded.

'What are you reading?'

The clipping was from 1944. There was a photo of a smiling young man standing next to a biplane, taken not long before he was killed in action. Next to it was a guy with a Hitler moustache, arms folded over his chest. He didn't look like a person somebody would mourn. There were more like it—war stories and faded obituaries stuck together in a seemingly random way—but when I looked closer, I could see that Silence had cut the clippings into the shape of headstones. He'd created a graveyard. From a distance, the clippings blurred into a dirty, yellow pattern; up close there were all these interconnected stories, overlapping, joined by an event or a person or an emotion.

Further up on the landing wall, he'd stuck down advertisements with women wearing flouncy skirts, posed with household appliances.

'That's the anti-feminist section,' I joked.

Silence shook his head. *Mothers*, I thought he said.

Carrie stomped past, overtaken by Darcy, who was trying to get to the bathroom first.

Darcy dropped her toothbrush on the stairs.

Carrie picked it up and brushed her hair with it.

Darcy screeched and threw a punch.

Carrie deflected it with a forearm the size of a leg of ham. She dropped the toothbrush down into the stairwell and dusted off her hands. 'My work here is done,' she said and continued to the bathroom, unchallenged.

Silence rolled his eyes and began cutting out another headstone.

The university was closer, bigger and more daunting than I had imagined. I couldn't have missed it, even if Silence hadn't come with me. Some buildings just look academic. The sun was lazy and warm. Students were stretched out on the lawn with books on their laps.

It was obvious I didn't belong.

I stopped in the middle of a walkway, jittering about like a haywire compass, getting in everyone's way.

Eventually, a man trying to pass me with a cleaning trolley asked if I needed help. He directed me to an old, stone building.

Inside, the ceiling peaked like a cathedral. Rainbows of light poured through high, stained-glass windows and the floor squeaked underfoot. The ceiling was ornate and beautiful, but from eye level the room became ordinary, divided into grey, compact cubicles with desks and computers. Everyone seemed to be busy.

'Excuse me,' I asked a woman moving paper around behind a long counter. 'I'm trying to contact someone who used to work here.'

'Name,' she said, peering over the top of her glasses.

'Professor Green.'

'First name?'

'I don't know.'

'There are three Professor Greens here.'

'Oh.'

The woman resumed her paper shuffling and in desperation I placed the photo down on the counter.

'He looks—looked—like this.'

She pushed her glasses up the bridge of her nose and looked down at the photo. I counted nine seconds before she answered and I felt nauseous for all of them.

'Yes, he teaches here.'

The man existed beyond that square of paper. 'Where can I find him?'

'I'll check. Wait here.' She went to a desk, picked up a phone and dialled.

I was a nervous, jangling mess. When she came back, I was leaning on the counter so I could stay upright.

'He's on leave. I can't give you his contact details, but if you write your name and number down, I'll put it on his desk,' she said.

I took the pen and Post-it notepad she gave me and

scribbled, *Friday Brown.* I didn't have a number, so I wrote, *Vivienne Brown's daughter.*

She read the note and raised an eyebrow. 'He'll know who you are?'

No. I don't know. I hope so. 'Yes,' I said. 'Thank you.'

I went outside. Disappointment mingled with relief. Then I realised I would just be a name on a piece of paper to him. He might screw it up and throw it away. The element of surprise would be gone—I would never be able to see his face when I said Vivienne's name, I'd never know if his first reaction was an honest one or a practised denial.

A few seconds later, the woman left the building too.

I went after her. I wanted to tell her I'd made a mistake, to ask her to destroy the Post-it note.

She stopped and chatted to a man along the way.

I waited.

When they parted, the woman went into another building.

I followed, but I hung back in the foyer.

The woman trotted down a corridor and tried the third door on her right. She jiggled it, tutted, then continued to the end of the hallway. She reached up and slipped her hand into a wooden pigeonhole.

I figured it was just as easy to take the Post-it note myself.

The woman left through the sliding door.

As I passed the office she'd tried to open, I glanced through the glass window. And stopped. My eye was drawn to a pin-board on the wall just inside the office. I pressed my face up to the cold glass.

Professor Green was a popular guy. Always smiling, often with his arm slung around people's shoulders. There were dozens of photos of him with his students, some obviously taken a long time ago. I scanned them all. There were none of Vivienne.

His desk was untidy. There were books and papers and even a half-empty coffee cup, as if I'd just missed him.

When I saw the family photo propped on a shelf, it was like a door slammed in my face. He had four boys. A beautiful wife. A tyre swing in the backyard. He was smiling and he managed to put his arm around all of them.

I felt sick and foolish.

Maybe, over the years, I'd dreamed up the intimacy in Vivienne's photo, imagined that they had some kind of epic romance. He hadn't been pining away for Vivienne; in fact, he'd been loving someone else. And they had plenty of children to prove it.

I moved away from the glass. A ghostly impression of my face faded and disappeared.

There were dozens of letters and magazines stuffed into his pigeonhole. I found my note, the latest in a sea of yellow and pink. When I pulled it out, a few others came with it:

Congratulations, a baby girl is such a blessing, Jill x.

Finally, a little girl. Well done, mate. Brent.

Best wishes to you, Caroline and the boys, Ivy and Jack xx.

I tried to laugh it off. Friday Green had a bad ring to it, and there were a few lame jokes I could come up with about swapping one coloured surname for another. Anyway, if there had been a space for a daughter in that family, clearly the opening had been filled.

I screwed up the notes and dumped them in a bin outside.

Chapter Ten

When I left the university, I looked for Silence in the glass-house with the fish. I looked for him in the shadows of trees, in the train station, on the street. I checked his hidden stash, but there were leaves piled up over the box and the empty wallets and purses seemed undisturbed. I saw his face in every slouched, hooded boy but it was never him.

I'd known him for barely two weeks, but I needed his devotion, especially after the Professor Green thing. I knew it was just loneliness and I wondered how many more days I could survive feeling that way, like my heart had caved in and just existing was too much effort.

The secret garden was starting to bloom but the ground still crackled with fallen leaves. Barefoot, I scuffed through the piles from one side of the park to the other.

Silence didn't show.

I sat outside near one of the brick-arched entrance gates near a bus stop. Not too close that a bus driver would stop, not too far away that I looked like I had nowhere to be. I parked my boots next to me. The footpath was warm from the sun, worn smooth by a trillion feet.

From beneath a rose bush, I dug up a piece of chalky shale embedded in dirt. It was fifteen different shades, from pale ochre to a deep magenta. I drew a circle that became a burning sun and a slice of desert sky. The shale was so soft it melted onto the concrete and when it wore away to a stump, I dug up more. Traffic became a distant hum and above it I heard the insistent whisper of a memory.

I started to write.

At first I couldn't remember the words—Vivienne's voice had started to fade along with her face—but, one by one, the lines of her old bush poem came back to me.

> Three roads there are that climb and wind
> amongst the hills, and leave behind
> the patterned orchards, sloping down
> to meet a little country town.

I wrote two lines in each square, leaving room for people to pass without smudging my work. Each word had depth, as if I'd gone over and over it with a few different colours.

> The road is rough—but to my feet
> softer than is the city street;
> and then the trees!—how beautiful
> she-oak and gum—how fresh and cool . . .

The first dollar came after I'd completed six squares. It landed with a ping and bounced into a bush. I thought the lady had dropped it by mistake and I scrambled after her and tried to give it back.

She smiled and shook her head. 'I'll read the rest on my way home,' she said. 'It makes me want to skip work.'

I tucked the dollar into my pocket and kept writing. Four more verses, and I couldn't recall the last lines but it didn't matter—by the fourteenth square I had nineteen dollars and fifty cents, including a five-dollar note handed to me by a young mother with twins in a double pram. Some people pretended to pass without looking, but I could see their eyes, trying to read, while their chins pointed straight ahead.

The sun was making me feel sleepy. My legs tingled from sitting for so long on the hard ground. My brain hurt from thinking. I learned fast that if I sat in the fifteenth square, by the time my audience had read the other squares they felt obliged to throw me a coin. So the money continued to pour into my cupped hands and the embarrassment—the feeling that I was a beggar on a street corner—passed.

After two hours I had fifty-three dollars and thirty cents.

I composed a menu in my mind. I wanted a bowl of steaming chicken and sweetcorn soup that didn't come from a can, and a plate full of battered fish and chips soaked in vinegar. I would finish with a punnet of chocolate-dipped strawberries and a tall glass of iced tea. Maybe even a bag of hot, roasted nuts.

Bree was right. This moneymaking thing was easy.

The sky was starting to fade out and the flow had eventually slowed; everyone was zipped into jackets with their briefcases and handbags swinging and the line for the bus was long. I was still hungry, but past the point of fantasising over a three-course meal. I was reluctant to leave.

It took about half an hour to walk home. *Home.* How quickly I'd got used to the idea that a rat-infested squat on the cockroach side of town was home. I bought a soggy hotdog from a vendor in the mall and chewed it without really enjoying it.

What's a hotdog made of? I asked Vivienne, once.

Pig, chook, lots of parts, she said.

Which parts?

Lips, beaks and arseholes, she replied.

I smiled to myself. It only lasted a few seconds, but I was conscious that I had dredged up a memory of her and it hadn't torn me apart.

I drank from a tap in somebody's front yard to get rid of the taste and rinsed my hands.

The others were already at the squat, except Silence and Bree. The kitchen was warm and buzzing and the usual fare was spread out over the door-table: chips and loaves of bread, cans of soft drink and a huge bottle of tomato sauce.

'Darcy's got laundry tomorrow,' Arden said. 'Make sure all your dirty clothes are in the bag.'

Darcy whooped and looked around with a smug expression.

'It's my turn,' Carrie said half-heartedly, through a mouthful of chips.

'Close your mouth when you chew. You look like a cow,' Arden snapped.

Joe pulled up a crate and gestured for me to sit down. He offered a bag of chips.

I shook my head.

Arden draped herself over Malik, lifted his T-shirt and dipped a finger into his belly button. He looked like he was enjoying himself until she pressed too hard and he doubled over.

'Did you check out the car?' Arden asked him.

'Yeah,' he said. 'Too easy.' He grabbed her and tried to kiss her but she shrugged him off.

'The plates?'

Malik grunted and tried again.

'You okay?' Joe said to me. He offered a slightly bruised pear and I took it.

'I'm okay. Have you seen Silence?' I bit into the pear. It was overripe and too soft, but it tasted like an orchard in my mouth.

'I think he and Bree are picking up some stuff,' he said. 'Arden's talking about moving. We've been here too long already.'

'Where will you go?'

Joe shrugged. 'If she knows, she's not telling. She's pretty good at finding places nobody else wants.'

My pulse was jumpy. I could feel it throbbing in my neck, flickering behind my left eye. When one door closes, another was supposed to open, wasn't it? Fifty bucks wouldn't get me far. I'd just got used to the idea of hanging around for a while.

'Oh,' I said. 'I might be moving on too.'

Joe's head swivelled. 'Hey, you're coming with us, aren't you?'

I didn't get to answer.

Bree and Silence came up through the cellar door. Bree handed a green shopping bag to Arden.

Silence trudged in behind her like a world-weary traveller. He leaned over and planted a kiss on my cheek, then, as if he'd realised he needed to downplay the moment, he did the same to Joe.

Joe wiped the kiss off with his sleeve.

'Silence loves Friday,' Carrie sang. 'Silence has a girl-friend,' she broke into chorus. Then she clutched her heart. 'I'm so sorry, Darce. You must be devastated.'

Darcy spat, 'Dream on, Carrie.'

'No,' Carrie said. 'If I was dreaming I'd be on a plane to Majorca and they wouldn't find your body.'

'Up yours.'

'It's not like that,' I said. I knew I sounded defensive.

Arden stalked me with her cat-eyes. *What is it like, then?* I read in her expression. She put her hand under Malik's T-shirt, rubbed slow circles on his chest, then moved it further down.

God, why does she do that? I thought.

Nobody else seemed to notice.

I wanted to react, to tell her it bothered me, that I believed sex belonged in the bedroom behind a closed door. Or to tell her that it didn't bother me at all, that I wasn't shocked or embarrassed. But I didn't really know how I felt. I just knew we were playing a game, and I was losing, because I didn't understand the rules. So I looked away.

Silence seemed tired, sad. He went upstairs.

I watched him go and ignored the urge to go after him. I didn't want to run, not with Arden watching. My skin was hot and prickly so I asked Joe for another pear.

'Sorry,' Carrie said to nobody in particular. She started clearing up leftover food, scraping chips and crusts into a plastic bag.

'What did I miss?' Bree asked.

'Nothing,' I mumbled. I risked a glance.

Malik was smirking at me, eyes heavy-lidded, while Arden's hand moved in his jeans.

I couldn't stand it. I ran to the bedroom and threw myself on the mattress. Arden's dirty laughter followed and my head ached. The blanket that Silence had given me was infused with dust and made me itchy all over.

I put my arm over my face and tried to imagine it was dark. I fantasised about stinging hot water in a bathtub so deep my shoulders and knees were under at the same time. I wanted to hitch out of the city and pick up where Vivienne and I had left off, in a town with salty air. I'd lie about my age and pull beers in the day; in the evenings I'd sit on a beach and drink glasses of wine and wait for morning. Maybe, while I was sitting there, I'd meet a guy. I'd smile and he would sit next to me and we'd wait for morning together. Or we'd sleep tangled and he'd wake first and brush sand off my face. He wouldn't care that I'd never wear a dress. He'd be all mine, not somebody else's, and he'd never have to sneak away before morning.

I felt myself slipping and jerked awake.

Outside, light was fading and streetlights were coming on. A piece of newspaper was peeling away from the window. Through the triangle, I saw the silhouette of a woman on the second floor across the street. She lifted a child above her head; she pulled him close to her chest. They were a two-headed creature. Together, entwined.

The black hole was sucking me in. Was this what Vivienne felt, those times she whispered that we were leaving? Was it her way of fending off the notion that nothing would ever be good again?

This was my inheritance—forever chasing stars.

'You okay?' Bree asked from the doorway.

Compassion was the worst thing to offer to someone like me.

'Yes,' I barked, and she went away.

Chapter Eleven

Our big adventure began at nine o'clock that night.

I'd fallen asleep, curled up with the blanket over my face, only waking when the sense of someone watching burned through my oblivion.

'Get ready,' Arden said. 'Put something warm on. It's cold out.'

In the kitchen, Bree sat by herself. She looked lost—not her usual smiling self.

Carrie kept cleaning dishes as if world order was at stake if she didn't get the mugs lined up for morning. I saw Silence on the stairs, briefly, before Arden dragged me away. We went down into the cellar.

'Where are we going?' I asked.

'Consider it part of your induction,' she said.

I followed, doubling my steps to keep up with her.

A few streets from the squat, Arden hailed a taxi. She sat right next to me in the back and I felt the push-pull force of her. She was reining her emotions in, keeping them close. She pinned her hands between her knees and stared straight ahead through the windscreen. She wore dark-denim jeans, her customary trench coat and high, thick-soled boots laced up to her knees. Her dreads were stuffed under a black beanie.

'You look like a member of the IRA,' I said, immediately wishing I could take it back. My stomach churned.

'You look like you're about to puke,' she said. Then she had one of her moments of light and grabbed my hand. She rubbed circles with her thumb on my palm, studying my fingers. She aligned her hand against mine and compared them, her fingers so long and thin they overshot mine by a couple of centimetres.

'You're like a doll,' she said. 'I saw a movie once where these tiny people lived inside a house with normal-sized people. They hid in the walls and they only came out at night, or when the others were sleeping.' She released my hand and breathed on the window. *Hah.* She drew a series of connected stick people in the condensation.

'Sounds like a kids' movie. *The Borrowers*?' I remembered the old movies Vivienne and I used to watch to get to sleep.

'No, it was weird. More like a horror movie. I can't remember what it was called. My parents were watching in the lounge room and I sneaked out of my room and hid behind the couch. I was about seven, I think.'

'*Chucky*?'

'Nope. Whatever it was I'll never forget how those tiny people fucked up all the big people's lives. And I got the biggest arse-kicking for sneaking out of bed.'

'I hope the little people won,' I said.

'Left here,' she told the driver.

'Why the taxi? Is it far? Where are we going?'

'Soon,' she said.

'Arden? That tattoo on your back. What does it mean?'

'It means what it says.' Her expression was blank and her fingers drummed a beat on the seat. 'Next right.' She nailed a thought and shared it. 'Just so you know, if you hurt any one of my kids I'll destroy you.'

'Why would I hurt anyone? How could I?' I said weakly.

'Because you're not committed. I can tell. You have one foot already out the door. We stick together.'

'I'm just trying to figure out how I fit in.'

'Just stay or go, it's that simple. You won't survive in the city alone. I think you know that. You're not street. We have each other's backs, but you're not watching anybody's back but your own, are you?'

I knew there was some truth in what she was saying, but it all seemed like badass, B-grade, homegirl hokum to me.

I sniggered.

Arden's hand whipped out and smacked the back of my head.

'Hey . . . ?' Anger flared but I copped the smack, rubbed my head and slid down in my seat.

'Here's your chance. Prove yourself, country girl, and you can make your own mind up if you want to stay or go. Otherwise, I'll decide for you.'

Arden got the taxi to pull up at the top of a wide, well-lit street. She gave the driver a fifty, waited for the change and told me to get out.

I stood in the milky glow of a streetlight and wondered where we were. Bugs swarmed around the light and I could see my breath in crystals. The houses were large, set well back from the road in leafy gardens. Most had high fences and wrought-iron gates. Warm yellow light spilled from several windows and the air was pungent with the smell of spring flowers. I felt like the little match girl, standing half-frozen in the dark while the families inside were toasty and warm.

'Come on,' said Arden. She strode off, shoulders square, hands dug deep in her pockets. Rage was so close under her skin, she seemed untouchable.

I followed.

She led me past four or five houses before she decided on one. She slowed outside a red-brick two-storey house that looked like it had been transported from a southern plantation. Lanky white columns flanked the entrance and a driveway bordered with a low hedge curved like a sad mouth at the front. Two rooms were lit downstairs.

She paced past the house once, twice, and cocked her head, listening, while I waited in the shadows.

'I like this one,' she said.

'I'm not going any further until you tell me why we're here,' I hissed.

She seemed to look right at me but a space beyond held her focus.

The situation slid out of my control.

'See that pillar at the end, under the tree? I'll give you a leg-up. It looks like that tree joins with the other one, the big one, see?' She pointed, running her finger along with one eye squinted. 'That big one has a branch that runs parallel to the ground. If you stay on that branch the sensor lights shouldn't come on. You'll be able to reach the roof, so you can drop down and climb up past the window on the right. The one with the blinds open. Okay?'

Blood throbbed in my ears. Arden sounded like she was speaking underwater.

'What . . . ?'

'Go over the top of the roof and straight down the other side. Look for the smallest window.' She held her hands about forty centimetres apart. 'Bathroom windows are never locked. Go in head first, not feet, or you'll get stuck.'

'I . . .'

'Listen. This is your chance. Prove yourself.'

'This is a *test*?'

'We've all done it. Bring me something pretty.' She drew a band around her ringless finger.

'You want me to break in? To *steal* something . . .'

'Keep your voice down,' she muttered. 'Go for the main bedroom. '

'I can't . . .'

'If you say can't, you can't.' She looked me over and found me lacking.

'What if an alarm goes off?'

'Abort.'

'But there are lights on. What if there's somebody home?'

'There's nobody home. No cars.'

'But what if . . . ?'

'Don't worry. I wouldn't send you in there if I didn't think you could do it. I've got your back,' she said and gave me that drilling stare.

I knew she meant it. And some pathetic part of me wanted to win her favour because she seemed to have all the answers. I wanted to ask her questions I would have asked Vivienne. Arden was the strongest, most real thing I had.

'Okay,' I said.

She cupped my face with her cold hands and kissed me gently on the lips.

I froze, stunned. Her lips pulsed with warmth and life when I expected more ice. It wasn't attraction I felt, but a connection that ran deep like she'd plugged into a socket in my brain and we were both lit up from the same energy source. I would have done anything for her.

It was in this fog of invincibility that I strode to the brick pillar and braced my hands on the top. I bent my leg back in an L-shape and Arden hoisted my featherweight easily. I sat on top of the pillar and unlaced my boots.

'What are you doing?'

'I can't climb with these on,' I said. 'I need to feel under my feet.'

I kicked off the boots and swung my leg over a branch that bowed dangerously under my weight. I shuffled along, legs wrapped around it like I was straddling a horse. It levered me up and levelled out as I crawled closer to the main trunk of the tree. Leaves brushed my face and a bird fluttered out of reach. I heard the intake of my own breath each time my foot slipped on the smooth bark—but I never really believed that I'd fall.

Arden was below.

I crossed over to the next tree, the biggest. There, I needed to go up, not just across. There were no decent footholds and I had to perform the monkey-bar swing with my hands.

I felt at ease; all my doubts were without substance and my fear had gone. There was only exhilaration. It gave me extra strength and when I reached the roof of the house, I was smiling, warm, out of breath.

I was grace. I was in control. I was . . . alone.

When I looked down, Arden had disappeared.

I jumped. The gutter groaned under my weight as I pulled myself up onto the sloping roof. The tiles were dry. Yellow lichen gave me traction as I clambered up and over the pitch.

There were two small windows on the other side. Mentally, I measured the opening of the closest one. I decided that my body and hips would fit, but my shoulders could pose a problem.

Head first, Arden had said.

I pushed the window and it opened without resistance. I put both feet through the opening and shuffled my hips. Once I was halfway through, I saw what she meant. My back was arched to breaking point. I had no force of my own, only gravity to keep me moving. With my arms above my head I was wedged half in, half out. The sharp edge of the window frame sliced my back. Sweat formed an icy layer on my skin.

Shit.

Through sheer will, spurred on by the threat of spending the night there, I pressed my shoulder blades together and wiggled them through the space. Near dislocation, my bones stretched the muscles past a point they'd never been before.

I gasped as I slid through, whacked my head on the sill, caught my wrists on the bottom of the window and landed with one foot in toilet water.

The seat was up. I put it down and sat there for a minute until my muscles stopped screaming. Muddy blue puddles pooled on the white tiles as I made my way to the door. I closed it quietly behind me.

I was in a hallway. My feet sank into plush carpet. I could just make out the shape of a doorway in the dark. I turned the handle and felt around for a light switch but I couldn't find one. I took a few steps, hit my shin against something hard and toppled onto a bed.

When my eyes adjusted, I could make out a tall dresser, side tables, the bed. The room smelled of expensive perfume and furniture polish.

I slid open the first drawer of the dresser. My fingers found satin and lace. I closed it and ran my hands along the top. Glass bottles clinked together and fell. I set them upright and opened the second drawer. There, I found the unmistakable shape of a jewellery box. It was unlocked, half open and spilling over with trinkets.

The first one I touched was heavy, so I figured it was only cheap costume jewellery. I didn't want to take anything valuable. I yanked and it started a chain reaction; one by one, other necklaces caught and dragged and slithered into a pile on the floor. I ripped the heavy necklace free, scooped the rest up and stuffed them back into the box.

I tried to leave the room as I found it. I smoothed over the creases on the bed and buffed the dresser's knobs with my T-shirt. In the hallway, I fumbled for the toilet door and turned the handle.

It wasn't the toilet. It was a bedroom. The faint glow of streetlights bled through the slats of the blinds and I could see a bed. And a person on the bed. Faint music came from his headphones. He was lying there, naked to the waist, wearing only a pair of jeans. His eyes were closed. One leg was crossed over the other and one foot tapped. His chest rose and fell evenly while my lungs were plunging and sucking like bellows.

I knew who had left the toilet seat up.

He opened his eyes.

We exchanged a look like a shooting star—brief, intense, over.

I ran for it.

My feet skidded sideways on the wet floor and my legs went out from under me. I landed hard on my backside, flung out my arm, slammed the toilet door and locked it. I scrambled for grip like a dog on a linoleum floor—pedalling hard and going nowhere, leaving half-moon turtle tracks in the slush. I twisted and landed on both elbows, yelping. If I hadn't been so scared I would have laughed at my clumsiness.

I stood slowly. *Breathe. Think.*

The door handle moved one sinister rotation before he must have realised I'd locked it. He didn't jiggle it. His composure made me more terrified. I backed up slowly and wound the necklace around my fist.

What do you do when you open your eyes and see a barefoot intruder standing in your doorway? He should have yelled or reacted, shouldn't he? Weird. I thought maybe he was priming for a run-up. *What if he had a key?*

I stood on the toilet seat and managed to crawl back through the window, even though my arms and legs were jelly.

Out on the roof, I was exposed, caught in the million-watt

glare from the floodlights next door. Half blind, I tried to climb back over the top of the roof without rolling off.

Getting back onto the tree was a hit-and-miss affair. *Miss* when I swung my leg over the branch and slipped, *hit* when it flung back and smacked my face. My eyes watered and my lip swelled.

Where the *hell* was Arden?

I was about two metres away from the fence when the porch light came on. I risked a glance back.

The guy was standing there, scratching his head. He'd taken the time to put on a shirt. He looked stunned.

I vaulted onto the footpath and took cover behind a bush.

'Jesus. What happened to you?' Arden said, emerging from the shadows.

I jumped. 'There's someone home,' I whispered. 'Go! Just *go*!'

Arden laughed and followed when I ran off. She overtook me without even trying, boots clomping. She was gasping for breath and holding her side. It was only when we eased up and stopped about three blocks away from the house that I realised she was laughing.

I had left my boots standing on the brick pillar. Like bloody Cinderella.

Arden put her arm around me and drew me close. She prised my fingers apart and extracted the necklace. In the light it was hideous—a garish mix of blood-coloured stones set in cheap, chipped silver. A heavy silver crucifix dangled in the centre.

I massaged my palm. The shape of the cross was imprinted on it.

Arden stroked the stones, then slipped the necklace over her head. She tucked the cross between her breasts.

I knew it was the thievery, not the bounty, that pleased her. But when she kissed my forehead and wrapped her trench coat around my shaking shoulders, I decided that guilt was a small price.

I was back, safe, under her wing.

Chapter Twelve

The next morning, my boots were sitting at the foot of my mattress as if they'd walked home all by themselves.

I sat up. Looked around. Was it a joke? Did Arden go back to get them?

Carrie snored softly. Bree was lying on her back with her arms folded under her head, coat-hanger style, smoking her breakfast cigarette.

'You'll burn this place down,' I said.

'Pfft,' she said and flicked her ash onto the floor. 'Where did you and Arden go last night?'

I ignored her, sat up and stretched my aching body.

'What happened to your face?'

I touched my swollen lip. Overnight, it had split and I could taste dried blood. I catalogued my other wounds: scratches on my arms, a throbbing tailbone, a scrape on my upper back. Raw and sore all over.

'Reconnaissance and retrieval mission.' I shrugged. The boots sat there like an accusation.

'You don't have to be like the rest of us,' Bree said in a serious tone.

'I don't know what you're talking about.'

'Yes, you do.' She lit another cigarette. 'Welcome to the Dark Side.'

I cupped my hands over my mouth and gave my best impression of Darth Vader breath.

Bree smiled and cocked an eyebrow. 'What's that?'

First *Peter Pan*, then *Star Wars*. Maybe my upbringing wasn't as culturally barren as I thought.

'Shut up or get out,' Carrie grumbled and rolled over.

Bree went downstairs first.

I pulled on my jeans and a T-shirt and followed. The guilt and fear of the night before was still stuck to my skin. I could hear Arden laughing in the kitchen.

'How did my boo . . .' I started.

It was obvious now that my boots didn't get there by themselves.

The guy was there. The bare-chested guy from the house. The bare-chested guy from the house I broke into, and stole from. He was so tall he made everything around him look like dollhouse furniture. Elbows and angles stuck out as if he'd only ever grown up, but not out. He was pale, dark-haired and unremarkable, sipping coffee from Arden's mug like he belonged there.

Arden was relaxed, sitting cross-legged on a crate.

Bree was smiling a lot and refilled his coffee without being asked.

Darcy sat on the floor with her knees up to her chest, one arm wrapped around them. For once, she kept her nasty looks to herself.

'You're a girl,' the guy said and stared at me.

I crossed my arms over my braless front, shoved my hands into my pockets, then folded them back over my chest. I didn't know what to do with them. They felt like leftovers, or an untucked shirt. Had he called the police? Is that why he was there?

'I was asking Arden who the boy in my room was last night. Except you're not a boy.'

'Obviously,' I snapped.

Arden laughed. There was something deeply satisfied about that laugh.

'I didn't think you'd be there,' she said to him. There was no apology in her tone. 'I didn't know you were back.'

He leaned forwards on his elbows. 'How about you tell me next time you want to break in and I'll save you the trouble by opening the front door,' he said.

They knew each other. My skin prickled. I covered my confusion by making myself a coffee and, when I'd recovered, I sat down at the table. 'Who's he?' I blurted.

'Wish,' he said carefully. 'Who are you?'

'Friday,' Bree answered for me. 'She's new.'

'Wish. What kind of a name is that?' I said.

Wish smiled. His face changed from unremarkable to miraculous.

I smiled back as if he'd tapped a reflex. He could have been a set mousetrap and I'd still have reached out and touched him to see how he felt. How do you go from ordinary to fascinating with one lopsided smile? Then he opened his mouth and I was annoyed all over again.

'Friday. That's a boy's name, isn't it?'

'It's good to see you,' Arden interrupted. 'I've missed you.'

I looked around for Malik. There was an invisible, twanging cord between Wish and Arden. I wondered if Malik knew; he didn't seem the type to share.

'I've missed you, too,' Darcy said. 'Are you coming back or what?'

'No, he's not,' Arden snapped. 'He has a higher purpose now.'

'I'm over eighteen,' Wish said softly. 'The rules have changed.'

'Your rules or theirs?' Arden said.

'Both.'

Arden nodded. She spread her fingers. 'I know, I know.'

I put my hand up. 'I have some questions. Like, why did you ask me to break into his house when you could have knocked on the front door?'

'That's no fun,' Arden said, laughing.

Wish looked at me and leaned across the table. 'I have a question for you, too,' he said. 'Did you ice this?' He touched my split lip with his finger.

In my head I was whispering, *No, no, no. He's going to touch me like that, then disappear.*

My mouth said, 'My real name is Liliane.' Infantile. Forgettable.

'Nobody cares who you really are.' Darcy got up, dusted off her pants and stormed out.

She pushed past Silence, who hovered on the bottom step. He was brushing his teeth, lounging in the doorway, drooling foam all down the front of his hoodie. Still gripping his toothbrush in his cheek, he walked over to Wish. They bumped fists. He turned to spit in the sink.

'How's it hanging, buddy?' Wish said. 'It's been a while.'

Silence asked a question using his finger-puppet language.

Wish obviously got it. 'No, I'm not back. I just came to retrieve something.' He gave Arden a hard look. 'I know she took something for you.'

'So?' Arden shrugged. 'It's just junk. Nothing special.'

'And where's the fascist bully-boy?' Wish stood and looked around. His mouth twisted.

Arden drew herself up to her full height. She was still a few centimetres shorter. They faced off.

'I need to talk to you. Privately.' She headed up the stairs and beckoned for Wish to follow. 'Don't worry. Malik's not here.'

He followed.

There was a bad brew of emotion in my belly. I watched them walk upstairs and in a sad part of my mind I imagined them, entwined, on Arden's mattress.

It was their business, not mine. There was no valid reason for me to feel sick about it.

Silence gave me a smile and busied himself making breakfast. He and Bree exchanged a loaded look.

I needed air. I went down into the cellar and slipped outside.

Darcy was there, poking a stick into the soupy surface of the pond, fishing out dripping strands of slime.

The pond gave me the heebies, so I went the long way around it, through the tall grass.

Darcy barely noticed.

I exited the trapdoor and sat out in the alley with my knees to my chest. *Time to go, Liliane Brown*, I heard in my heart. A breeze whipped through the tunnel, out of nowhere. It sent leaves tumbling.

I don't believe in ghosts. I don't believe that Vivienne is still here in another form. I don't.

A leaf floated up and landed in my hair. It was perfect, still green, fallen too soon.

Darcy came through the trapdoor about ten minutes later. She sashayed off on high heels, swinging a strappy handbag as if she was on her way to a garden party and I wasn't even there. Suddenly she stopped side-on and looked back. There were several bald patches on her scalp the size of dollar coins.

'You don't belong here with us,' she said.

'Don't I know it.' Under my breath.

'Just go, why don't you?'

'Am I such a threat to you, Darcy?' I stood up and brushed dead leaves off my backside. I tried to keep my cool and not look like I was completely without gumption at the same time. What I really wanted to do was rip some more of her hair out.

'Don't flatter yourself. You're no threat.' She started pulling at her own hair.

'If you hadn't taken my money I would have gone by now,' I said.

'What money? I don't need your money. I have wads of the stuff.'

'And how do you get it, huh?' I stuck my tongue in my cheek and poked it in and out. It made a disgusting, sucking sound. I wasn't proud of myself.

She tossed her bag onto the ground and stalked towards

me. 'You're a real bitch under that little-girl-lost act, aren't you?'

'You started it.' I planted my feet and braced for impact. In her heels she stood a head taller. I was braless, shoeless and thinking about someone else.

As if I'd summoned him, Wish ducked through the trapdoor.

I forgot all about Darcy—I looked at his mouth, searching for a sign that he'd been kissed.

Darcy's expression erased itself. She smiled and toed the dirt.

I tried to stay calm, but I snorted. I leaned against the fence, slid down and started laughing. I had to hold my side because it hurt; it was giving me a stitch to laugh that hard. I couldn't seem to stop.

Wish and Darcy gawked.

Wish's mouth twitched. He picked up Darcy's bag and handed it to her.

'What's so hilarious?' he asked.

I couldn't answer. I had no rational thought left in my head.

Of all my beginnings, this was the worst. Even if I could delete the part where he thought I was a boy, and the part where I left my boots standing on his fencepost, I'd still be left with this:

I am Friday Brown. I buried my mother. I ran away from a man who buried a swimming pool. A boy who can't speak has adopted me. A girl kissed me. I broke and entered. Now I'm fantasising about a guy who's a victim of crime and I am the criminal. I'm going nowhere and every minute

I'm not moving, I'm being tailgated by a curse that may or may not be real. They call me Friday. It has been foretold that on a Saturday, I will drown . . .

'She's a lunatic,' Darcy said and tapped her head with a finger. 'We're supposed to be quiet. Shut up, you *freak*.' Her bald patches looked like the crop circles in the backyard.

The thought set me off again. My face ached. I was near tears.

'Oh, God, make it stop,' she threw over her shoulder as she stalked away.

Wish walked with Darcy to the end of the alley. He kept looking back at me like I was a car crash—but he was smiling.

The odd thing was, while Darcy and I were squaring off and spitting venom, all I could think was that finally I felt something. I was alive. And when that laugh came up in my throat, it was downright confounding. I could feel myself coming back, like a ghost materialising, absorbing others' energy. Maybe I was the one who was see-through.

And Wish. His touch. Seeds of obsession. I was Vivienne's daughter to the core, and suddenly there were more reasons to stay than to leave.

I spent the afternoon with Silence.

He took me to a hostel where they let me have a three-minute tepid shower. I used shampoo that left me feeling itchy and smelling like a toilet-block air freshener. We wandered the streets and shared lunch in the park. Our conversation was easy, if a little one-sided. He made me laugh some more, and whenever I laughed, I could feel the million criss-cross cuts on my soul starting to heal.

On the floor of a gazebo in a memorial rose garden, I drew the shape of a snail's shell and decorated it with stones and flowers.

There were no coins, but Silence watched and clapped when it was finished.

In Silence's secret garden, I showed him how to climb, how he had to plot his ascent like advance moves in a chess game—one foot in the wrong place could ruin your whole strategy and the descent could get scary. Up high in a tree, we dropped prickly pods on people strolling underneath; I hung upside down with my legs hooked over a branch and made enough noise for us both. Later we ate ice cream in a paddleboat and I barely thought about the void underneath. I could swim, after all. Like a goddamn fish. Even *with* boots on.

At one point I caught Silence staring. He was looking at me like I was something precious he'd found.

I'd missed being looked at that way.

Chapter Thirteen

The next night, Arden was behaving badly. She couldn't sit still and a few drinks didn't calm her down either. She found something to criticise in everyone, even AiAi, who couldn't be offensive if he tried. At ten o'clock she banished AiAi to bed and informed Bree that she was babysitting. She told the rest of us to get changed.

'We're going out,' she said. 'Arden needs to party.'

'Shit,' Joe said to me. 'When she talks about herself in the third person like that, look out.'

Darcy rolled her eyes and bolted upstairs to use the bathroom first.

I was wondering what to wear, but then I was offered a public makeover, courtesy of Carrie. She made me sit on the kitchen counter while she did my make-up. She ran her fingers through what was left of my hair, using a handful of stuff that looked like congealed fat. She worked carefully on my face while Silence watched. He looked worried.

After an eternity, Darcy emerged wearing red stilettos, an oversized leopard-print shirt and not much else. When I got to the bathroom I held up a small battery-powered lantern that we left standing in the hall. The mirror was covered in a sticky film of hairspray, but even the airbrushing didn't prepare me for how I looked.

There was nothing of me left. Everything belonged to someone else. I was an alien with Cleopatra eyes. Two blue glitter teardrops dripped beneath my left eye and I had a slick, pale blue mouth. My hair had been pressed into a lopsided Mohawk that curled like a frozen wave.

When I went back downstairs, Arden looked me over. 'Darcy, give her your silver dress,' she ordered.

'No way. She's not having any of my stuff.'

'No, thanks,' I said.

'Darce. Pretty please. Help the androgynoid look like a girl,' Arden pleaded. 'You can have extra drink money.'

Darcy reluctantly handed over a shimmering, knee-length dress that, paired with my boots, completed the look I wasn't after. I waited for the others, standing so the dress didn't crease. No expression, so my face wouldn't crack. My skin felt set in concrete.

The club was underground. Entry was down a steep flight of steps, past a bouncer with overblown biceps, through double doors with handles the shape of a crucifix. The bouncer had yellow plugs stuffed in his ears. Music louder than anything I'd ever heard before was pumping out into the night. The whole building had its own pulse. *Bam, bam, bam.* I pressed my hand against the wall and the beat passed through me like a kick from a cattle prod. A neon sign wrote itself in molten, red-lava letters, then erased and started again—*Le Freak*.

'You're going to love it,' Joe reassured me. 'It's party time, it's Saturday, all the freaks come out to play,' he sang to the tune of *It's raining, it's pouring*. He had his usual bib 'n' brace pants on, but he'd gone all out with a tight, purple shirt.

Freak, all right. When we left the squat I felt like a walking corpse, dressed up for Halloween. But I fitted right in. In fact, I was less freaky than the other Halloween characters lining up outside. I tried not to stare.

Arden wore spiked heels and skintight Lycra pants. Her dreads were twisted into a knot on top of her head and she had fake eyelashes with miniature peacock feathers on the ends. She looked like a Vegas showgirl. Slow blinks kept the eyelashes from falling off. It made her look sleepy.

Arden drew a line down the bouncer's chest with her nail and batted her peacock-eyes at him.

Carrie went first, pumping her fist in the air. Darcy looked underage—for that matter, so did I—but the bouncer just held the door open and let us in.

'God, it's been forever since we went out,' Carrie said. She barged through a crowd of people lining the corridor. 'Coming through. Scuzi. Beep, beep. Fuckin' *mooove*. Carrie needs a drink.' She stopped by a kissing couple and yelled, 'Get a *snorkel*!'

Darcy had been practising her model-walk. Instead of sophistication, she managed to pull off the little-girl-dressed-in-mummy's-clothes look. She had to keep tugging her shirt down so it covered her backside. Most of her patchy hair was tucked under a red beret.

'What do you want to drink?' Carrie yelled.

'Beer,' I said. It was the easiest to say over the noise.

Arden leaned over an iron balustrade and surveyed the action.

The dance floor was a sinkhole in the middle of the club. Two levels of bars and standing room surrounded it. Nobody appeared to be dancing, even the people on the floor. There was a lot of writhing and jumping and fist-pumping, but not dancing. Not the kind I was used to anyway.

Carrie came back without the beer. She had a holder with plastic test tubes lined up. They were filled to the top with purple goop and I imagined they were giving off toxic gas.

'Here.' She handed me one. 'Heart-starter. Clear!' She threw her head back and the goop glugged down her throat.

Arden did the same and took another. She dropped the empty tube over the balustrade into the crowd below.

'What is this stuff?'

'Just drink it,' Arden challenged. She spotted Malik coming towards us and turned away, her mouth tight. She said something I couldn't make out and strode off.

Carrie pulled me by the elbow. 'Come on. Trouble in paradise,' she said in my ear.

Silence and Joe commandeered a booth. The table was covered with stacks of empty plastic cups and sticky rings. I slid in next to Silence. Something cold and wet seeped through the back of Darcy's dress.

Are you going to drink that? Silence mimed, pointing to my test tube.

I shook my head and handed it to him.

Carrie and Darcy followed Arden down to the dance floor. Joe started talking to a guy who seemed to want to smell his shirt and after a few minutes of flirting they edged off in the direction of the exit.

Silence wasn't into it. He slouched down in his seat and polished off the remaining tubes, one by one. There seemed no point trying to have a conversation with him and I didn't feel like drinking.

'I'm going to the toilet,' I told him.

He shrugged.

'What's wrong with you?'

He flicked his hand.

'Is it me? Is it because I broke into your friend's house? Arden didn't say she knew him. I didn't know.'

Silence turned suddenly and raised his hand.

I jerked back, but he was only reaching out to pick at the glitter teardrop on my cheek.

He peeled it away, rolled it into a ball and dropped it into an empty tube.

'You don't like my new look?'

He answered by ruffling my hair viciously. The wave came crashing down.

'Is that better? Are you happy now?'

He looked so serious. There were dark smudges under his eyes like bruises. That he couldn't talk was one thing— that he didn't want to was another.

I felt stung and bored and sober. I had that homesick feeling that I remembered from sleepovers: waking up in the night and wanting your mother more than anything—far, far more than you wanted to be that kid who doesn't make their parent come and get them in the middle of the night.

I got up and weaved through clusters of people. It reeked

in there. Sweat and too many clashing layers of aftershave and perfume.

The toilet wasn't any better. I waited for ten minutes in a line that went almost back to the bar, going nowhere, until I realised that girls were pushing in at the front. When I finally made it to a cubicle I stood in toilet water that wasn't in the toilet and reached for paper that wasn't there.

If this was Arden's idea of fun she could keep it.

I heard Carrie over the jabber of girls. 'Comin' through. Gotta spew.' The door next to me slammed.

I washed my hands and waited.

When she came out, Carrie was smiling. 'Thanks, ladies,' she said.

'Are you sick? Do you want to leave?' I asked.

'Course I'm not sick,' she laughed. The girls waiting in line glared. She put two fingers down her throat and did a fake retch. 'Oh, yuck. I didn't wash my hands. Come on. You're missing the show.'

'What show?'

'The Arden and Malik show.'

Arden was up on a podium. She was swinging around a pole that might have been for dancing, or a prop to hold the sagging ceiling above the stage. She'd lost her jacket and her peacock eyelashes were gone, too. There was something wrong with her. Her movements were graceless and jerky, like a puppet's. Her jaw was slack but the tendons in her neck were rigid.

She smacked a kiss onto the unsuspecting DJ and bowed. The crowd in the sinkhole cheered and clapped.

Malik appeared at the foot of the podium and tried to

grab Arden by the foot. She lashed out at him with her spiked heels.

'Jesus. What was in those shooters?' I shouted.

'Just booze. I think she needed to let herself go tonight.' Carrie yelled back.

'Does she do that often?'

Carrie shook her head. 'It was probably seeing Wish again.'

'What do you mean?' I asked but she didn't answer.

Malik was getting aggressive, trying to capture Arden and reel her in by the hem of her pants. As the crowd pushed and pressed up against the podium he started swinging his fists. The crowd fell back. A bouncer said something in Malik's ear and hauled him off in a stranglehold.

Arden gave the bouncer the thumbs-up and continued dancing.

'It's going to be a long night,' Carrie said and headed off back to the bar.

'I'm going to get some air,' I shouted after her, but she didn't hear. I stumbled out.

Chapter Fourteen

In the dark side street I gulped cold, night air. I looked left, right, chose left, and walked a little way past a stinking bin and two men, walking and smoking.

'Sweetheart,' called one of them wearing an unbuttoned white shirt.

'Leave her,' said the other, gripping a bottle.

White Shirt unzipped his jeans and took a piss, right there, in plain view.

I passed an alley, the Jack the Ripper kind, complete with dripping gutters and chimneys coiling steam. I could just make out a couple, kissing, up against a wall. A maybe purple shirt with puffy sleeves. *Joe getting lucky?* I thought and smiled. I was tired in my bones and my head was still thumping with the echoes of bass.

The two men weren't far behind me, so I sped up. Ahead, there was a main street with more lights and more people. My blood was pumping so hard I couldn't feel the cold, except in my fingertips.

I checked behind me but the guys had disappeared.

In the distance, laughter, and in that laughter, hate.

I stopped. It went quiet—the kind of quiet that comes before disaster.

A guy hobbled out of the alley clutching his stomach, half fell, recovered and started running.

'Joe?' I called. 'Is that you, Joe?' My voice sounded wobbly and uncertain. 'Are you there?'

There was a yelp. A crunching thud, like the sound of an animal hitting a bull bar. Another. More laughter and breaking glass.

'Joe!' I yelled.

I ran past the opening to the alley because I couldn't bear to look or hear any more.

'Can you help?' I pleaded with the bouncer but he just opened the door like an automaton, earplugs jammed in tight.

It felt like forever until I found Carrie, long minutes wasted scanning the writhing crowd when I could have—should have—done something to help Joe while I was right there.

Carrie was dancing by herself, waving her arms around like a washing machine, clearing a space around her.

'It's Joe,' I gasped. 'Outside. Guys in the alley.'

'Cool,' Carrie said vaguely. 'Joe likes guys.'

'No, they're beating him up!' My words couldn't get out fast enough, tripping over one another. 'Other guys. Not the one he was kissing. We have to help him.'

'Oh, shit,' Carrie said and lunged off towards the toilets. 'Find Darcy and Silence,' she said but I followed her, pushing through the line-up.

Carrie yelled, 'Arden! Come out. We need you. Where's Malik?'

'Gone,' Arden called back in a dreamy voice. 'He started

123

swinging and got chucked out.' She sounded pleased with the outcome. 'I'm not finished partying. You guys go if you want. I'm having a good time.' She flushed and came out of the cubicle, still pulling up her pants. She staggered and caught herself by hanging on to the edge of a basin. She looked tall and dangerous in her heels. The girls in the line fell back.

'It's Joe. You've gotta come. Now.'

'What's wrong with Joe?'

'Some guys caught him doing a Brokeback Mountain against the wall outside. They've got him,' Carrie said.

Arden casually applied lipstick.

Carrie was aghast, waiting.

'They're hitting him,' I said. I was crying. 'We have to call the police.'

Arden looked at me with disgust and pushed me out of her way. She slipped off her shoes and carried them, broke into a sprint, elbowing people aside. Carrie and I followed. When she got to the double doors she slammed through, taking the bouncer by surprise. He grunted and stepped aside, then resumed his position, arms crossed and legs apart.

'Down there,' I pointed.

It was too late.

In the dark, Joe was a crumpled mess in the gutter, his arms curled around his legs as if he was still trying to fend off blows. His purple shirt was spattered with blood, his face puffy and grotesque. There had to be blood. After those sounds I heard there had to be lots of it, but the sight of it was still shocking.

'What did they look like?' Arden snapped.

124

'He needs an ambulance,' Carrie said.

Darcy and Silence turned up and stood nearby with their hands over their mouths.

I sat down in the gutter next to Joe. I touched his face. It was bursting, his eyes swollen shut and his lip split in two places. He groaned and when I lifted his shoulders he rolled his head into my lap.

'I'm a lover, not a fighter,' Joe said in a high voice and tried to smile.

'*What did they look like?*' Arden screamed.

'Big guy, white shirt and jeans. Another one with a bottle of bourbon. I don't really know. They'll be gone. We need to get him to a hospital,' I said dully.

'Stay with Joe,' Arden said to Carrie. To me, she said, 'You come with me.'

Reluctantly, I let Joe go. Carrie dipped her shirt into a puddle and started to clean his face. Her tenderness made me cry harder.

We paced the street. I searched the crowd. Arden watched me for any signs of recognition.

'Stop crying,' she said. 'Crying doesn't help Joe.'

'They're gone. I can't see them anywhere. They probably got in a cab.'

'Keep looking. Pigs like that always hang around to watch.'

She was right. They were sitting in a green car parked across the street. Eating kebabs. I could see Joe's blood on the big guy's white shirt. He held his fist up and inspected his knuckles. The other man laughed.

'That them?'

'Yes. I think so. What are you going to . . . ?'

But Arden was gone already, striding barefoot along the wet footpath, crossing the road, doubling back behind the car. She reached the rear bumper and leaned on it as she slipped on her stilettos.

I had my hands over my face, but I watched through my fingers.

Darcy flopped down next to me on the bench and tucked stray hair under her beret. She glanced at me and smirked at my expression.

Silence slipped up behind me in his ghostlike way. He touched my shoulder and raised his eyebrows.

'I don't know,' I said to his unspoken question. 'I can't watch.'

'Watch and learn, country girl,' Darcy said.

Arden climbed up on the boot of the car. Her weight made the rear end dip and the guys' heads whipped around. Her heels made terrible scraping sounds on the metal and I could imagine the shiny green paint grinding off under them. She levered herself up onto the roof and stood there like a warrior princess, hands on her hips.

Darcy, Silence and I climbed on the bench for a better view. People were stopping to look as word spread that something was happening.

Both guys got out of the car.

'Get down, you crazy bitch!' White Shirt yelled.

Arden ignored him. She danced. Tap dancing. Her heels left hailstone dents in the roof and each step was punctuated by a sound like a bullet hitting a tin can.

'Jesus, help me get her off!'

126

Darcy laughed and clapped, clearly still drunk.

Silence was transfixed and smiling, his bad mood forgotten.

I bit my lip, unsure what to do.

Arden tapped out her rhythm with her arms above her head like a flamenco dancer.

The two guys circled the car and reached across, snatching at the air, trying to grab her. One got a grip on Arden's ankle and she came down hard, passive. He reeled her in, dragging her down across the bonnet. Arden wound up and kicked out. *Riiip.* She caught his cheekbone with her heel and he let go. He fell backwards, hit the gutter and clawed at his face. Arden rolled off the bonnet like a stuntwoman and landed on her feet. She whipped off her shoes and went after the guy on the ground, swinging her stilettos. *Smack!* Another whack to his wounded face and he dropped again.

A growing crowd gathered around. Arden was outnumbered and they seemed content to watch.

White Shirt was livid. He stood, breathing hard, probably deciding how things would play out if he hit a girl.

Arden decided for him.

She took a low, fast run-up and swung her shoe in a looping arc that landed sweet under his chin. He clutched his throat with one hand and tried to hit her with the other. Missed. The motion carried through and he turned his back to her. Arden dropped her shoes and climbed aboard, legs wrapped around his waist in a death grip. She had one arm hooked around his neck and with the other she punched him, flat-fisted. *Whack, whack, whack.*

White Shirt howled, spinning around in a useless attempt

to shake her off. He beat at the back of her head, but she wouldn't let go. She had him and he knew it.

Silence pointed a finger past my nose. There was a police car pulling up, blue lights blinking, further down the street.

Arden saw it too.

Darcy yelled, 'Cops!' and the crowd started to break up.

Arden let go. She dismounted as if she'd broken a brumby; she picked up her shoes as if she'd just been for a walk along the beach.

'What the fuck?' said White Shirt, his face already swelling.

'You know what!' Arden yelled. She pointed at the blood on his shirt, probably more his than Joe's.

Her finger stayed there for a long time, a witch's bone that quivered ever so slightly. Then she loped off. Stopped. Dragged her heel along the side of the car, leaving a ragged silver scar in the paintwork.

I looked at Silence. I wasn't sure if the expression on his face was horror or admiration.

I felt awe. My heart was doing double time and my jaw was wired open. It's not that she was brave—she *was* brave—it was her conviction. The way she waded in and extracted revenge like that. It made me feel small. Not in size, but small like . . . inconsequential.

Darcy was already gone.

'Go, go, *go*!' Arden screeched and flew past.

Silence didn't need a second invitation. He took off after her, leaving me dithering, wondering what would happen to Carrie and Joe if we left them behind.

The police officers had already collared White Shirt. The

few onlookers left standing around were gesturing in our direction.

I ran.

Back at the squat we waited for an hour before a call came from Carrie.

'They waited for us,' Arden said. 'They're on their way in a cab. Joe's okay.'

She smiled at me. That unexpected, beautiful smile. It felt like a benediction.

Arden went upstairs and after ten minutes of ping-pong arguing, she and Malik started making up.

I put my fingers in my ears.

Bree boiled the kettle—it had the same effect.

'Don't you just love happy endings?' she smirked.

Darcy didn't make it upstairs. She passed out in the hallway.

Silence waved goodnight. He touched my face where my wounds were still healing and in his eyes and touch there were questions I didn't understand. The violence had left me feeling fragile. I was at breaking point. I had nothing for him, why didn't he get that?

'Goodnight, Silence,' I said.

There were bloodstains on the front of Darcy's silver dress. One more reason for her to hate me.

Bree put a steaming mug in front of me and sat down.

'You did a good thing. Getting help for Joe.'

'I didn't do anything,' I said miserably. 'I could have stopped it sooner, but I was too scared. You should have seen her, Bree. She just went for it. She took out those two men like *that*.' I snapped my fingers. 'We all sat there on the other side of the street and *watched*.'

'Yep. That's Arden for you.' There was pride in her tone—and something else.

'What do you mean?'

'Told you she'd do anything to protect us.'

'Anything?'

'Anything.' Bree said. 'And that's why you always want her on your side.'

Chapter Fifteen

It had been nineteen days since Silence had found me in the train station. I was starting to feel less like I was stuck and more like I belonged. I was earning my keep by chalking all the loose thoughts in my head on the footpath. Some were my own. Others were wisps of recollection, snippets from poems Vivienne used to recite when she was in the mood. Poetry, the others called it, but I knew better. Poetry had rhythm and reason, and what I wrote had neither, but the punters seemed to like it. Some days I could write four or five in a few hours and other days I sat empty-headed for ages while traffic swirled around me.

I still felt alone. I still fended off grief every day, but it didn't take me by surprise any more. It was a dull ache all over, not an acute physical hit every time I thought of her.

If it wasn't for the fact that the others saw him too, that he was made of flesh and bone, I would have suspected Silence was my invisible guardian angel. Since the attack on Joe, he'd started sleeping in the room I shared with Carrie and Bree. The first night he crept in, I was unnerved. The second, I was resigned. By the third I was comforted by his presence and I missed him if he wasn't there. We found peace in each other and nobody else seemed to think it was strange that he watched me all the time.

I thought he was waiting to see when I'd leave. Without him. That was what he expected—to be left behind.

Sometimes he knew what I was thinking before I knew it myself. He left me food when I was busking. Offerings, like a cat might leave on your doorstep—a cinnamon doughnut, a bunch of grapes, a bag of nuts, a fresh bread roll.

On the day I met Alison Dunne, it was a large pretzel, still warm. I looked around but Silence had been and gone.

Intense morning sunshine had beckoned more people outside than usual. They were stunned and blinking, as if years had passed and they were waking from a long sleep.

Days like that brought out the best in people; in a little under an hour I'd made thirty-eight dollars. But by midday the sun was overhead and I'd fallen into shade. There was too much foot traffic outside a gallery, squeezed between a couple of cafés, too many shoes scuffing through my words, leaving them smeared and unreadable. I started packing away my chalk and prepared to move to another spot.

I lingered a few minutes too long, mesmerised by a painting in the gallery window—a woman, standing still in a city street while people jostled past. She was rendered in black and white as if she hadn't been finished. The rest of the streetscape was in vivid colour. Her face was expressionless and her feet were anchored in concrete. The brushstrokes were thick and glossy as butter; it was the kind of painting you itch to touch.

The artist had so perfectly captured my feeling of

132

isolation—of being different, motionless, while everyone around me was moving—I reached out. I pressed my hand to the window. My palm left a faint, chalky imprint on the glass, like it had been dusted for fingerprints. I saw the reflection of someone just behind me, a young woman. She was staring at the painting too.

I gave her a quick smile and made room.

'It's pretty,' she said.

I nodded.

'Makes you want to touch it.'

'Hmm.'

'Do you paint?' she asked.

I shook my head.

'Do you do anything?'

It was a pointed question from someone I had never met. I frowned and looked at her more closely.

She was in her early twenties, dressed smartly in suit pants and a matching jacket. Her hair was cut blunt, dyed a colour too red to be real. She held a briefcase-style handbag that looked heavy enough to be carrying bricks, and her shoes were plain black, flat and scuffed. Cheap shoes. There was a newspaper tucked under her arm.

'Are you living on the street?'

'What?'

That was like asking if you'd ever wet the bed. I took it as personal and offensive, even though it was just a straight-up question with a straight-up answer. I was wary and I backed away.

She reached out and touched my arm. 'Don't go. I want to ask you some questions. If that's okay?'

'I'm in a hurry,' I said.

There was something about her that made me squirm. Her eyes were too blue and direct. She was looking at me as if I was something she wanted to unravel.

'Look, I'm sorry . . . maybe I should explain who I am?' She sighed like I should have known who she was, and handed me a business card. 'I'm Alison Dunne. I'm a journalist.'

'That's not what the card says.' It only had her name and a picture of a typewriter. 'You look a bit young to be a journalist.'

'Actually, I'm an intern,' she said quickly. 'I'm writing a profile piece on some of the city's homeless.'

'Do they let interns do that?'

She blushed and seemed uncomfortable.

I held out her card. 'I can't help you.'

'Keep it. Maybe I can help *you*.'

'I don't think so.' I picked up a stray piece of chalk that was too worn to use again and flicked it into a rubbish bin. 'You have a good day.'

'Wait. Why won't you talk to me? I want to know why you would choose to live on the street. Tell your side of the story.' She fell into step behind me.

'Stop following me.'

'If you tell me your story.'

'What story?' I said over my shoulder. 'I don't have a story. What makes you think I'm even living on the street? And what makes you think it's a choice for some people?'

'Some people,' she said. 'But not you.'

Something in her tone made me stop.

She opened the newspaper and snapped out the crease. She licked her finger between pages. It reminded me of Vivienne, thumbing through a book of maps, singing *eeny-meeny-miney-mo*.

'This is you. You've cut your hair, but it's you.'

She showed me a smaller version of the train station photo, next to a précis of the saved-baby story. Relegated to page fourteen, but still there, weeks later. It was accompanied by an article about the dangers of sloping platforms.

'That's not me,' I said.

The sly look came back. Her red fringe hung so perfectly straight I wanted to hack a big V in it with a pair of sharp scissors.

'So, if that's not you . . .' she opened the paper to another page, '. . . and this isn't you, then tell me why there are two people who look exactly like you taking up space in the paper this week. Look.'

I felt the sudden ache of shock. My hands were instantly clammy.

MISSING, it said in black, fat letters. Smaller: *Liliane Brown, 17 years, 157cm, dark brown hair, grey eyes.*

The print underneath was too small to read without leaning over the bloodhound's shoulder, but there was no mistake. The girl was me. The photo was taken two years before, when I still had some idea of who I was and where I was going and who I was going there with. My hair was so long it ended out of the shot. My gaze was steady and knowing, which was weird, because back then I didn't know anything. Not about death or about losing everything I had that defined *me*, about love—nothing at all.

'Do you realise how much it costs to put a half-page ad in a newspaper?'

I shrugged.

'So, who's trying to find you?'

I smiled at her. She seemed caught off guard and took a step back.

It wasn't exactly a revelation; I knew who was looking for me. I knew exactly who could afford a half-page ad, who was rattling around in an empty mansion, who thought he owed a debt to his dead daughter and runaway grand-daughter. I figured he had too much time and money and guilt. In a city where it should have been easy to disappear, I'd turned into a billboard.

The bloodhound's cogs were turning. She was stuck between digging deeper and letting me speak, trying to figure out whether her best strategy was attack or retreat.

'What would you say if I called this number and told the police I'd found you?' She tapped the bottom of the ad.

'I'd say that the whole point of disappearing is not to be found.'

'Okay, so what if I don't tell anyone. Instead, you tell me your story?'

'I'd say what I said before.' I leaned close and breathed in her ear. '*I don't have a story.*'

I gave her credit for persistence. She chased me for a few blocks, but eventually gave up. Following Silence around had given me a crash course in jaywalking, slipstreaming and evading capture. I outran her in no time.

When I finally stopped running, I realised I still had her homemade card clenched in my hand.

I tore it in half and tossed it. The breeze caught one half, the half with her number, and blew it back. It stuck to my shoe, but I shook it off.

Chapter Sixteen

I dreamed about water.

I was the clueless girl who opened the door that she shouldn't, who ignored all the signs telling me to leave it closed. There was the cinematic suspenseful music, the close-up of my hand turning the handle, the sound of my heartbeat in my ears. My hair was long again, whisper-soft against my bare back, and I was naked. The door beckoned, yet repelled.

I opened it, stepped through, let it slam behind me.

I was standing in a long, grey corridor with another closed door at the far end. There were five people, like wax mannequins, lined up along the corridor, arms outstretched. Their faces were blank, no eyes, noses or mouths. Four held objects, offerings: a bundle of clothing, a knife, a key and a pair of boots. The fifth held out an empty hand.

I knew instinctively that I could choose only three and that I had to use them in the correct order, like a game of strategy. I heard a steady *drip, drip, drip* and felt bulldust under my feet even though the floor was cold, cold concrete. A chilled draught wound itself around my legs. There was a hand in the small of my back, pushing me towards the other end of the corridor. When I turned around, there was nobody there.

I chose the key, of course. I chose the clothes, because I was cold. And I chose my boots.

There were four skirts, seven blouses, three pairs of stockings and one Sunday hat—I put them all on and immediately felt a weight, not just physical, as if all the good had been sucked out of me. I put my boots on and laced them tightly to mid-calf. The key was in my fist, solid and certain, but when I tried to fit it into the lock it shattered into four rusted, metal screws.

I felt no fear. Only fury.

I kicked the door as hard as I could but it was impenetrable. I beat it until my hands were bleeding and I realised that I was alone. Creeping vines had grown over both doors and the ends were coiling around my ankles. The mannequins were gone, the pressure on my back released.

In the silence, I heard a *click*. A latch being released. I went back to the first door but as I got there it locked again. *Click*. The other door unlocked itself. I ran to it but the same thing happened—*click*.

I positioned myself in the middle of the corridor and took off my boots. I stripped off the clothes and left them in a pile. Lighter. Nothing to weigh me down. But it made no difference, I was still too slow. The doors locked themselves just as I grasped the handle, every time.

Bawling, I collapsed, choking in bulldust I could feel but couldn't see. Dust that then began turning to mud—water was seeping like dark blood through the cracks beneath the doors, rising, up, up, to my chest, to my chin, to my face. But I couldn't breathe because I had no eyes no nose no mouth . . .

I woke. That's when you're supposed to feel relief that it's just a dream and even though the dread lingers, you can savour it because it isn't real. And I could have stayed safe in that realisation if I hadn't sat up and turned around.

My pillow was damp. It might have been the sweat of fear, but there were several long hairs on my pillow that I could have sworn weren't there before. They were mine. I reached up and touched the stalks on my head—still short.

It was as if a hole had been punched between worlds.

The others were still sleeping. I knew I had woken myself with a noise—a gasp or a moan—but nobody had stirred. I staggered upstairs to the bathroom, dry-mouthed and panicky. I glanced sideways at my reflection and found nothing familiar—cropped hair, dilated pupils, pale as death. I splashed freezing water on my skin and the pipes rattled all through the house.

I tiptoed down to the kitchen. I wanted some time to myself to shake off the disorientation, but Arden joined me after a few minutes.

'Hey,' she said, eyes still puffy with sleep. 'You're up early.'

'Bad dream,' I said and cupped my hands around my steaming mug.

'Wish asked about you,' she said, out of the blue. She cocked her head, as if she was trying to decide whether she cared about that, or not. She reboiled the penguin kettle and held a flattened hand over the steam. 'Looks like he's finally getting on with his life.'

'I didn't know you were . . .' I stopped. I let her talk. I'd made up some smooth explanations in my mind, like they were neighbours, he was just an old boyfriend, a relationship that didn't work out. Funny, the spin you can put on something to avoid the truth. The last thing I wanted to suspect was that they were connected by something that couldn't be broken.

'It's hard, seeing him again,' she admitted. It sounded flippant, but there was an edge of emotion. 'When I left home the first time, he wanted to take care of me, make sure I stayed out of trouble.'

'Why did you leave home?'

She gave me a sharp look. 'It was leave, or suffocate. The old man's a cop. The worst kind. A control freak. Used to lock me up whenever I got out of line, you know, slap me around a bit.'

'I've never had a father,' I confessed. 'It was just me and my mum.'

'Well, you're lucky,' she said. 'I think I could have been close to my mum if he hadn't kept getting in the way. She only ever stood up for me once and he made sure it was the last time. Knocked her silly. That was the first time I left, when I was fifteen. He's dragged me back a few times, but I think he's given up now.'

'Hence the tattoo?' I asked. 'No more tears?'

Arden smiled. 'It sounds like a shampoo ad when you say it like that.' She tossed her hair. 'There comes a time when you decide you're done playing the victim. It just came a bit sooner for me.' She sipped and winced. 'Ouch. Too hot.' She looked relaxed and happy. Softer, as if sleep had rubbed away her sharp edges.

'So, what did he say?' I ventured. I had to ask.

'Who?'

'Wish,' I said, stumbling over that single syllable.

She sat across from me and rested her chin on her hands. Stabbed me with her stare. 'Nothing Wish wouldn't say about anyone else. He was worried that I took advantage of you. He said you looked lost.'

'Really?' I choked out.

'He said you were pathetic, if you must know. So is that what I did? Did I make you do something you didn't want to?'

'No,' I lied out of pride. I rephrased it to convince myself. 'It's no big deal.'

'Wish wants to save everybody,' she said. 'But he and Malik hate each other. It's impossible. I can't have them both.'

Carrie and Darcy wandered in.

Arden closed up.

A few minutes later AiAi was bouncing off the walls and Silence was brooding and Joe was trying to make conversation with anyone who'd listen.

I felt squeezed out. I went to our room and made my bed, quietly, so I wouldn't disturb Bree.

She woke anyway, blinking and groaning.

'Sorry,' I said.

'S'okay.'

I picked up another long hair from my pillow and wound it around my finger until the tip turned purple. When I released it the sudden flow made my finger throb. I dressed slowly because my hands weren't working properly, fumbled with my laces, one of them so frayed it snapped. I rethreaded it and tied a minuscule bow that barely held.

'Where did you go last night?' Bree asked.

'Shower. At the Y.'

'No, after that. I woke up and you weren't here.'

'I was here all night,' I said. 'Right there, next to Silence.'

'Whatever you say.' She winked.

'No, really,' I protested.

I remembered the dream and wondered if my subconscious could spirit my physical being away, if I really wished I was somewhere else.

I found Silence on the stairs again, papering the walls.

'What's up?' I asked him.

He flashed me his notebook. He'd been writing. There was a page full of scrawl, a neat, tight first sentence that turned into lopsided scribble, as if he'd written it in the dark. The final sentence ran off the paper.

I sat on the step next to him.

'Can I see?'

He shook his head and glanced furtively at the wall.

I looked up. There was a page of his writing plastered over the top of his hero clippings.

I am nothing.

I feel like nothing.

I want my life to matter.

What if one day I'm gone and nobody ever knew I existed?

'You're quite the philosopher,' I said gently.

He grabbed my arm and squeezed it, a sudden move that made me flinch.

'What? What is it? Has something happened?'

He shook his head fiercely and pressed a fist against his temple, as if there was a voice inside his head.

I felt the same frustration and helplessness that I used to feel when Vivienne started rolling down her slope, throwing our gear into a suitcase, flipping her thumb on a highway somewhere. Why did everyone have to be so goddamn *needy*? I knew that feeling of panic, too. I was hard-wired to run when I cared too much.

I prised his fingers from my arm and stood up. 'Look, I don't understand. I can't help you. I don't know what you want from me—I'm barely holding it together myself.'

He slumped. Snapped his notebook shut. Squeezed his eyes shut.

'I have to get going. I'm still short this week. Will you be okay?'

Silence nodded but I knew he didn't mean it. Still, it was enough for me to disengage, to walk away from him. I felt guilt, followed by relief that I could still do that. Walk away.

At about nine, we all left the house and headed off to 'work'.

What started in the spirit of freedom was beginning to feel like a cycle of pointless wandering. Incarceration in a wide-open space: no bars or locks, but a prison just the same.

The city was cloudy and grey. The people were moody and miserable and I spent ages trying to write something inspiring. I ended up with a numb backside and three stilted lines. Nobody gave me money.

On a whim, I went to the university and hung around for a few hours outside the library building. I lolled on the grass with students, mingled with the swarm between classes.

I bought a coffee in the student cafeteria, thumbed through books in the library and smiled at strangers. I gave myself a new name, a new address, a new look, a new personality, a new past.

For three and a half hours I pretended to be someone else.

Chapter Seventeen

By early afternoon I was back at the squat. I felt jumpy.

I punched the trapdoor open and it swung back hard, into my shoulder. The grass was flattened all over the backyard. Dying off. A workman stood on a ladder behind the house next door. I ducked and tried to slink past, but he spotted me. He waved and, a reflex, I waved back.

In my absence, a towering stack had appeared in the cellar, under a tarpaulin in the corner beneath the stairs. A battered jerrycan was tipped on its side and the air smelled strongly of petrol.

I ran my finger around the nozzle and sniffed.

I had hoped the house would be empty but Arden rarely went out during the daytime and Malik always slept then.

Darcy was in the kitchen, making a coffee. She jumped. 'Shit. What are you doing here?'

'What's all that stuff in the cellar?' I asked.

'How the fuck should I know?'

'Charming.' I spun on my heel and went into the bedroom. It struck me that the house was just as dusty, rotten and mildewy as when I'd first arrived, but by now I was used to it. I couldn't smell it any more. It was the smell of blankness. Emptiness.

As usual, Silence and Bree had left their beds unmade. Carrie's and mine were made. A corner of Silence's notebook was sticking out from under his pillow. I pulled out the notebook and flipped through the pages. It was nearly full and the last few blank pages were scarred with outlines of words from the pages before. Silence had a whole lot more going on in his head than he could say out loud. His frustration was there on every page; in places the pen scored right through the paper. Some phrases stood out more than others:

Today I caught Darcy and Malik together when Arden wasn't here. Darcy isn't the same any more.

He didn't elaborate on what he saw them doing.

Carrie said her teeth hurt and she wishes she had her old ones back.

I found another girl in the train station. We saved a baby. Darcy doesn't like her. I like her. She looks so much like Amy.

Amy? His sister?

Friday showed me how to climb a tree. The world looks different from up there.

Joe sleeps like a dead person. I don't feel safe. I can't sleep without someone watching over me.

Was that why he'd started sleeping in our room?

Nothing.

I am nothing.

On the last few pages, this was his recurring theme, as if he'd fallen into a place of darkness.

Reading his words left me feeling unsettled. So many gaps to fill in. I tucked the notebook back under his pillow.

I jumped up to stick the peeling corner of newspaper back onto the window, but I couldn't reach.

A hand stretched above my head and I caught the whiff of male underarm.

I fell back.

Malik stood there. He pushed the loose corner back onto the Blu-Tack and turned around. He was wide awake, obviously had been for some time, and he reeked of petrol.

'Hey,' I blushed.

'Hey,' he said.

'Where's Arden?'

He rolled his eyes towards the ceiling.

'Sleeping?'

'Nuh.'

My skin was crawling. He stood directly between me and the door, wearing an empty stare that screamed sociopath.

'Well. I gotta . . .'

Malik put out a hairy arm to stop me. He looked me over crudely.

I was flustered and sweating. It was like I was trapped underneath, trying to break surface tension. My vision was smudged, my hearing distorted. I was panting and he took it for something else.

Malik's jeans were partly unzipped as if he was halfway through dressing or undressing. When I made eye contact his pupils dilated until they were whole.

I took another step back and measured the distance between my foot and his crotch.

Arden appeared. 'What's going on here?' she asked. Her eyes landed on me, ran up and down, darted to Malik, back to me again.

Darcy sidled up behind her in the hallway.

'Jesus, Malik. Lay off the sniff,' Arden said.

I was so grateful to her for coming when she had that I staggered past Malik and stood next to her.

Arden's fist shot out and connected with my jaw.

I flew backwards. I landed on my side on top of Carrie's mattress. The release of tension followed by the shock of her punch made me burst into noisy tears.

Malik sniffed. He zipped up his jeans and stomped out.

Arden stood there a moment longer, barely moving. She said calmly, 'You'll be all right.' As if I deserved punishment but she hadn't meant to hit me that hard.

Darcy looked shocked. She stared after Malik with an expression of distaste.

The pain set in a few seconds after they had left the room. Aching, throbbing, and the sensation that some of my teeth were in the wrong place. My bite was off. I wiped away tears with the hem of my shirt and noticed that my zipper on my jeans was also riding low. Is that what Arden had seen? Is that what she'd thought?

The punch, Malik, Silence's notebook—it was all too much. I'd never been hit. Not ever. Even when Vivienne was furious, she'd never reacted like Arden just had.

I stuffed my things into my backpack. I gave in to the despair that had been threatening to spill over for weeks. There was no point trying to keep it inside. Maybe that's how it had felt for Vivienne—all those times I'd thought she was at her lowest, it hadn't been that at all. She hadn't been draining away, she'd been spilling over.

*　　*　　*

It took hours to find Silence.

In a city that big, it should have taken even longer. He was a creature of habit, so I checked his favourite places first. The first time I went to the glasshouse he wasn't there, but an hour later, he was. I caught him trying to scoop the fish into a jar. His balance was precarious, his sleeves wet to the elbow. His hair too, from trying to peer through the murk.

'What are you doing?' My question squeezed out between gritted teeth; my jaw felt wired shut, out of alignment. 'Arden hit me.' I hadn't meant to spring it on him like that, but it came out before I could think.

Silence had caught one goggle-eyed goldfish. He tipped it out. It dived tail-first and disappeared. He watched it swim free then turned and hurled the jar at the square, greenish panes of the glasshouse walls. The jar shattered, but the panes held up.

'I'm okay.' I looked around but there was nobody nearby. 'I can't stay. For real, this time.'

I know, he said on a sigh.

I was thinking, *It's too late, I'm already attached.* I hated goodbyes.

Silence held up his hand. There was a spark in his expression that had been missing for some time. *I'm coming with you,* he signed.

'But I don't know where I'm going.' I tried to stop the surge of excitement I felt.

I don't care. I'll come with you.

'Me and you against the world, huh?'

He smiled. *Me and you.*

*   *   *

We put off returning to the squat until it was dark. Silence bought hamburgers and we ate as we walked. He swapped his tomato for my onion and he gave me his hoodie when I mentioned the cold.

When I hesitated outside the cellar window, he held my hand.

Arden met us at the top of the cellar stairs. She launched herself at me. I cowered and nearly fell, but she was hugging me, her embrace a vice. I was stiff and unforgiving but she folded me into her.

'You're back,' she purred in my ear.

It sounded like a threat.

She stepped away from me and my heart did a stage-dive.

Wish was there. He was playing cards with Joe, whose face still looked collapsed in places, who still struggled with the stairs and moved like an old man.

Carrie and Darcy watched as if there was a thousand acres at stake.

Wish high-fived Silence and eyed me with friendly curiosity and not much else.

Barely moving her lips, Carrie said, 'There's beer in the sink.'

'Chug-a-lug,' cackled AiAi.

Silence grabbed a bottle out of AiAi's hand and smacked him on the top of his head.

AiAi, drinking? Arden would never allow it. I raised an eyebrow but Arden seemed not to care.

'Leave him alone,' she said and twisted the top off a fresh one. 'It's only beer. Don't be a killjoy. Look, it's the old crew all together again. Cheers.'

The others followed with a chorus of clinks.

I went to the bedroom and dumped my backpack. I could stay there and sulk, or I could join in and go through the motions. Maybe even have a conversation with a guy who made me feel all thumbs and two left feet, instead of behaving as if I was an asylum inmate like I had the last time I saw him.

Except he'd said I was pathetic.

I wasted time rearranging my bed, changing into cleaner jeans and a T-shirt.

Back in the kitchen the air smelled like an old keg and everyone's voices were louder than Arden would usually allow. It was like she'd scrapped all of her rules.

Bree wasn't there. Malik wasn't either and that suited me just fine.

I helped myself to a beer, even though I didn't much like the taste, and sat next to Carrie.

'Here she is,' AiAi said as if somebody had just asked where I was.

'Do you want me to deal you in?' Wish said. He shuffled and split the deck like a pro.

'Don't do it,' Joe butted in. 'He counts the cards. If this was Vegas he'd get dragged off with a bag over his head.'

'I don't know how,' I said. 'I'll just watch.'

'Story of her life,' Darcy snorted.

Wish dealt two cards each to himself, Darcy, Joe, Carrie and AiAi.

AiAi immediately turned his cards face up and showed everyone what he had.

'Not yet, numb-nuts,' Joe told him and flipped them back over.

I watched Wish's face as he dealt. Sure enough, he seemed to be cataloguing the cards as they were revealed. He told everyone to place their bets—with bottle tops—and scooped the pile towards him when he won.

I drained the last of my beer. 'Who wants another one?' I plunged my hand into the ice-filled sink and dredged up a couple of bottles.

Silence was sitting in a corner, sucking on his inhaler. He said something to Arden. She crouched next to him, talking in a low voice. He shook his head suddenly, violently, as if a bug had crawled into his ear. Arden grabbed his chin and turned his face to hers, slapping his fingers away when he tried to communicate.

I put my hand under the ice again. Fished out two more.

When I looked across again, Arden and Silence had gone.

'Where'd they go?'

Darcy shrugged.

'I'm shattered,' Carrie said and pushed away from the table.

'Me too,' yawned Joe.

Wish scraped up the deck and accepted another beer. He turned his attention to me.

I forgot all about Silence.

Chapter Eighteen

Darcy and I were waging a battle of wills.

If it had been Carrie or Joe still standing, I would have gone to bed hours before—but it was Darcy. Wish and Darcy and me. All of us almost sober and sleepy at an hour that was closer to morning than night.

Wish said he'd had one too many beers to drive home. Darcy was grim and determined, incapable of speech.

My eyelids felt like they were being pulled shut by invisible threads. Dry mouth, hot cheeks, aching bladder—I wasn't a good beer drinker. I could feel diamond-shaped imprints from the crate on my butt.

Wish had done most of the talking—about joining the Army Reserve, about starting his electrician's apprenticeship, about missing Arden and the others—until he ran out of things to say.

None of us had spoken for about five minutes when he said, 'Darcy's asleep.'

I looked over. Her head rested on her hands and she was snoring quietly. Limp hair hung over her face, her mouth so slack and childlike I couldn't imagine anything nasty coming out of it.

'I might crash, too,' I said. 'I wonder where the others went?'

'Dunno. Arden's always been nocturnal. She's probably clubbing with Malik.'

'But she took Silence with her. And why would she leave if she invited you over?'

'She didn't invite me,' he said. 'I just came.'

I believed him.

'She said . . . never mind. Did you really say I was pathetic?'

Stupid mouth. Stupid, stupid mouth.

'What? Pathetic, no. I said you were lost. I knew it the moment I saw you standing in my bedroom doorway. Like you'd just stepped into another dimension.'

'I was in shock,' I said. 'Arden didn't tell me she knew whose house it was.'

'Well, she wouldn't. That would spoil her fun, wouldn't it?'

'You mean she knew you were home?'

'She knows where my bedroom is, if that's what you're asking,' he said. 'The light was on. She knew.'

'That was an accident. I went to the wrong door. But why would she do that?'

'Why does Arden do anything? She's a force of nature. Other people just get swept up with her. When you get too far away from her she yanks your chain. I should know.' He sounded bitter.

'So why do you keep in touch?'

He looked at me with a quizzical expression. 'How could I not? I love her. Always will.'

'Oh,' was all I could say. It winded me. I'd danced around the definition of them, together, and now there it was. Plain and simple.

'We haven't really seen each other much, not for at least six months. I just brought your boots back. Arden never used to be like this. She needs to go home, face her demons.'

'She told me a bit about her family.'

'You would have got the "my father is an abusive cop-bastard" version.'

'Something like that,' I admitted.

'It's not so black and white.'

'Nothing ever is.'

'Arden's version will change depending on who she's telling,' he said. 'And I never said you were pathetic. So how did you end up here?'

'I'm between dimensions right now,' I joked.

He loved her. Always would. It didn't get much more black and white than that.

Wish leaned across the table and ran his finger along my jawline, where Arden had hit me. For a second, my vision shimmered and if I hadn't already been sitting, I would have fallen. He traced the slight swelling, still there. Suddenly it didn't hurt at all.

'How did you get this one?'

I thought of Arden's fist. 'Can't remember.'

'Liar.'

'It doesn't matter.'

'It does to me.'

'I wonder where Arden went?' I glanced at the cellar door.

'Don't change the subject. She'll be fine, she always is.'

'It's not her I'm worried about. And what was the subject?'

'You. This.' His finger had a rapid pulse.

I looked at Darcy sleeping, wondered what we were going to do with this super-charged energy between us. With Darcy there it felt illicit, dangerous. Thrilling. It was me he wanted. I was tired of being alone. Tired of being me—timid, sexless, unremarkable me.

Darcy didn't stir.

Wish was waiting for me to start something. Holding his breath.

I thought of Arden, how she danced Malik on her string. I remembered how Vivienne never had to ask. I wanted that indescribable thing that made them female and powerful. I thought that if I hadn't been born with it in my marrow, I could maybe try it on, wear it for a while, see if it fitted.

My heart was pounding. I kneeled, crawled under the table and surfaced between his knees.

He lifted me easily, like I weighed nothing.

I felt like I was slipping. There were only rules to break, taboos to challenge, and nothing else mattered. There was a dragging sensation in my lower belly. It was unfamiliar, yet still belonged—and it was taking me over. I stood between his legs, I leaned down, and he kissed me. It was a hello kiss, slow and deep. For the first time since forever I had something solid and real to hold; I could feel his bones, his ribs, shoulderblades, his hips. His lips. His hands traced light circles on my back and ran up to my neck. He was holding back. Was he afraid I'd break?

He stood up and we staggered into the dark hallway, joined

in too many places to count. The papered walls were rough against my back where he lifted my shirt. It was so dark. Too dark to see his face, so I traced his eyes with my fingertips. He closed them. Went by feel. My bra unsnapped and hung loose. Warm hands with a cool air chaser. Goosebumps wherever he touched. I tried to breathe normally but it wasn't possible.

It was so far from anything I'd ever experienced; those few awkward, sticky moments in fogged-up cars with guys who didn't even notice when you'd gone, when you were nothing but a sordid rumour the next day.

I would be chasing that feeling forever and, because I didn't want it to, I knew it had to end. I wanted to be alone with him. Not like that. Not with Arden in his head.

'Wish . . .' I let my hands fall to my sides. I willed them to stay there.

'I know,' he said and his hands fell, too.

He leaned his forehead against mine. We breathed each other's breath and pulled apart. I expected pain, as if a vital organ could have gone with him, but all I felt was cold and tired and empty. And confused. I'd taken what I wanted, but what would it cost?

We went back into the kitchen.

Wish looked at Darcy, still sleeping. He smiled ruefully and kissed her lightly on top of her head. 'Thank you,' he whispered to her. 'Tomorrow night,' he said to me in a low voice. 'Can I pick you up? Take you for a drive somewhere? Away from here?'

I loved that he had to ask, that he wasn't sure of my answer. 'What about Arden?'

'What about her?'

'Yes,' I answered, because he'd said what I wanted to hear.

As soon as he was gone, I felt the wrongness of what we'd done. I saw the inevitability of it, too. I was my mother's daughter, destined to run, and to be with a guy who would never be mine, except for a moment. And I knew that it wasn't a good fit; I could never be a taker.

My eyes were already closing when I crawled into bed.

'Good night?' Carrie murmured.

'Goodnight.'

'No, that was a question. Did you have a good night?'

She must have heard us in the hallway. 'Yes,' I smiled.

'Be careful,' I thought she said, but I couldn't be sure because my mind was already drifting.

Wish.

I wish.

I woke too soon, yanked out of a deep sleep by the sound of pounding feet on floorboards. Carrie bolted upright at the same time. We looked at each other, still groggy, trying to make sense of what was going on.

'What the . . . ?'

Silence tore into the room. He headed straight for the corner and slumped against the wall, bleak-eyed, staring. His skin was grey, his breathing rapid. There were bits of grass and leaves in his hair. His mouth was wide open—he looked like he was screaming but there was no sound.

I gathered my wits enough to go to him but he pushed me away.

'He needs his inhaler,' Carrie said. 'Where is it?' She rummaged through his things, scattering underwear and toiletries all over the floor.

I reached under his pillow and pulled out his notebook. I offered it to him.

'Tell us what happened,' I said. 'What's wrong? Are you hurt?'

I handed him his pen but he dropped it. He was shaking too much to write.

Joe shambled in, rubbing his eye with a fist. 'What's going on?'

Carrie tossed me the inhaler. I slipped the nozzle between Silence's lips and cupped the back of his neck, the same way I'd seen Bree do it. It took four blasts before he took some in.

'Talk to us,' Carrie whispered. 'Where's Arden?' Louder. 'Say something!' She reached out and shook him.

At her touch, or on hearing Arden's name, Silence stared at the doorway.

As if she'd been conjured, Arden appeared wearing her commando-style garb, black beanie bulging with her dreads stuffed underneath. Her eyes were red-rimmed, but still so direct they burned.

Her voice didn't waver. 'Get some sleep,' she said to Silence. 'The rest of you—pack your things. Get something to eat. Keep the noise down. I'll tell you what's going on later.'

'What about him?' Joe said, pointing to Silence.

He looked semi-catatonic, but when Arden strode over and hauled him up by the front of his hoodie, he struggled.

'Get it together!' she hissed. She shook him, hard. 'Stop it!' Then—*slap*—across his face.

Silence crumpled. Not because of the slap—it wasn't that hard—but because his legs wouldn't hold him up.

Arden turned to me. 'Keep an eye on him. Stay with him until the rest of us get some things sorted out.'

'Why me?' It wasn't the looking after Silence part I objected to—it was the way she kept barking orders.

'Because there's nothing else you can do.'

'But . . .' Silence grabbed my hand and squeezed it. I opened my mouth to say more but the pressure increased.

Carrie nudged me. 'I'll go get him a drink of water.'

Arden pulled off her beanie and shook her hair free. For a few seconds it resisted, a knotted halo of snakes, then it unwound and fell down her back. 'It'll be okay. Everything's going to be okay.'

I wondered who she was trying to convince.

In the kitchen, AiAi sat in a corner on a crate, looking lost.

'It's all right, mate,' I reassured him, not because I knew what was going on but because he needed to hear it from somebody.

Arden kept going with the orders. 'Darce, go find Bree, will you? She needs to be here, too. I need everyone back here as soon as possible. Like, yesterday.'

Darcy nodded. She bolted upstairs.

'What's going on?' I asked.

'We're leaving,' Arden said, not looking at me. 'Everything's good to go.'

'Where are you going?'

She ignored me and sat down at the table. She placed her black box next to her and opened the padlock, pulled out a pen and notebook and started writing a list.

Carrie walked in. 'Is this it, then? We're really going?' she said.

Joe, Malik and AiAi came to stand alongside her, a row of disciples.

Arden slammed down the pen. She was like a cobra, hissing and weaving. 'We have to leave. I need money, whatever you have stashed. I know you all have a stash, but we need it now. And your phones. Leave them here on the table.' She glared around.

I lingered around the edges, catching scraps of hushed conversation.

'Friday. Are you coming?' Arden followed me with her eyes.

The others stopped their pocket-searching and stared.

I shook my head but I couldn't find my tongue. 'I can't,' I said eventually. I hated my voice and the smallness of it.

'Suit yourself.' She went back to her list, wrote a few words, then looked back at me. 'And Silence is coming with us.'

'What if . . . ?'

'Ask him. We talked about it. We've been together for two years—he's not about to run off with someone he's just met, is he?'

She was right. We hardly knew each other. I had to get out of there.

Silence was lying on his side, on my mattress, facing the window. His shoulders were heaving.

Quickly, quietly, I shoved all my things into my backpack. I rolled up my swag.

I sat by Silence for a while. I held my hand on his shoulder until his breathing slowed. When I left him, he was asleep. He drew shuddery breaths and sighs leaked from him, the kind that come after crying so hard there's nothing left. But he was asleep, and peaceful, his face streaked like a dirty window after rain. I covered him with my blanket and left him.

In the confusion, nobody noticed, nobody saw when I crawled out through the cellar window with my stuff, nobody stopped me when I let the trapdoor swing shut. I avoided the usual route through the maze of alleys, afraid I would run into Darcy or Bree. I felt immense relief when I hit the main road and followed the flow of traffic into the heart of the city.

It made sense not to care too much. Once I'd scraped up enough for a bus ticket, I would leave the city. I wrote it off as a wrong turn: Silence, Arden, Wish, all of it. Wrong turns just added more to who you are.

I didn't know that they also add to the toll you must pay to go back.

Chapter Nineteen

I found a pristine patch of footpath outside Parliament House. I turned my back to the morning sun, chose a purple stump of chalk and honed it to a point on the kerb. A man in a suit gave me a dollar for nothing but being there.

I lifted my face to catch something of the morning, a sound or a feeling, just a couple of words to start, but I got stuck on Silence's desperation. It was catching, I should have known. When he grabbed at me like I was some kind of saviour, I saw Vivienne. Her last clutch at life, and my retreat, scrabbling backwards in horror, in case she took me with her. It had leached into me anyway and it was stuck to my hair and my clothes and my skin.

He was fine, I thought. Snoring still, probably. He was better off with them. Safety in numbers and all that.

I tilted my chin, closed my eyes. Spring. The cool breath of it, the damp edges. I couldn't concentrate. All I could think was that Silence had said he liked autumn best, when the leaves let go. He'd liked to cover himself in fallen leaves in the Botanic Park, then leap out at tourists.

I smiled to myself.

A flurry of pedestrian traffic. A woman pushing a pram invaded my space and I ducked left. My head thumped against a man's leg. A piece of chalk was crushed and dragged, then thrown out from behind a heel like a hit and run victim. I was invisible. It must have been so much worse for Silence, without his voice.

The thought of leaving without telling him why I had to go was more than I could bear. Maybe this time I could stand a little desperation.

I packed up, leaving the footpath unmarked.

I hopped on the free loop tram but the driver kicked me off because I wasn't wearing shoes, so I jogged the rest of the way.

At the top of Jacaranda Lane, I realised that something was happening. My mind had been elsewhere and there were signs I had failed to notice.

People were walking in the same direction as I was. More than I could consider a fluke. Dozens. Shielding their eyes against the sun and looking up. Murmuring in low, shocked voices and shaking their heads in disbelief, like a scene from the Apocalypse. Two police cars flashed past, lights strobing, sirens switched off, followed by a fire engine that scattered the crowd with a booming honk.

I was caught in the current, blending with onlookers. Running scared, but not away from the terrible thing, towards it. The air was acrid, a warm, dense layer. My throat was full of it. One man had a handkerchief pressed over his nose and mouth like a surgical mask. I was shaking with terror so swift it arrived minutes before comprehension.

The squat was burning, exhaling twin plumes of smoke up into the sky. Dragon's breath.

I knew it was deliberate. I didn't know if anyone was still inside.

When I got closer the smell was overpowering. The old house was lit up from the inside like a Halloween pumpkin. The firemen's hoses were aimed at the houses on either side, as if they'd decided the squat was past saving.

'Was there anyone inside?' I gasped to a female police officer.

She shook her head—but only as a warning not to go further—and spread her arms wide. 'Move back. All of you, move back, please.'

The police had cordoned off the middle section of the street with barricades. I couldn't get through. I backed away from the growing crowd and legged it back down the street to the alley. The narrow access had blocked any vehicles but there was a lone fireman wearing a mask, wandering through the haze at the far end.

He spotted me and shouted something I couldn't make out, but it was clear he wanted me to go back.

I dropped my stuff at the end of the alley and pressed forwards, pushed my hands against the trapdoor, felt the rush of heat as air sucked through the opening. Coughing, choking. I put my hands over my face and breathed through my fingers. I had to see for myself. If I could just look through the cellar window. If the pile of stuff under the tarpaulin was gone, I'd know for sure that they had got out.

I was no closer than the pond before the radiant heat was too intense. My skin felt as if it was shrinking and peeling. The smoke was too thick, my eyes were watering, vision was almost nil. I stepped back, spun around and tripped over the edge of the pond. Something slick and slimy writhed against my leg. A black eel, lying stricken on the singed grass, gills flapping. Four bloated, dead fish were floating on top of the green water.

I crawled backwards but the eel's flat shark-eyes were staring at me. I sucked and held a lungful of breath. I shuffled back and picked up the eel, sinewy and pulsing, felt its dying weight, slung it into the water. It sank without swimming.

Just as I realised that one breath was not enough—too much smoke and not enough oxygen—strong hands gripped under my arms. The fireman dragged me through the trapdoor and dumped me onto the ground.

He tilted his mask and yelled in my face. 'You crazy kid! What the hell do you think you're doing?' Then, 'Are you okay?'

I coughed and nodded. 'My friends were in there.'

'There's nobody. We checked. It's unoccupied.'

'No, street kids. Homeless kids.' I was crying, but I knew they weren't in there. Arden wouldn't have torched the place without an escape plan.

'There's nobody. It's empty. You need to get checked out. Let's go.' He hauled me up and handed me my swag and backpack.

'I'm fine. Really.' I shrugged him off. 'I'm leaving. Promise.'

He looked at me doubtfully and slipped his mask back on. 'Get out of here before the whole place comes down.' His voice was muffled.

The fireman gave me a five-finger countdown and I took

it. I headed off, rubbing my stinging eyes. My hand came away streaked with black.

I picked up my things and walked away.

I had a long shower at the Y, ignoring the pacing time-Nazi, letting the warm water flow until it finally ran clear. When I got out I was jittery and dizzy. I sat down on the cool tiles until it passed, wrapped in a threadbare towel. I dressed slowly, mechanically, and even though I was clean on the outside I could still taste smoke and ash.

'Do you have a spare bed for the night?' I asked the woman.

'Full,' she said. 'Try the youth hostel on Brixton Street.'

Standing outside on the footpath, feeling lost, hungry and afraid, I remembered Wish.

He would pull up outside the squat later and find a taped-off square, a heap of charred remains where there'd been a house. Would he know with the same certainty that the fire was deliberate, or would he think the worst? How could I find him? I searched my exhausted mind for an address, a direction, any lingering memory from the taxi ride to his house, but all I could remember were fragments of useless detail.

This is what you wanted, I told myself. *To be alone. To keep moving.*

People passed, cars honked, traffic lights beeped—the incessant beat of life on fast-forward when I was stuck on pause.

I wandered past a café and smelled burnt cheese. It turned my stomach even though I hadn't eaten in ages. My body felt impossibly light—I must have lost three or four kilos in those few weeks—but my thoughts were becoming clearer. I decided to go back to the squat. I would wait for Wish, and when he came we'd go for a drive as if we were still on the brink of something new and the last few hours had never happened.

I started walking.

Vivienne once told me that I came out sideways with a monkey on my back and screamed non-stop for the first year of my life. Then, one day, I stopped. I slept for fourteen hours straight and during that time she didn't check on me, not once. She said that she went through the five stages of grief in that time—denial, anger, bargaining, depression and acceptance—but not once did she check to see if I was still breathing. Because even though she was imagining the worst (only the most dire of circumstances could have kept me quiet for so long, she presumed), for her own sanity she had to delay the moment that either a) she found me choked to death by the curtain cord, or b) I opened my eyes and my mouth and recommenced screaming. Those hours were the most tortured yet exquisite she'd ever experienced, she told me.

I never really got her reasoning until that moment.

The squat had been razed. Only a section of interior wall was still intact, lying flat but whole. The clippings were smoke-stained but hardly singed by the fire. Everything else was gone. A fire engine was parked outside but the firemen were leaning against the truck, swigging from thermoses, chatting. The hoses were wound in coils, put away. A few residents were arriving home. They stood in a huddle across the street and stared in shock at the aftermath. A man pointed at me and I wondered if they knew we'd been hiding in there at night, while they were eating three-course meals, tucking in children, staying warm.

I walked a lap of the block. The rear alley was drenched; my feet sank deep in the sodden leaves and clumped ash. When I got back, there was a flimsy strip of tape strung between two stakes along the council strip. The firemen had left. It was almost dark.

I filled up my water bottle from a garden hose and sat on the kerb outside the neighbouring house. Everything was still and empty.

An hour passed. My legs were stiff and my fingers numb. I put on an extra layer of dirty, ash-grey clothes even though they stank. With every car that passed my heart beat faster, and when it wasn't him, I felt the sudden dip of disappointment like my stomach was leaving through my feet.

Another car crept past. I shrank into myself. I stopped hoping. Part of me didn't want him to see me like that. I breathed on my hands and tucked them under my armpits to keep them warm.

Then, at the far end of the street, I noticed a figure. Heading in my direction. Features in shadow, but with that familiar, loping, alley-cat stride. So tall, long-limbed, with a smile that could make the whole world seem different when nothing had really changed. When the figure was close enough, I could see that smile, and I felt relief so sharp it hurt. I blinked back tears.

'Hey, you knew I'd come. Didn't you?'

I didn't. But you have to get on the first boat that sails past, Vivienne always said. You never know when the next one's coming.

'I knew I'd find you here,' Arden said and slung a long, pale arm around my shoulder. 'I knew it.'

PART 2

DUST

Thoughts become words,
words become deeds,
deeds become habits,
habits become character,
and your character becomes your destiny.

Chapter Twenty

Carrie told me later that it took Malik under an hour to steal the car and switch the plates. They were waiting a few streets away, engine running—it was a Toyota troop carrier with big steel racks on top. It had obviously been off-road—sweeping arcs of mud, dried to a dusty crust, were sprayed up the sides and someone had written *wish my wife was this dirty* with their finger in the film obscuring the rear window. A caged trailer was hooked to the back, stacked full with stuff. Inside the car it reeked of diesel and cigarettes.

When I got in, Carrie screamed, 'Road trip!' then chattered on like nothing much had happened, filling in the blanks since I'd left without pausing for breath.

Bree reached over the seat and brushed the back of her hand across my cheek. Silence gave me a slow, sad smile and clapped his hands. The two gestures didn't go together and gave me no clue how he was really feeling.

'Found her,' Arden said. 'Don't say I never give you anything.' She winked at Silence.

She tried on a *Keep on truckin'* cap that she found in the glove box, then pulled it off and sniffed it. Disgusted, she lobbed it out the window and did the same with a few

CDs that didn't meet with her approval. She took off the crucifix necklace I stole for her and hung it from the rearview mirror.

Malik had tied down as many sleeping bags as would fit and they'd crammed the rest into the space in the back. All the other gear sat on our laps or under our feet.

Silence hung his head and picked at his fingernails. I tried to catch his eye but he wasn't looking. We sat four across on the back seat: me, Darcy, Silence and Carrie. Three in the front: AiAi straddling the gearshift, Malik driving and Arden in the passenger seat. Joe and Bree hid in the back, lying low.

The first hour was quiet and tense as Malik drove too slowly and too carefully out of the city. When we hit the open road, Arden wound one window down just a crack. We were doing over a hundred and the air throbbed through the opening, giving me an earache. I pressed a hand to my ear to relieve the pressure.

As if she could read my mind, Carrie opened her window to create a passage of air.

Darcy's leg was pressed hard against mine and I tried to move away, but there was nowhere to go.

Arden put on a CD that she found stuffed in the overhead parcel shelf. She turned the volume up loud and sang tunelessly.

It was a song I hadn't heard for a long time. Leonard Cohen's 'Hallelujah'. Vivienne had loved it—the Jeff Buckley version—and I couldn't hear it without imagining a tortured man walking into a river to end it all. She'd joked that he was a long-lost relative of ours.

There was an ache in my chest. Tears were running down my cheeks. I had only ever had one eye that cried—the left, as if I was half committed to the act—but now there were twin streams and I couldn't stop. I wound down the window and hung my head out. My tears skidded off like raindrops on a windscreen.

'We had a dog that used to do that,' Carrie said looking over at me. 'His lips used to flap like this.' She pinched her lips and lifted them. Her fangs gleamed. She put her head out of the window and waggled her lips up and down.

I smiled at her. I knew she'd seen me cry, but she wasn't telling. I was grateful for it.

'Put the window up unless you're gonna puke,' Arden said.

I fell asleep with my head on Darcy's shoulder, too tired to care.

The moon followed us the whole way. The landscape was nothing I hadn't seen a thousand times, but you'd think AiAi had never seen a cow before, the way he yelped every time we passed a farm animal. Halfway through the night, after long hours of nothing but pitch-dark plains and the occasional farmhouse, Malik pulled into a 24-hour service station.

Arden gave Carrie some money and a bag and told her to stock up on drinks and chips.

Malik filled up the tank and scraped dead bugs off the windscreen.

I climbed out to stretch my legs. When I walked past, Malik flicked the gunk he'd scraped off in my direction.

Arden gave me a look.

The others got out, too. We used the toilets, then mooched around in the car park. Apart from a few truckies in the restaurant, we seemed to be the only living creatures out there.

We dawdled, reluctant to get back in the car.

'How much further do we have to go?' Darcy yawned and stretched her arms so far behind her back she looked double-jointed.

A double-B road train passed and whipped up a flurry of dust and styrofoam cups.

'It's all starting to look the same to me,' Carrie chimed in. 'Road, paddock, tree, cow, road, paddock, tree . . .'

As for me, it felt like heading home.

Malik drove for a couple more hours until morning. When we passed a rundown caravan park, Arden yelled at him to stop. She seemed transfixed by the rusting metal archway, the peeling paint, the sad little caravans parked in rows. The park sign read 'Ploser's Family Caravan Park'.

'I think I've been here before,' she said.

'They all look the same to me,' Joe answered.

'I want to have a look.'

Over the next couple of hours we took turns sneaking showers using a key that Arden 'borrowed' from a teenage boy. Some money changed hands. I showered with Carrie chattering incessantly in the next cubicle while the water ran grey from my filthy hair and skin. Afterwards, we played pool and pinball in the communal games room and ate melting chocolate from a vending machine.

Arden sat apart, watching us.

Silence stayed away from her.

'I know I've been here before,' she said to no one in particular when we were leaving. 'I'm sure my parents brought us here when I was a kid. Maybe we always want to go back to the last place we were happy.'

She didn't seem to need an answer. As we took turns sneaking past the office, she pulled out a thick, black marker pen from her bag and crossed out the 'P' and the word 'family'.

Chapter Twenty-one

The troop carrier limped in at dusk.

Behind us, the sky was bleeding out. A derelict black-and-white sign hung at an angle, complete with a bullet hole and a smear of something brown and unmentionable. *Murungal Creek*, it told us, glowing neon in the headlights. Dust and half-light set a milky cast over everything. The road snaked away, crumbling to nothing, past ancient river red gums that reached up into the deep, dark blue.

When the dust cleared, we were all crawling over each other to peer through the windows. To see what had drawn Arden to this place.

It was a town left behind.

Buildings leaned like tombstones; walls gaped with cracks. There was a double-storey white building on a corner that could have been a pub, a tin shed with a bowed porch, several identical squat houses that looked like they'd been pressed out of the same plasterboard mould, and a regal church with a soaring spire. Piles of slate and rubble in between, lesser things, reclaimed by the land.

We got out of the car, stretching and groaning. There seemed more than nine of us now, unfolded. I took a gulp of pure air that wasn't somebody else's exhalation. It tasted of eucalyptus.

There were signs everywhere. *Keep Out. Trespassers Prosecuted. Private Property.* Tags, too, garish and out of place. Old water tanks crusted with rust, jagged fence posts linked with drooping wire, shuttered windows and the taint of green, the spreading, noxious green of rot and rain.

'This is it,' Arden sighed. 'It looks just like the picture. You know how sometimes the pictures are just too perfect? Not this, though. It's *exactly* how I thought it would be.'

I remembered the postcards on Arden's wall. *This* is what she'd been planning?

'There's nobody here,' Joe said. 'It looks like a godforsaken ghost town.'

'It *is* a fucking ghost town, you knob,' Arden snapped. 'I told you guys all about it.'

'You said we were going to find our own place.'

'This is even better—I got you a whole town.'

'It's a *ghost town*. What's the point? There's not even a pub.'

Arden sighed. 'There probably was one a long time ago. We can make our own pub. That's the whole point. We can do whatever we want.'

'You can't just claim a town and move in,' I said.

'Why not? Obviously nobody else wants it,' she fired back. 'And it's a hundred kays from anywhere. Perfect.'

'There's no power,' Darcy said. 'How will we boil the kettle?'

'Jesus!' Arden exploded. 'We'll survive. We always do.

Here or back there,' she pointed to the distance. 'What's the difference? I'll tell you what—here, there's just us. Nobody else. No one to tell us what to do. We don't have to creep around or watch our backs.'

'The difference is we're a hundred kilometres from anywhere and that makes me nervous,' Joe admitted. 'How are we supposed to make money or buy what we need?' There was a chorus of nods.

'We have a car.'

'A stolen car. How long before we're picked up?'

'Malik switched the plates. Nobody will know it's stolen. And I have money,' Arden said.

'That's our money, too,' AiAi said, his bottom lip sticking out.

'Of course it's our money,' Arden placated him. 'We have plenty of the stuff. This is what we've all worked so hard for. Our own place. All we need to worry about right now is where we're all going to sleep tonight. Then we can get started and fix this place up.'

'Yeah, let's call it "Shithole Makeover". Then we'll just nip down to the hardware store and pick up everything we need,' Joe said. 'We're in the middle of *nowhere*, in case you hadn't noticed. The last piece of civilisation we passed through had a ten-metre tall friggin' monument to a *sheep*. That's gotta tell you something about the locals, don't you think?'

'Shut up, Joe,' Malik said through his teeth.

I think we were all grateful that Joe was voicing group opinion. What the hell were we doing there in an abandoned town? It was picturesque and peaceful, but people didn't just up and leave houses and churches and livelihoods for no good reason.

'What does it mean, Murungal?' Malik asked. *Muh-run-gal,* is how he said it.

We all turned to Bree, figuring she'd know more than the rest of us with our mongrel pedigrees and shallow histories. I wanted to hear her say it, with her warm rolling consonants like a mouthful of cobblers.

Bree looked up. Sunset was rolling in, a distant shore in the sky. She lit a cigarette. 'Why are you asking me? How the fuck would I know?' She exhaled, slit-eyed against the smoke.

'Murungal,' I say. *Moo-roong-garl.* 'It means . . .'

Arden cut me off with a dirty look. It turned into an expression I hadn't seen before—as if she'd come to a conclusion and was filing it away in her steel-trap mind, for later.

Bree stalked off to inspect a boarded-up window.

'Sorry,' I shrugged.

'What does it mean?' Silence rasped behind me.

'Well, let's get unpacked, shall we?' Arden interrupted. She sounded like a schoolteacher. 'What's first?'

'Food,' said Malik.

'Food,' seconded Carrie.

'Beer,' said AiAi.

Arden snorted. 'No, *shelter.*'

'Well, take your pick,' Joe said and gestured at the collapsing buildings.

'Water,' I said, under my breath.

I could tell by looking that there wasn't much of that here. It had rained, a lot and recently, but the red dust had soaked it up like a dry sponge. Boring through metres of rock would have been the only way to dredge a drop back. There was an old windmill missing two blades but it didn't look as if it had turned a single rotation for a century. A full twenty-litre water container was stashed in the back of the car but I figured that might last us a day, two at best.

'We need water,' I said loudly.

'We have water,' Arden said.

'Well, how long are we staying?'

She looked at me as if the answer was elementary and I was stupid. 'We've been planning this for a long time.'

'Then we need more water.'

'So do a rain dance. Come on, let's get unpacked. We'll worry about it tomorrow.'

'It's going to get cold. I'll make us a fire,' I said. It was more to give myself something to do than anything.

Silence, Darcy and Malik looked at me as if I'd just beamed down from a UFO. 'What?' I shrugged.

I headed off past the buildings into a dense cluster of scrubby gums, scraped together an armful of thin, dead branches and made a pile in the clearing next to the church. AiAi helped—or hindered—by dragging the biggest, still-green branches he could handle. The sticks I'd collected were damp, but they'd burn well enough once they got going.

A smouldering half-sun floated on the horizon and soon there would be little or no light, only a crescent moon. The cold was creeping in. I stopped to catch my breath and stared at the opal-streaked sky.

Joe might have called that place godforsaken but I could see a whole lot of proof that if there was a God, He'd been there. I'd missed it—the way the outback lit up in dying light. The stillness, the colour. Out there, a quiet moment to yourself could feel like forever, but at the same time you were reminded that your entire life so far was barely a blink.

In the background, Darcy and Carrie started bickering and I was yanked back into the present. The others had unpacked the car and stacked everything on the ground near the church entrance. I should have told them to leave it all in the car; it was a dewy night and it would all be wet in the morning. Not that Arden was ever in a mood for advice.

I scraped out a shallow basin in the dust using an old hubcap and ringed it with glowing-white chunks of limestone rock. Then came the Blair Witch pile of sticks in the centre, ready for the flame. It was a ritual I could do in my sleep—there was something almost religious about building a fire.

AiAi whipped out a lighter and tried to ignite the sticks. I let him go for it, confident that it wouldn't catch, so he couldn't burn himself.

There was a plentiful supply of old mallee stumps close by. It told me there hadn't been too many people around to build a campfire. I found a good half-dozen and started hauling them back to the fire pit. Often there's just a small, telltale piece sticking out above the ground but underneath there's a whole knotty, gnarled mass. Mallee burns long and slowly through cold nights.

AiAi followed me around.

'Kick them,' I told him. 'They're like icebergs—all hidden underneath. If it's dead and dry it'll come loose. If it won't come up it's probably still growing.'

He kicked, too hard, and rubbed his foot.

I laughed and he didn't seem to mind. He wandered away with his hands in his pockets, scouring the ground.

Silence joined me. It was the first time we'd been alone in the same space for a while.

'You okay?' I asked.

He nodded and mirrored my actions, kicking stumps, but with a lot less enthusiasm.

'Did you know she was going to bring us here?'

Yes.

'A place to call her own.' I snorted.

Silence made the same sound in his throat and we laughed together.

'Do you think you'll ever tell me what happened to you the other night?

His smile froze. He nodded, a tiny movement. *One day.* He looked over his shoulder at the others.

They'd discovered the fire pit. Darcy and Carrie stomped around it in a bad parody of an Aboriginal dance.

Bree stood off to the side with a blank expression that said a lot.

'Let's light this sucker,' I said and grabbed his hand. 'Come on. I just need some newspaper.'

Arden, it seemed, had thought of everything. That tarp in the cellar had hidden a cache of camping and survival gear that could have stocked an underground bunker in preparation for Armageddon. A couple of eskies full of food, another full container of water, nine army-green swags, more fuel, cans of insecticide, chairs, a portable stove, even bulk packets of toilet paper. I counted seven slabs of beer and four heavy-duty torches. Apart from a layer of road-dust, everything looked brand new, the tags still on.

But no newspaper.

'The toilet paper will do it,' I said.

Silence pressed his notebook into my hand.

'Cool,' I said and flipped to the back of the book.

Silence snapped it shut and shoved it towards my chest. 'Burn it,' he said, quite clearly.

'No.' I tore out a few blank pages and handed it back to him. 'You might need it.' I screwed the pages into twists and stuffed them into the cracks beneath the pile of sticks. Soon, a racing flame was taking hold.

Arden watched our exchange with tight lips. She had a beer in one hand, a plastic cup in the other. She saw me looking and said, 'Rainwater. The tanks are full of the stuff. See? Mother nature provides.'

'Don't drink it,' I said quickly. 'It needs to be purified.' I got busy building up the fire with larger pieces of wood.

'It's clean,' Arden said and held her cup up to the flickering light. 'Crystal. We used to drink from our rainwater tanks all the time.'

'These tanks probably have rust or shit or dead animals floating in them,' I said carefully, without looking at her. 'Quickest way to gastro and dehydration out here.'

Carrie, squashed into a deckchair, turned and spat water into the dust. 'You said it was okay to drink.'

'Listen to Bear fucking Grylls,' Arden sneered. 'Look.'

Arden tilted the cup, poured a tiny amount between her lips. She held the mouthful for a microsecond, the barest hesitation, then she swallowed. 'Ah,' she gasped. She grabbed her throat, made a gurgling sound, fell into Malik's lap and went limp.

AiAi looked around at each of us before he realised it was an act. He laughed.

After burnt baked beans and too many beers, the next few hours were a comedy of falling-down pee-stops in the dark. Carrie stumbled back with spattered jeans, scratched arms and an expression like an axe murderer was on her tail. Darcy made Joe go with her and hold the torch.

The fire burned down to a pleasant glow.

'Where are we going to sleep?' Darcy slurred.

'In the church,' Arden said. 'It's the only place with a decent roof.'

Nobody spoke. They were all looking at me. Even Darcy.

'I'm just going to sleep out here,' I said.

I rolled out my swag a few metres from the fire and arranged my bag and pillow. The canvas was so old, so deeply ingrained with dust and ash and oil, that water rolled right off.

The others followed, until the campfire was surrounded. Malik did the same but set up his swag further away from the rest of us.

Arden sat on the bonnet of the car for ages, smoking, alone.

'If I need the toilet in the night, will you come with me?' Carrie whispered and burrowed deeper in her sleeping bag.

'Sure,' I said.

Why she was so freaked out? It wasn't like the city. There was nothing out there to be afraid of.

Chapter Twenty-two

I loved the morning light the best. It seeped in, a one-way tide; it coloured in dark spaces until the land was flooded with silver light. The magpies' song began while it was still dark. I'd been lying awake for more than an hour. I sat up. My muscles were cramped and stiff and my head throbbed with the sudden blood-rush.

The others were still sleeping.

I crawled out of the swag, stretched out my kinks and looked for a private place to pee behind the church. I squatted on wobbly legs next to an old lean-to stacked with rotting wood. It had been cold overnight, but not enough to keep me awake. The landscape sparkled with crystals of ice and I heard the steady *drip-drip* of melting droplets on tin. Beyond the lean-to there was a beached, battered rowboat next to a pile of planks, a rusted axe poised mid-chop in the trunk of a tree, and a porcelain toilet bowl standing by itself in a circle of stones. A coil of barbed wire was a trap for tumbleweed. It was a scene frozen in time as if only yesterday it had been the land of the living.

I wandered a little way past what must have once been the main street, to where the rows of red gums cast looming shadows. Between them ran an almost-dry riverbed, about five metres across with smooth, pale stones and a few puddles the colour of black tea. The land was split in two: on one side rambling, twisted scrub and the bones of the town; on the other, bare yellow paddocks carved by a cattle fence.

It all felt familiar, as if I'd been there before. It was uncomplicated. I was at peace. I didn't feel the need to look over my shoulder; I could breathe properly and my senses weren't tripping over each other.

'We wondered where you were,' Bree said.

She had her sleeping bag wrapped around her shoulders and a beanie pulled low over her ears. 'Thought you might have been dragged off by a dingo.'

I shrugged. 'Just exploring.'

'Did you happen to find an ensuite?'

I smiled and slid down the riverbank on my backside. I pointed to a puddle. 'Look. Tadpoles. The eggs can survive without water for months, even years. Then when it rains, they hatch and the cycle goes on.'

'Amazing.' She smirked and followed me.

I offered a squirming tadpole. 'Isn't it? He doesn't know he's going to grow legs and lungs. The information's all there, waiting for the right time, packed in his DNA.'

I thought of Vivienne, her hands next to mine, turning a small creature so I could inspect it and be amazed. How she made everyday things seem like a miracle.

Bree pinned her hands under her armpits and shook her head.

'I heard there are caterpillars in Antarctica that defrost for just a few days at a time,' I went on, determined to raise her interest. I scooped another handful of water and let the tadpoles wriggle through my fingers. 'It can take them up to ten years to eat enough vegetation to pupate. Imagine that. Imagine if we could be frozen in ice for a whole year and then wake up and start eating like nothing happened. Makes us seem so fragile, don't you think?' I smiled at her but she was staring at the ground.

'Whoopie-doo.'

'What's wrong with you?' I asked. 'Didn't you sleep?'

Her mouth twisted. 'God, didn't you hear it? In the night? All that rustling and squeaking. I was lying there listening to it with my heart in here,' she pointed to her throat. 'Carrie too. Arden ended up sleeping in the car but that was probably because she was pissed off with Malik. What the fuck did she bring us here for?'

'There's nothing out here big enough to carry you off,' I laughed. 'Maybe a camel. Sorry,' I rambled on. 'But animals adapt. One caterpillar and one green leaf against a whole frozen continent. That tiny thing knows exactly what it's born to do and it survives against all the odds.'

'Look at you,' she said.

'What?' I smoothed down my hair. I knew I must look awful. 'What?'

'I don't think I've ever seen you smile.'

'Of course you have.' I blushed. 'I smile all the time.'

'Not from here to here.' She drew a line from one ear to the other with a finger. 'See, I'm just not feeling it.'

'Feeling what?'

'Whatever it is I'm supposed to feel. You know, some deep connection with the land, or whatever. What a load of shit.' She wrapped the sleeping bag around her shoulders.

191

'You're pretty hard on yourself.'

'I want to go home.'

'Me too. Wherever that is.'

Bree raised her eyebrows. 'Carrie said something happened with you and Wish.'

Self-consciously, I touched my lips. I thought about the false Friday Brown he'd kissed, and compared that image to the real me. But he hadn't turned up that night, so I decided maybe he wouldn't have wanted either.

'Nothing I want to talk about.'

'Come on, tell me,' she prodded. 'Did you catch the Wish fish?'

'More like he got away. *And* he stole my bait.'

She was shocked. 'Did you two . . .'

I got what she was thinking. '*God*, no. Bad choice of words. Nothing happened. I'm glad it didn't. He loves Arden.'

There was a distant pop, then another, like something exploding.

'Well, why wouldn't he?' she said. 'Come on. I smell food.'

We walked back to the campsite.

'You're ruining this for me,' Arden was yelling, her hands on her hips and her feet apart. Her insult wasn't aimed at any one person; it was flung wide like a net. She had her back to us but spun around when she heard us approaching.

'The fire's going out,' she accused. 'And you'd think somebody would know enough to open the fucking cans.'

Carrie retreated behind the car.

Silence was sitting up, still inside his sleeping bag. It looked like it was bleeding orange sap. The dirt surrounding the campfire was sprayed with baked-bean buckshot. A couple of gaping, blackened cans bubbled and spat in the dying coals. A sickly, sticky odour made me screw up my nose and cover my mouth.

AiAi returned from wherever he'd been, zipping his jeans. He gauged Arden's mood, then slunk away.

Bree and I turned to look at each other.

Her mouth twitched and one deep dimple appeared. 'I'm not that hungry,' she said.

'Me neither,' I agreed.

We giggled and Silence, who looked like he was wearing most of the exploded beans, laughed too.

Arden stalked off.

A few minutes later, she was dragging junk out through the door of the old church, making a pile of iron sheets and planks that would have to be moved again anyway.

Malik helped, stripped bare to his waist.

In the end, nobody could stomach beans for breakfast.

I grabbed a piece of stale bread and toasted it on the end of a stick, then ate it dry.

AiAi did the same. He burned three pieces before he got a colour he liked.

I stoked up the fire and rolled my swag, then followed Carrie and Silence into the church.

'Shit,' Carrie said under her breath. 'This is worse than I thought.'

Even Arden's determined efforts had not made a dent in the mess. Fire had ravaged the church once—maybe more than once—and the air tasted stale and smoky. Most of the pews were more or less intact but they were charred and brittle, breaking apart. The whitewashed walls were covered with graffiti, dripping with yellow stains. There was no glass left in the windows. Birds had moved into the rafters and a one-eyed crow watched us from above, head tilted, its good eye aimed down. Our footsteps echoed on the scarred wooden floor, black with dirt, grease and burns.

Arden broke from her frantic pace and wiped her arm over her face, leaving a clean, pink spot on her nose.

'Don't just stand there,' she snarled. 'If we all pitch in it'll be cleaned up by tonight.'

'No fucking way am I sleeping in here,' Carrie said and squashed a spider with her foot. 'I'll take my chances out *there*.' She jabbed a thumb over her shoulder.

Silence wheezed agreement.

'How about you, country girl? Scared of a few spiders?' Arden challenged.

'Just the redbacks,' I conceded. 'But if we bomb the place, that should fix them.'

Carrie laughed. 'Now there's an idea. Let's blow the place up. Looks like it's been bombed already.'

'I meant spider bombs. Those cans of insecticide.'

'I've started a list of everything we'll need,' Arden said, waving a piece of paper. 'Let me know if you think I've forgotten anything. Malik and I will do a run tomorrow morning.'

'We need more water,' I reminded her.

'Oh, shut up about the water, will you?'

Near dark, we were all filthy, bleeding and exhausted. Arden's vision was a long way from being realised and the air was still choked with dust. We'd cleared a large space, enough for living and sleeping. Six rows of pews were gone, ripped apart and stacked up for firewood, the rest wiped clean and lined up along the walls for seats.

Much to the others' disgust, Arden and Malik laid out their swags to claim the raised platform where the preacher's pulpit would have been. I wasn't too bothered. Up there, the floor seemed fragile.

The other buildings were beyond hope. The pub was a wreck, a house of cards ready to fall in on itself. It was plain dangerous to go in there. The squat, plaster houses were nothing but walls—no roof, no floor. We'd found a few useful things—a shovel, a crowbar, a dresser and a rickety table—but most of the half-buried artefacts that looked promising had disintegrated on touch.

We looked like a group of dirty savages, collapsed around the fire. I smelled burnt toast again but, thankfully, no beans.

Joe was smoking on the steps, alone. I went over.

'I'm in mourning,' he said, showing me his empty packet.

'Arden's going shopping tomorrow,' I said. 'I'm sure she'll get more for you.'

'She said we all have to give up,' he said, miserable. 'Part of her vision for a better world. But there's nothing else to do out here.' He crushed the packet and dropkicked it into a bush. 'Where are you going?' He gestured towards my torch.

'I just came to see if you were okay. Come over by the fire. It's freezing over here.' I switched on the torch and flashed an S.O.S. on his face.

Joe squinted and waved me away. 'I want to sleep for a month. When I wake up, I want this all to be over.'

I sneaked into the church and pilfered two cigarettes from Arden's packet, which was sitting on top of her precious tin. The tin that I supposed had money in it. I wondered how much she had stashed away, how long she'd been saving up for her plan to take over the ghost town. I picked the tin up, felt the *thunk* of something shifting inside, jiggled the lock, then put it back carefully inside the impression left in the dust.

'Abracadabra, alakazam,' I said to Joe. I reached behind his ear and pulled out one cigarette. I held it under his nose.

He inhaled the scent of it, a cheeky smile on his lips. I handed him the second one and he gripped my hand for a moment.

'I'm going to call a referendum,' he said seriously. 'I'm pretty sure we all want to get out of here. How will you vote?'

I shrugged. 'Even if you get enough votes, do you really think it'll make a difference? Sounds like Arden's put a lot of effort into this.'

'I was hoping the fact that she has to shit in the woods like all the other bears might change her mind.'

'It probably will. Give her a few days.' I was enjoying myself. I felt more at ease, more *sure* of myself than I had in a long time.

Silence materialised. He tugged at my sleeve.

Joe got up, lit a cigarette and took a long, blissful drag. He sighed through a stream of smoke. 'Yeah. A few more days. We can all survive that.'

Chapter Twenty-three

Joe, Silence and I wandered back to the circle of fire.

Carrie had her hand deep in a bag of Doritos and AiAi sat cross-legged on the ground between her legs, drinking beer again.

'We're telling campfire stories,' Arden said.

'It was disgusting,' Darcy said. 'Malik said how this family had their house broken into and all their stuff was taken. But not their camera. So, when they took the film in for processing they found all these pictures of the burglars mooning. And when they zoomed in they could see the family's toothbrushes stuck up their arses. And they had been using them since the burglary.'

'It isn't true. It's an urban myth,' Joe said. 'True stories are even creepier.'

'I've got one,' said Carrie. 'Our next-door neighbours went away for a few days and somehow our other neighbour's dog got into their backyard and killed their rabbit. It was all covered in dirt and slobber. So this woman is horrified that they'll find out and she takes the dead rabbit, washes it, blow-dries it, and makes it look like natural causes.'

'Gross,' AiAi slurred.

'I'm not finished. So, the neighbours get home and they

tell my mum that the weirdest thing happened—their rabbit died the day before they left and they buried it in the backyard. And when they got home it was back in its hutch.'

'Freaky,' Arden said.

'Another urban myth,' Joe argued. 'Notice how everyone always said it happened to someone they know?'

'Bah, humbug. It's true,' Carrie said, but she sounded unsure.

'I have one,' I volunteered. 'This is a true story.'

'Go on,' Arden said and swigged her beer.

I told it just like Vivienne told it to me. The setting was almost the same: a dying fire, ghostly gums all around, bitter cold. The hairs on my arms were standing up and I had the keenest sense that with Vivienne gone, this was my story to tell. My history. Campfire stories were in my blood.

'We lived in a two-roomed hut,' I began, and their orange-glowing faces all turned to me.

I was three years old. Vivienne and I were there all alone, nineteen kays from anywhere, her man away droving. There was bush all around, flat land with no horizon. We had an ugly, yellow-eyed dog called Croc. He was ten generations of mongrel, but he was whip-smart and he wasn't scared of anything.

One afternoon, Vivienne was hanging wet sheets. I was playing by the woodheap when a metre-long red-belly black snake shot out, writhed past my feet, and went under the house.

'Snake!' I yelled and pointed at the gap between the house and the ground.

Vivienne snatched me up with one hand and a heavy, club-ended stick with the other. We waited, but the snake didn't appear. Vivienne set a saucer of milk near the gap to entice the snake out. For hours, Croc eyeballed the gap where the snake had disappeared, but it didn't show itself.

A thunderstorm formed overhead and we went into the hut. The sky was churning, purple and black, and a single bolt of lightning struck the woodheap. It sparked and started to burn, but a torrent of heavy rain doused it. Vivienne took me and Croc into the kitchen. She put me high up on the wooden table and told me to stay there with Croc crouched on guard beneath.

Vivienne could withstand more than this; the land was cruel and her life had been lonely and tough. With nothing but her stick and her yellow-eyed dog, she fought bushfires and floods and fended off loners who knocked at her door, vagrants without conscience. A drifter had chopped and stacked her woodheap in exchange for food and she'd given him extra as thanks, only to discover he'd built the woodheap hollow.

Once, when I was sick, she rode our ancient mare hard for thirty kilometres to get help, with me draped across her lap. The old mare dropped dead and Vivienne walked the whole way home with me on her back.

I fell asleep on that hard table, while Vivienne and Croc stood vigil, their eyes on the corner.

Near midnight Vivienne was reading, attuned to the slightest noise and every quiver of Croc's tail. Thunder boomed and wind rushed through the gaps of the old hut; lightning flared, illuminating the room. The fire burned low and Vivienne dozed with her hand on the stick. Her eyes were drooping, but still she waited for that devil snake to show itself. Croc dozed, legs twitching, chasing snakes in his dreams.

Almost morning. Weak, grey light poured through the curtains and Vivienne needed to use the outdoor toilet. She couldn't hold on any longer. Out of habit, Croc followed her. She lay the stick next to me on the table and closed the door quietly behind her.

But the soft click of the door and the sudden silence woke me. I slid off the table, onto the floor, still half-asleep.

My mother and Croc were missing. I was alone, only three years old.

But I wasn't alone. An evil pair of bead-like eyes glistened at the gap between the wall and the floor. The snake inched out, testing danger with its tongue, then slid out further.

I reached up for Vivienne's stick.

Further.

I raised the stick above my head and brought it down before the snake had a chance to retreat.

Whack!

I hit the snake with the clubbed end of the stick. It smashed down and broke its spine near the tail-end of its body, but there was still nearly a metre of angry snake, moving, darting at my bare feet with pinkened fangs.

Whack!

I severed its spine halfway, but still it came. I backed into the corner and raised the stick again.

Vivienne opened the door. The snake had three enemies and didn't know which way to go. Its rear half was limp *and useless but its single-minded dying wish was to inject venom.*

Croc advanced on one side, his yellow eyes gleaming with deadly intent. He'd killed hundreds of snakes; he'd die by snakebite, never old age, as snake dogs do.

Croc darted in. His jaws clamped down behind the snake's head and he snapped it like a whip. The snake landed belly up, flipped itself over, and kept coming.

Vivienne snatched the stick from my hand and brought it down near the snake's head. She missed. Croc slashed the snake with his teeth but it was still too quick. Vivienne hit again and skinned the end of Croc's nose.

She scooped me up under her arm and swung again, one-handed. She dropped me onto the table, but the momentum carried me up and over the side. I rolled onto the floor, gasping, and opened my eyes.

The snake's mangled head was centimetres from my cheek.

Croc gathered his body to launch but Vivienne had him held by the collar.

'Friday Brown, do not move!' she said.

The snake stared at me. If it wasn't just a dumb creature with a half-smashed head I'd have sworn it was dragging out those final moments, summoning every last drop of venom, loading its gleaming fangs, for me.

Vivienne stayed Croc and bent low under the table. Slowly, she opened her fingers like pincers. She held her hand poised over the snake's tail, ready to grab should it strike. Croc hunkered down next to her, set to spring.

We stayed like that for what seemed like forever. The sun

came up, a huge burning orb. A golden shaft of light poured through the window and cut like a laser across the floor.

Still Vivienne waited.

The burning beam crept onwards, across the dusty floor and over my leg, my arm, my face. It hit the snake full on. In slow motion, it blinked, and Vivienne struck. She clamped down on its tail, dragged the snake backwards and summoned her yellow-eyed dog.

Croc had the final say. He'd die by snakebite—but not that day.

Croc crushed the snake's head between his teeth. He carried it to Vivienne and, when he dropped it at her feet, Vivienne picked up the carcass with her stick and threw it onto the fire.

'We sat together, the three of us, and watched the snake burn until there was nothing left,' I finished.

It was Vivienne's story, but now I'd made it my own. Vivienne had never been able to say with any surety what had happened in that room while she was gone, and the truth is, I couldn't remember any of it. By making the story complete, it left me feeling like I'd finally taken ownership of my own memories. With her gone.

Darcy and Carrie were speechless, gripping each other's arms.

Malik's perpetually bored expression had softened into something like mild interest.

Silence was staring at me like I was the new Messiah and AiAi was wide-eyed, his beer tipped over and soaked into the dust.

Arden sighed. 'That's a great story.'

'Thanks,' I said. I waited for her smile to tell me she meant it.

'What happened to the dog?' AiAi asked.

'I . . . I can't remember. He died, I guess.'

'And it's a true story?' Arden shifted in her deckchair until she was leaning forwards, her elbows pinned together on her knees, her chin in her hands. Watching me with an expression that was far too intent. 'You're sure?'

'My mother told it to me. Many times.' I hated the bubble in my throat. I hated that my voice had to squeeze past it to get out.

'Did she really?'

'Yes, she really did,' I said, puzzled.

'Fascinating, don't you think,' she said, 'that the snake blinked. Snakes don't have eyelids.'

Malik barked a laugh.

'What?' In the back of my mind I knew this was fact. A fact that bored a hole through the middle of Vivienne's story—and my memory.

'I meant that the snake was blinded,' I stammered.

It didn't matter anyway. The moment was gone. The memory was flawed. I was left with a sense of loss.

Arden wasn't finished.

'I've heard that story before,' she said. 'I can even tell you who wrote it and what it's called. It's called *The Drover's Wife* and Henry Lawson wrote it and if your mother told it to you and said it happened, that makes her a liar. And a thief.'

Darcy snickered and put her hand over her mouth. 'I knew she was full of shit.'

Joe said, 'Shut up, Darce,' and wouldn't look at me.

Arden smiled. 'Sorry to be the one to burst your bubble. Hey, like I said, it was a good story.'

I was suddenly light-headed. I felt sick.

In the quiet that followed, I saw my life in flashes. Every campfire tale that Vivienne had told, every edge of me that was defined by a memory, all the glittering recollections that stacked up to make me who I am—they were revisited. Not in a fast-forward, 'you're about to die', flickering-vignette kind of way. It was more like seeing a magician's act, exposed. I wasn't a kid any more, the one who believed without question. If I was honest, I hadn't been for a long time.

In that moment, doubt finally extinguished belief.

I saw Vivienne's invisible wires, the smoke and mirrors, her sleight of hand. It sounded like a good story. Why didn't she just tell me the real version? I hated her. I hated her for leaving me, for leaving me half done, for leaving me out of the joke. I was nothing, and it was her fault.

I tried to stand but my legs had no substance. I blinked away tears but my chin wobbled. For something to do I grabbed a beer, opened it and slugged a mouthful. It was warm and gassy, unpleasant.

Bree watched me, her eyes dark and shimmery. 'AiAi, pass me a beer.'

Joe said, 'You know, you could say the same about every staunch little Christian. Doesn't make them any less a Christian just because the Bible is a bunch of far-fetched stories that lasted more than one generation.'

Carrie nodded. 'What about the Dreamtime?' She glanced at Bree. 'Sorry. No offence.'

Bree just shook her head.

Silence's features twisted into such intense fury he looked ten years older, a whole lot taller. He walked over to Arden and pointed his finger at her. 'You're mean,' he rasped. 'I hate you.' He broke into a fit of coughing that doubled him over, but his finger stayed there.

Arden flinched, recovered. She grabbed his finger and curled it under, then threw his hand away. 'I'm just being honest. Get that out of my face.'

Malik stood and shoved Silence hard in the chest.

Silence landed on his back. He propped himself up on an elbow. His jeans were stained red with dust.

Carrie and I moved to help him up but he pushed us away.

He smiled at Arden, pointed his index finger again, and drew a line across his throat.

'I hate you,' he hissed.

Chapter Twenty-four

We needed something good to happen.

Sleep was restless, tangled. It turned out the church didn't really count as shelter, not with so many gaps and missing windows. The wind started at around midnight; it sucked and blew and played the old church like a woodwind instrument. I woke often. So did the others. We staggered into a washed-out morning and a fine, misty rain.

Arden and Malik left early to get supplies.

'Looks like we're stuck here for a few more days.' Bree watched them leave. 'Imagine if they didn't come back? We'd probably die out here and nobody would even know where to look.'

'Nah,' said Joe. He looked up. 'Don't forget the eye in the sky.'

AiAi took him literally and scanned the clouds.

'People probably come here all the time,' I said. 'Photographers. History buffs. I don't think we're truly isolated.'

'Not like your hut, huh?' Darcy sniped. 'Bet that was a long way from anywhere.'

'Hey, Darcy. Something for you.' Carrie pretended to reach into her back pocket, then flipped out her middle finger.

Joe laughed.

Silence mooched past us without a glance, his hands in his pockets, hood pulled tight around his face.

'I'll see if he's okay,' I said and went after him.

I followed him all the way down to the dry riverbed. Except it wasn't dry any more.

'It's flowing!' I said. Fresh water—here was our good thing. 'It could be melting snow from far away. Or maybe there's an underground spring somewhere.'

The tea-coloured puddles were gone, washed away by a trickle that skipped over rocks and carried on.

Silence nodded and prodded the surface with a stick. It was clear and only a few centimetres deep. We could wash properly and the water would be safer for drinking than the stuff in the rusting tanks.

'Hey, Silence. We could build a dam. Then it'll be deep enough for a bath.'

I took off my shoes. Rolled my jeans up to my knees. The water was icy and tickled my feet. I carried pile after pile of round, smooth stones in my T-shirt and started stacking them to build a wall across the river.

At first, not much happened. The water found its way between the stones and trickled away. Then, as the wall grew wider and the stones settled into each other, a small lagoon of calm water pooled around my feet.

Silence watched from the bank, his arms looped around his knees.

'Are you going to help me, or what?'

Reluctantly, he started to untie his laces. He skidded down the bank and inched into the water.

I wondered if he'd ever paddled his feet before, the way he was looking at them, as if they were alien parasites attached to his body.

Suddenly he sat in the pool, soaking his clothes. His teeth clacked together, but he was smiling. He washed his clothes while he was still in them, kneading and squeezing, until the pool was clouded with dirt.

'Good idea. But wouldn't it be better if we took them off?'

Silence looked up at me. He mouthed a challenge.

My teeth were chattering too, but I wanted so badly to be clean.

I took off my T-shirt, leaving my skin-coloured bra. It had been white, once. I pulled down my jeans and threw them over the other side of the wall where the water rushed through. I sat next to Silence in the pool and drew my knees up to my chest.

'Strip,' I told him. 'I am *not* going to be the only blue person in this river.'

He hesitated, then pulled his hoodie up slowly over his shoulders. He struggled—it was waterlogged and got stuck.

I reached over and peeled it gently over his face. I tried not to look. We were shy with each other. He turned his face away. I looked elsewhere, anywhere but at him. I tossed the hoodie onto my pile of clothes and sat back down. It was inevitable that we did look at each other, eventually.

What I saw. Oh, what I saw.

Silence's pale, boyish arms and body were marked with vicious, red circles, raised, knotty scars that formed a map of pain. His chest was white and slightly concave. A couple of ribs protruded so sharply they seemed ready to burst through his skin. On both inner forearms, matching vertical scars ran from his wrists almost halfway to his elbows.

I reached out my hand and ran a fingertip over one of the circles. They were all small and round, exactly the same size, randomly scattered, like he'd faced a firing squad and lived to walk away.

'Did you do this to yourself?'

He shook his head, *No.*

I released the pent-up pressure in my throat by clearing it. I was relieved, but it didn't last.

Silence claimed the scars on his wrists as his own. *I did this.*

But I knew that, even then. Those scars were personal, by a person who had nowhere else to go but oblivion.

'I . . .' I couldn't speak. My eyes were filling up and my vision was blurred.

It's okay.

This kid, with scars and a history that sickened me, was looking at *me* with compassion. He'd lived a life of terror and come through it with his heart open. His blue eyes were welling up too, but it was *me* he was upset for. A faint blue hue outlined his lips. He reached out with a cold hand and clamped it over mine.

It's okay.

But it wasn't. It was pretty far from okay.

'Vivienne used to say that sometimes the best you can do is try not to be one of the bastards,' I said.

I wished it was that simple. I used to believe in karma. If it existed, the innocents would be safe in palaces and the bastards would be picking each other off in the streets. Silence wouldn't have been stealing and his ribs would be in the right place. AiAi wouldn't rattle when he walked and Joe could kiss whoever he liked.

'We can start over, somewhere. I won't leave without you. But I can't stay here. That's what we were going to do, anyway. Weren't we? The night before the squat burned down?'

Silence looked sharply over his shoulder. He withdrew his hand and dragged it to and fro under the water as if he was conducting a symphony.

'What happened? Why can't you tell me?'

He shook his head and, in the shadows, his cheeks looked hollow.

The water was too cold to stay there for much longer. We wrung out our clothes and hung them over a branch. Where the pool overflowed we bowed our heads and rinsed our hair, then climbed up onto the bank. Sunlight made camouflage patterns on our chilled skin and soon my blood was flowing again.

Out of the shade, the heat was intense.

'Where have you two been? Why are you all wet?' Darcy asked.

'Take me there,' Carrie said and held her filthy shirt away from her body. 'I don't care if cows have shat in it or fish have fucked in it—wherever it is, take me there. Oh my God, you're so *clean.*'

Within a few hours, despite everyone having a bath in the pool, we were dusty again. The trees along the river were draped with dripping clothes. With Carrie and Joe's help, we raised the dam wall high enough to hold back a metre of water. I boiled litres and litres of the stuff and refilled both water containers while Darcy sat and watched.

A box of muesli bars and a few packets of chips were the only edible food left. Everything else had been mauled by bull ants, thousands of them, in our clothes, our beds—everywhere. I poured petrol down into the nests but they were relentless.

'Jesus, it's hot,' Carrie complained. 'We seriously need to get out of this hellhole.'

'I concur,' Joe said. 'On both points.'

We'd been lucky. It hadn't been that hot yet, but that day there was a taste of the summer to come. There was nothing to do but chase the shade. Darcy's nose and shoulders were pink and raw. Joe had a wet T-shirt tied around his head. I'd forgotten how changeable the land was; one minute, it was green, and the next, brown. If you listened, you could hear the bush crackle and retreat.

When Arden and Malik finally got back in the late afternoon, they were mobbed. The one thing I asked for—deodorant—they managed not to get.

Arden eyed the refilled water containers and raised an eyebrow.

'We have a creek now,' Carrie said.

Arden reached in the back of the troop carrier and hauled out a box of spring water. 'Here. You wanted water, you got water,' she said, and heaved it in my direction. The cardboard split, the bladder inside burst, and litres drained away into the thirsty ground.

Mud spattered up my legs.

'We need more water,' Arden mimicked me. 'Bloody drama queen.'

Chapter Twenty-five

That night we cooked our first real dinner.

Arden had bought two chickens, which we roasted in a cast-iron camp oven. It was too new, nothing like the battered old pot Vivienne and I carted from place to place. Malik didn't season it properly and wouldn't listen when I tried to tell him how to do it. Half the meat burned and stuck to the bottom. We wrapped potatoes in foil and cooked them slowly, buried in hot coals. I mixed flour, salt and water and kneaded a lump of damper dough. It rose like it was supposed to and even tasted a bit like heaven. If everything had a slight charcoal flavour, no one complained. Dessert was toasted marshmallows and vodka and cranberry from a cask and, for the first time since we'd left the city, we were halfway to thinking that life was good.

Arden was trying too hard with Silence. She served him extra food and topped up his drink after every mouthful. She put her hand on his shoulder like she was dipping a toe in water, testing—and he shrugged her off. She asked him a question and he ignored her.

I watched them circling each other and wondered exactly when she had lost his devotion. It ran deep in him, as it did with the others, but he'd turned hard and unforgiving. It hurt her, I could tell.

'Want to go for a walk?' I asked him after we'd cleaned up. I was at that point where alcohol makes you feel like everything's right with the world. 'Come on.' I picked up a torch and trained the beam on a distant clump of bushes. Something flapped and skittered away into the night.

No way. Silence made a spider with his hand and walked it along his arm. He shook his head again.

'Chicken,' I nudged him.

When I set off along the winding track that ran past the pub, he followed.

Near the edge of the bush, where the trees started to thicken, there was an old water tank perched on a lopsided framework of stilts. A ladder was propped up against it. The tank seemed sound enough, but when I tapped on the outside it rang hollow.

'It's not connected to anything,' I said. 'I'm going up.'

Silence shrugged and held the torch when I handed it to him. He heard a noise in the space under the tank and bolted up the ladder after me.

The roof of the tank was about four metres above the ground. It was covered in a layer of eucalyptus leaves and twigs. There was a square opening with a screwed-down lid on the far side.

I used a leafy branch to sweep a space for us to sit.

'Look. You can see for miles from up here.'

We could see the warm halo of the campfire, the shadowy mounds of distant hills and brilliant, scattered stars above.

214

The tin was still warm against my back when I stretched out, my hands cupped behind my head.

Silence looked over the edge and sighed. He dropped down next to me.

'It's okay. It's perfectly safe,' I reassured him.

A far-away creature called a long, plaintive moan. A rogue current of air parted the trees like an invisible serpent.

Silence was rigid beside me.

'Silence?'

Yeah.

'That stuff you wrote. About being nothing.'

Yeah.

'I don't think you're nothing.'

He grabbed my hand and held it.

'You know, since my mother died, I've been trying to figure out who I am and where I belong,' I confessed. 'All I have is a bunch of stories and memories that aren't even real. And that kind of leaves me feeling like nothing, too. So, I get it—why you would feel like that.'

Silence squeezed my hand.

He was looking up at the stars, but not, I think, because they were so close they seemed suspended between earth and space. He was still, not blinking, because his eyes were filling up like that dammed pool and he was trying to hold back his tears. But the water always finds a way through, even when you pile those stones high and deep—eventually it finds a way.

Silence pointed his finger and drew lines between the stars, one by one.

'They're ours tonight,' I told him. 'If someone like you

can come from this,' I touched his hidden scars, 'then there's hope for all of us.' I let my hand fall away. 'But not Darcy. She's beyond hope.'

He laughed. The movement made his tears spill over.

I wiped them away with my thumbs and leaned over him to press my lips to his wet cheeks, one at a time. I never would have believed I could kiss a boy that way. I thought there were only two types of kissing: the passionate, rip your clothes off kind, and the dry, chaste peck you gave an elderly person because it was expected. But there was another kind of kiss. The kind that sealed a moment in a time capsule, forever: a small moment that branded my soul.

Silence sat up. He found a stick and scratched his name in the layer of dirt on the top of the tank. He formed the letters carefully, but they were small.

I thought of Vivienne and me, on a beach somewhere writing our names in the sand, and I told him what she had told me.

'Write big,' I said.

I put my hand over his and together we wrote in large, deep letters: *Silence was here.*

'Who was Amy? Was she your sister?'

I didn't mean to ask him that. Not when he was so broken.

He nodded and smiled. Thumped his heart with a fist. *My sister.*

'What happened to her?'

He spread his hands. *Gone.*

With some effort, he told me.

They'd left home together two years before, when Amy was sixteen. Silence was thirteen. Amy had changed her mind at the last minute—she didn't think she could take care of him. She gave him money to go home, said he should stick it out until she found a place for them. She got on a train and disappeared.

Silence never went home.

The train station—it was so clear to me at that moment. Darcy. Me. Silence haunted the train station where he'd last seen his sister. He picked up lost girls.

A thought hit me.

'Silence, who are you, really? What's your name?'

'Lucas,' he whispered. It was almost a question, as if he was calling out to someone he used to know. 'Lucas Emerson,' he said more clearly.

'I'm Liliane Brown,' I told him. 'Pleased to meet you, Lucas Emerson.'

We shook on it.

A beam of torchlight cut through the dark, blinding us.

'What are you doing up there?' Bree called.

'Hanging out,' I said. 'Hey, Bree—what's your real name?'

I shone my torch over the edge. Her face was spotlit.

She blinked, looked confused. 'Bree,' she said. She crawled up the ladder and peered at us both. 'Come with me, you guys. You have to see this.'

'What is it?'

'Just come.'

We climbed down from the water tank and brushed dead leaves from each other's backs.

Bree led us past the old windmill. It was spinning slowly,

creaking in the wind. Along the dirt road, past the row of red gums, to the edge of the river. Nearer to the bank, the rushing sound of wind was louder. Bree's torch grew dim and flickered out.

'Shit.' She smacked it against her leg. 'You go first,' she said to me. 'Down there.'

I directed my torch beam past the pale, scarred trunks of the gums, down into the riverbed, where the pool had been.

Had been.

My skin prickled. My nose started to drip. I wiped it with the back of my hand and concentrated hard on keeping the torch steady.

'See it?'

'I see it.'

The rushing sound wasn't the wind in the trees. It was the river. Its level had risen to almost a ruler's length clear of the top of the bank. The water was dark and I couldn't see the bottom. The current raced, dragging clumps of debris, spinning branches around and around then dragging them under and spitting them back out downstream.

'I came to see if the pool was still full, but it was gone,' Bree yelled over the noise.

I had been worrying about the lack of water, certain the Brown curse couldn't show itself out there on the edge of a desert a hundred kilometres from anywhere. Even with my doubts about Vivienne and her stories, that didn't explain why fear had my gut all twisted up like a balloon animal.

I took a step away from the bank. It was starting to soften

and crumble in places, as if the river was trying to cut a new path. As we watched, a piece broke away and dissolved, leaving a tangle of exposed tree roots. Where our lagoon had been that afternoon there was now a whirlpool of current.

I wiped my nose again.

'Your nose is bleeding,' Bree said. Her eyes were wide and fearful. She took the torch and shone it on my hand.

My wrist and thumb were smeared with red.

Silence was staring at the blood. He turned white and gripped a branch to steady himself. He seemed to be waiting for me to answer him, except I hadn't heard a question.

'It's only blood,' I said.

He nodded at the river.

'Oh, that. It's only water.' I could tell he wasn't convinced. 'It happened pretty fast,' I went on, trying to keep my voice steady. I pinched the bridge of my nose and cupped my hand to catch the drips. 'It could be raining a lot somewhere upstream and this is the run-off. I don't know . . . I need a tissue. It'll be okay.' To prove it, I stepped closer to the bank, leaned down and scooped a handful of water. The current was freezing and strong as a spa-bath jet. I rinsed my nose and my arms, but the more I added water, the more blood there seemed to be. I could feel pressure forcing its way up behind my nasal passage, into my ears.

Silence came up behind me and held onto my T-shirt as I leaned over.

'I'm okay,' I said, sniffing. 'We should go back and tell the others.'

'Maybe Arden will let us go home now.' Bree picked up a stick and threw it into the river. It spun crazily, dancing on the surface, then dunked and disappeared. 'Did we do this? By piling up the stones?'

I shook my head. The movement made me dizzy. 'There's no way we could have done that.' *It's me*, I thought. *It's the curse. I did this.*

But that was stupid. Irrational. We'd seen signs of it when we arrived—clumps of grass and leaves matted together, stranded up high in the cracks of the buildings. Old tide marks, like sweat-stains, on the walls. A picture-perfect postcard town, abandoned, for no apparent reason.

Murungal Creek. *Thunder* Creek.

That's the noise it made, the river—rolling and booming like storm clouds rubbing together.

Back at the fire, only Carrie, Joe and Darcy were still up.

'Don't go in there. Arden and Malik are going at it,' Carrie informed us.

'So, where's AiAi?' Bree said.

'Ah, shit,' Carrie smacked her forehead. 'He said he was going for a leak ages ago.' She stood unsteadily. 'Better go find him. What happened to you?' She pointed to the bloodstains on my T-shirt.

'My nose,' I said. 'It's nothing. It's stopped.' As soon as we'd come away from the river, the pressure had eased and the flow had slowed down. 'Which way did he go?'

Darcy looked at Bree. 'I thought he was with you?'

'Nope. Didn't see him.' Bree picked up the cask of vodka and poured from the tap straight into her throat.

Silence stared off into the dark.

I moved away from the fire and stepped into the sparse

shrubbery behind the church. I made a funnel with my hands. 'AiAi!'

Carrie came and stood next to me. She shone her torch into the blackness. 'AiAi!' she called.

'He wouldn't have gone near the river, would he?'

'How would I know? Who knows what goes through his head. Why, what's wrong with the river?' she asked.

'If he fell in he would've been swept away. It's nearly overflowing,' I said.

'No way!' She smacked her forehead again. 'Oh, shit.'

Across the clearing, the others had their torches flickering. Their calls bounced back.

'Surely he wouldn't take off by himself? He's afraid of the dark,' Carrie said.

'What's going on? What's all the noise?' Arden beamed us full in the face with her Maglite.

'AiAi's missing.'

'How long for?'

'Probably half an hour or so,' Carrie answered, shame-faced. 'Maybe more. I didn't really notice.'

'He'll turn up. Keep it down. I've got a headache and I'm trying to sleep.'

'AiAi. Is. Missing,' Carrie repeated. 'How can you even think of going back to sleep?'

'Easy.' Arden's colourless eyes didn't blink. 'I'm tired and my fucking head hurts.' She spun on her bare feet and left a trail of man-sized footprints in the dust.

Carrie looked at me with her mouth open.

'Come on. We'll find him,' I said and slung my arm over her shoulder. 'He can't have gone too far. AiAi!'

We did find him, not far away, crouched under a tree and looking miserable.

'I saw a snake. I think it was a snake. And Friday told me not to move and to be very quiet if I saw a s . . . sn . . . snake.' His teeth chattered.

'You did good,' I told him. 'Let's get you warmed up.'

Carrie piggybacked him all the way to the campfire and called to the others.

I was seething. My skin was crawling, like there were bugs under it. I burst into the church with my torch still on high beam. Arden was sitting up reading, Malik lying stretched out next to her, apparently asleep.

'We found him. I thought you'd want to know. Since you were so concerned and all.'

Arden jumped and stuffed something under the edge of her swag. 'Good,' she said. 'Tell the others to get some sleep.'

'You tell them.'

'What?'

'Tell them yourself.'

'Come here and say that.' She got up and assumed her combat stance. Her elbows stuck out at sharp angles. 'You shut your mouth.'

'Which is it? Speak or shut my mouth?' I was trembling and she saw it.

'Want me to shut it for her?' Malik drawled.

Arden ignored him. 'What's up your arse?'

'Have you seen the river? It's flooding. We need to get out of here. It isn't safe. AiAi could have died out there tonight.'

'Stop acting like you know everything. You make me sick,' she spat.

222

'We need to leave,' I said stubbornly.

'Remember what I said to you?'

'You say a lot of things.'

'About not being able to survive alone?'

'You said I wasn't *street*,' I said. I took another few steps towards her. With less distance between us I could see she was shaking, too. 'Well, I happen to think that's just a matter of location.'

'You can go,' she said in an offhand way. She smiled sweetly. 'You can leave. We'll drop you at the nearest town on the next supply run.'

'Silence, too.'

'If he wants to go with you. Sure. No problem.'

'Good,' I said, surprised that she would give in so easily. I should have known better. 'He will.'

'Really? You think so? You've known him for, like, five minutes. You don't know anything about him. Or me.'

'Yeah, you're a real enigma, Arden.' I turned and headed for the door.

'You have no fucking idea,' she said.

I stopped. Her expression was so smug I wanted to slap it off her face. I hissed, 'Silence tells me *everything*.'

Her gaze wavered. There was a tiny crack in her performance. A flicker of fear.

Chapter Twenty-six

The next morning was pale and clear. Not a breath of wind.

Silence and I packed our things and left our gear piled up in the shadow of the car. We'd slept outside by the fire, partly because I didn't want to be near Arden, partly because Silence was wheezy and the dust made his throat close over. That day there was a swagger in his step, a limping gangsta roll that made me laugh, which made him ham it up even more.

'Wish we were going, too,' Joe sulked. He was preparing coffee over the coals with the precision of a surgeon.

'Why don't you?' I asked him.

'Nah. I don't fancy hitching anywhere. It'll be easier, just the two of you. I'm a liability. I'll stick it out till she gets sick of being here. Can't be much longer. We'll catch you back in the big smoke.'

'Maybe,' I said. 'Some day.' I had other plans. We wouldn't be going back to the city.

Silence and I hadn't slept much. We'd whispered to each other and I'd told him stories about how it could be if we made it all the way up north. I told him about the rainforests, where the bugs were as big as your hand and slower than a rainy day; about the time I watched a cane field burn and it seemed like the whole planet was on fire; how riding out a cyclone in a weatherboard shack can take a year off your life for fear and give you two back for sheer exhilaration. I gave him accounts of my true life, the stuff I could remember. Not Vivienne's fairy-tale versions of truth.

In the dark, anything seemed possible. I wondered if I'd promised him too much, made it all seem bigger and brighter than it really was. What if my idea of freedom wasn't what *he* wanted? What if I was just like Vivienne, building castles in the sky?

While we were waiting, Silence, Bree and I checked out the river. It seemed to have stopped rising. A dirty, brown current meandered along, oily bubbles floating on the surface. The level was a little higher but without the fury of the night before.

By lunchtime, we were still waiting to leave.

Arden seemed in no rush. She dithered about, fired drill-sergeant orders for lunch and dinner, and ignored Silence and me as if we'd already gone. She had a saucepan perched too close to the flame and I could hear the contents sizzling.

'I thought you were dropping us off in town,' I said carefully.

'Next supply run,' she said without looking up. 'Not today.' There was a trip-wire tension in her body. Her focus on the intricacies of opening a can of corn was unsettling, her movements sluggish, as if she was drugged.

'So, tomorrow?' I pressed.

'Maybe,' she said vaguely. 'Yes, tomorrow. We'll see.'

Darcy sighed. 'I thought you were taking them today. I need some . . . you know. Girl stuff.'

'No. Too many chances. Stolen car. We'll wait,' she said in her strange, robotic tone.

I broke the news to Silence gently. His shoulders slumped. He refused to unpack his swag and sat on top of his pile of stuff like a roadside refugee. Carrie brought him a sandwich but he let it go dry in the sun.

Don't leave without me, he said fiercely.

'How can I leave without you?' I said. 'I'm not exactly going to flap my wings and fly out of here, am I?'

He dug around for his notebook and flipped to the back. He pointed to a blank page.

'What's wrong?'

Gone. He spread his hands.

'What's gone?'

He showed me the ragged butts where some pages had been torn out. Our eyes met.

'You can tell me later. You can write it all down again when we get out of here.'

He nodded. He walked over to the fire and made a great show of burning the notebook in front of Arden. It took a while to catch, then began to curl slowly at the edges. Blue flame ate a hole right through the middle and the book dissolved into ash.

Arden watched.

'Bored, bored, bored,' Darcy whined. She kicked a stump that didn't give and limped over to where Carrie and AiAi were playing cards. 'What's going on with him?' She poked a thumb over her shoulder at Silence.

Silence was still guarding his stuff even though the sun

was belting down, the patch of shade gone. It was his version of a protest, but it wasn't working.

Arden and Malik were hooking up the trailer, working around him.

'He's making a stand,' I said.

'Didn't ask you.'

'Give it a rest, Darce,' Joe said. 'It's boring.'

Carrie snorted, then cocked her head. She stood and put a hand up to shield her eyes from the sun. 'What's that?'

AiAi scampered up the bonnet of the troop carrier. 'Car,' he said. 'There's a car coming.'

Arden froze. She climbed up next to AiAi and surveyed the landscape. Her cogs were turning.

I stood on the bull bar. 'It's a long way off yet.' There was a cloud of dust on the horizon, moving slowly in our direction.

Malik let the trailer coupling fall to the ground. 'What do you want me to do?' he asked Arden.

She was breathing hard, nostrils flared like a spooked animal. 'Get the trailer hooked up now,' she said. 'The rest of you, start putting your stuff in the back.'

'What for?' Joe asked. 'We're allowed to camp here, surely?'

Arden turned. 'We're driving a stolen vehicle, you idiot,' she spat. 'Go, go, go!'

Malik fumbled, Arden swore. The rest of us threw everything in a dusty pile in the trailer. I kicked dirt over the campfire but it wouldn't go out. In desperation, Arden poured a whole container of water over the coals. A spiral of smoke and steam stained the sky.

'Subtle,' I said.

'Can you drive?' she yelled at Joe.

'Yeah, but not that thing. It's manual.'

'I can drive,' I said quietly, dusting off my jeans. *Give me the keys, Arden.* I wasn't sure what I'd do—take Silence and go, just drive off, leave her there to rot?—but I wanted the keys. The keys meant control.

Arden looked at me. She read resolution on my face. She didn't like it.

'I can drive,' I said again and held out my hand.

She glanced at Silence, still perched on his pile. He hadn't moved. He was looking at the distant trail of dust with a tiny smile on his lips, as if he was expecting company.

Arden wrestled with her decision. She stared at Silence. Swung her gaze to me. Judged the distance between us and the oncoming car. Flicked back to Silence. An expression of pure hatred passed across her face like the shadow of a cloud—then it was gone. She must have made up her mind— she handed over the keys.

'Take the others. Drive out that way.' She pointed to the river. 'Not too far, just out of sight. Park the car somewhere hidden in the scrub and wait for my signal. And keep quiet. Do *not* come back until I let you all know it's clear.'

'A cooee?' I smirked. 'Hey, you could send us a smoke signal.' *Get in, Silence*, I thought. *Get in.*

'Shut up and get going.'

I climbed up into the cab and started the engine. Bree slid in next to me and the others got in the back. I could barely reach the clutch, even with the seat fully forwards.

Get in, Silence.

He had his eyes locked onto Arden. Still guarding his post.

228

'Silence, get in!' I called.

He started to move towards the car.

Arden said something to Malik in a low voice. Then she leaned in the window. 'Not him,' she said. 'Insurance.'

At the same time Malik snaked an arm around Silence's throat and held him there. It was as effective as a collar—Silence gasped and wheezed and scraped divots in the dust with his heels.

'Go,' Arden said. 'He'll be fine. I want to make sure you come back.'

I hesitated, riding the clutch until the rear wheels spun.

Malik whipped Silence around and pinned him on the ground with one arm. He gave me a signal that I figured meant 'floor it'.

'Let him go,' Arden said.

Malik let go of Silence's throat.

Silence waved.

'Do what I say and he'll be okay.'

I put the car in first and eased off the clutch. It jerked forwards, dragging the trailer along behind. I looked back to see if Silence was okay but the car was spraying a cloud of dust. The town disappeared.

Third, fourth. I followed the road away from the town in the opposite direction to the approaching car. About a kilometre out, the gravel ended. Deep ruts scarred what was left of the track and the trailer bounced all over the place, dragging the rear of the car sideways.

In the back, AiAi made a bleating sound in time with the jolts.

'Jesus, shut him up!' Bree yelled.

I geared down. The car skidded to a stop.

AiAi whooped.

'Oi, redneck!' Bree leaned over the seat and slapped him. 'It's not funny!'

Darcy gave me a sly look. 'Arden thought you were going to drive by yourself, didn't she?'

'Don't be stupid,' I answered, still shaking. My heart was squirting blood around my body faster than my brain needed it. I felt dizzy.

'Would you have? Are you crazy?' Carrie said.

Joe warned, 'You're not doing us any favours, you know, getting her all riled up. She'll make us stay even longer just to prove her point.'

'This is stupid,' I said. 'Any normal person would have taken one look at that town and turned the car around.' I put the troopie back in gear and took off more slowly. Some of the holes in the track were half filled with water. I was worried I might bog the car, then we'd all have been stuck. 'All we wanted to do was leave. She has no right to keep us here when we want to go.'

'She said she'd take you on the next run,' Darcy said.

'I don't believe that,' I said, under my breath.

Bree heard, but she didn't answer.

'There,' Joe said. He pointed to an open gate that led into an overgrown paddock. At the far end, the land rose gently into bushland. 'They won't see us in there.'

The troopie navigated itself through the ruts and several times the steering wheel yanked so hard my thumbs were almost ripped off.

'Where'd you learn to drive a truck like this?' Joe asked.

'My mother,' I said. 'After driving her car, I can drive just about anything.'

Vivienne taught me to drive in her old EH Holden, when I was twelve. It had no rear seat, a column-shift gearstick that needed three hands to change, and a hole in the passenger-side floor so big you had to dodge roadkill or you could end up with a kangaroo carcass in your lap. Sometimes she would let me drive at night because the reflective lines gave her double vision. We torched it somewhere near Coonabarabran after the gearbox blew up. Vivienne said you had to honour your dead. We camped there that night around the smoking wreck. In the morning, Vivienne woke and realised she'd left her handbag under the front seat.

'There's not much of a track,' Carrie said. 'And it's pretty sandy up here.'

She was right. I stopped the car again and got out. I locked the hubs on the wheels and changed into 4WD. The car crept up a shallow incline, the engine screaming in low gear. We left obvious tyre tracks right through the centre of the grassy paddock. I drove fifty or so metres into scrub, taking out small trees and bushes with the bull bar, then I parked and we all climbed out.

'I'll go out and have a look from the paddock. See if we're visible,' Joe said.

'Joe, wait,' I stopped him. 'Before you do that.'

'What?'

'You're wearing a red T-shirt.'

'You're right.' He looked down at himself, then at my bare feet. 'You go, then. But you haven't got any shoes on.'

'It's okay, I can't feel anything.'

It was true. Days in the dirt had made them tough again. The sand underneath was as soft as cottonwool. I picked up a stick and bashed the weeds before I ventured into the tall grass. From the clearing, the car was well hidden, though I could see Joe and AiAi moving around.

When I got back Darcy and Carrie were rummaging in the back of the car.

'We haven't got anything to drink,' Bree said. 'There's plenty of food, but no water.'

'Yeah, Arden poured the whole container onto the fire,' I muttered.

A queasy rolling started in my stomach. Prickly numbness started in my fingertips, like the early signs of an insidious disease.

'There's warm beer,' said AiAi.

'Bored, bored, bored,' whined Darcy.

'Hopefully we won't be here for too long,' I said. I had to do something. Anything but think.

I sat up on top of the roof racks and looked back towards the road. A faint smudge of smoke still hung in the air in the direction of the town. I thought of Silence and the seesaw feeling grew stronger.

Afternoon passed and the scrub fell into shadow. We sat there, waiting, for hours. The inside of my mouth tasted like crumbled chalk. Flies swarmed the interior of the car, crawling over everything, and my arms were tired from swatting them away. The air was humid and heavy.

'Let's go back,' Carrie said. Her hair had started to grow out into a short afro. It was damp with sweat. 'I am not spending the night out here.'

'Well, you can explain that to Arden,' Darcy said. 'I didn't see a signal yet.'

Joe said to me, 'What do you want to do?'

I wanted to go back for Silence. But I also wanted to stay, just a little longer, even with all the flies and the dust and sweat. Out there in the bush, there was nothing more threatening than the darkening sky.

'I don't know,' I said.

If I had known, would I have gone back sooner? If there was an audible reshuffle and click every time my path was altered, some *Jumanji*-like close-up of a game-piece slotting into place, would it have changed our fate? It could have been that moment or a million before it; I'll never know.

So we waited.

Back at the ghost town, there was something malevolent. I could feel it. And I wasn't ready.

Chapter Twenty-seven

I was lying flat on the roof of the car. In my delirium, pieces of the sky seemed to be shuffling, rearranging themselves into shapes like teardrops and ice cubes.

I needed water. I was parched. I wet my lips with my tongue but nothing happened. *Water.* I sent a plea to the rain gods, if they were listening. I'd lie in the middle of that paddock with my mouth open, catching drops, until I burst like a water-balloon.

I laughed. Was it a hallucination? Did I imagine the feel of cool wet drops on my skin?

'Friday?' Joe. Flicking dregs from a beer bottle at me.

'What?'

'Are you sick? Are you going to be okay to drive?'

'I'm fine.' I held out a hand. 'I give in. I'll have that beer now. We should wait a little bit longer, I think.'

Joe climbed up and sat next to me.

I drained the warm beer. It had the same effect as swallowing a bucket of salt water but, strangely, my stomach settled down and I had some feeling back in my fingers.

'Do you think he's okay?' Joe asked what I was thinking. Is *he* okay? Not, are *they* okay? 'Who do you reckon was in that car?'

'I don't know. Probably just tourists,' I said and swung my legs over the side of the car. I jumped down. 'Carrie's right—we can't stay here all night. We should go back.'

Reversing the car with the trailer attached proved too much of a challenge. I drove straight forwards, through the scrub. The car escaped with a few branches stuck in the bull bar and a fresh dent in the driver's side door. AiAi jumped up and down like a lunatic until Darcy sat on him to shut him up.

'There hasn't been a signal,' Darcy warned. 'What if it's not safe?'

I drove with only the parking lights on, creeping along at a jogger's pace. As we got closer to the town, shapes emerged in the dying light: the silhouette of the church, its spire and cross, two figures huddled over the campfire.

'Do you see that?' Bree said, pressing her nose to the windscreen. 'Are they . . . ?'

'They've got the fire going again,' Joe said in a flat voice.

'Why the hell didn't they send a signal if everything was okay?'

'Well, maybe they tried and we didn't see it,' Darcy said.

Arden and Malik stood as we pulled up. Hunched shoulders, hands in pockets.

That cheery, orange glow filled me with rage. We were hiding, like fugitives, out in the bush, while Arden and Malik sat warming themselves by the fire.

And where was Silence?

I hopped out. I unlocked the hubs.

'Where have you been? I've been so worried,' Arden accused. Her eyes were black holes, her back rigid. 'We've been flashing the torches for hours. We thought you'd left us here.' She threw a look at Malik and he nodded.

'Told you,' Darcy said. 'God, how can it be so hot during the day and so cold at night?' She warmed her hands over the fire.

'Where's Silence?' Carrie and I said together.

My pulse had an unsteady rhythm that left me breathless.

'Where's Silence?' AiAi echoed, his voice edged with fear.

Arden pulled herself up to her full height.

Malik stood behind her and wrapped his arms around her waist.

'We couldn't stop him.' She stared at her feet and when she looked up again, her eyes were filled with tears. 'There was a car. A family. They'd taken a wrong turn. We told them we were camping. Silence was hiding, like I told him, but we gave them directions and when they went to drive off he came running out after them. He begged them to take him with them.' She sniffled and wiped her nose. 'They put his stuff in the back and drove off. I said, what about you?' She pointed at me. 'But he was upset and he said he had to go. He was missing Amy.'

She sank into a deckchair.

'You know all about Amy, don't you?' Arden peeked at me from beneath wet eyelashes. 'I mean, he told you *everything*.'

Was. She said Silence *was* missing. *Told* you everything. Past tense. It's the way she said it—not like it was something that happened a few hours ago, but like it was a footnote on an obituary.

'I don't believe you,' I said dully. There was an ache the

size of a fist where my heart should be. I felt like I was surrounded by strangers. 'He wouldn't.'

Carrie and Bree exchanged a look.

'He got in?' Bree asked. She chewed her nail.

'He got in,' Malik confirmed. 'And they drove off.'

'Look,' Arden sighed. 'I've been thinking. Maybe we should get out of here and go someplace else. It's not exactly working out the way I imagined, is it?' She gave a rueful smile. 'I'm willing to admit defeat.'

Joe held up his hand for a high five but I ignored it.

'No.'

'What do you mean, no?' Arden frowned. 'You're the one who wanted to leave.'

'Not without Silence.'

'He's gone!' she screamed. 'How many times do I have to tell you!'

'Leave her alone,' Bree said quietly. She stood between us. 'Let her get used to the idea.'

Arden muttered something under her breath. 'Go to sleep. We'll stock up tomorrow, plan our route and drop off our excess baggage.' She glared at me. 'Then we'll come back, pick you all up and head back the other way.'

My body felt electrified, like I was picking up current through my feet. Volts of frustrated energy and no way to release it.

I grabbed a torch and headed off in the direction of the river.

Bree and Carrie followed.

'He wouldn't have left without me,' I said, when we were out of earshot.

'Well, what do you think happened to him? I doubt very much he's lying in a shallow grave,' Carrie joked.

I played the torch over the trees. Their pale, naked trunks were scarred with initials. In the trickster light I imagined they were arms and legs, torsos, twisted in agony. The beam hit the water and diffused.

I was suddenly freezing. Iced water for blood. The river was higher, lapping at the edges of the bank. It looked like I felt: a few ripples on the surface but rolling and churning underneath. My dread was real even if Vivienne's stories weren't—this was the curse, staring me in the face.

'I know you don't believe me,' I said. I looked back at the distant circle of fire. 'And tomorrow I'll be gone.'

'I'll miss you,' Bree said.

Carrie agreed. 'Me too. When you get back to the city you'll find him back in the train station, or swimming with his fish. You'll see.'

I kept looking, furious that I was alone out there, alone in thinking Silence had never left.

Arden watched from the church steps, chain-smoking, backlit by a square of dim light.

I checked inside some of the houses, calling his name. I dared to tread the brittle porch surrounding the old pub, but the windows and doors were still boarded up. Only my own prints were left in the dust.

I followed the river about as far as I could downstream, until the thickening scrub grew too dense. Wherever piles of branches had snagged and collected, I used a long, heavy stick to paw through them and break them apart. Leaning out over that water, seeing the river toss trees like they were toothpicks—it was as close as I'd ever been to death.

When the torch battery died, I worked my way back by faint moonlight and the glowing doorway, feeling sick and defeated. I needed to sleep.

If Silence had been taken by that river, he was lost.

That night, the wind picked up. The old church moaned and creaked. Our swag configuration had changed and we were clearly divided into two factions: Arden's group of Malik, Darcy and AiAi crammed together up on the pulpit, while Joe, Carrie, Bree and I lay on the far side near the entrance.

I half dozed with my senses on high alert. A few times I imagined a voice—Silence's raspy voice, out there, calling for me—but the wind snatched every sound away and it was too difficult to make anything out. I sat up and tried to catch the faint ringing noise that was bugging me, to separate it from all the rest. I was aware of Bree, watching and listening, too.

Joe's watch glowed green in the dark. I leaned over, turned his wrist and tried to read it.

He lifted his arm and groaned, 'It's only eleven o'clock. Go back to sleep.'

'I can't.'

'Me neither,' Carrie groaned. 'I need to pee.'

'I'll go with you,' I offered.

Carrie passed me her torch. I fumbled and dropped it. The noise, a resounding hollowness, made me wonder if there was something under the floorboards of the church.

Outside, I faced away to give Carrie privacy.

I played the torch over the walls of the church and took a slow, measured route around the side. There were piles of junk all over the place. Everything sharp and jagged. In most places the walls weren't visible, hidden behind sheets of iron and rusting machinery.

On the second lap I found it. A hatch door. A timber-framed doorway that led underground. The opening was shrouded in broken cobwebs and flattened grass.

The sound started when she was doing up her pants—or maybe it had started earlier and we just couldn't hear it from inside.

Clang, clang, clang. Clang, clang, clang.

I froze and aimed the torch beam in the direction of the sound. It was eerie, like hearing a foghorn through mist. The light couldn't penetrate the clouds of dust and bounced back.

My stomach dropped.

Carrie stepped into the glare. 'Do you hear it?' she said, her face white and pinched. 'It sounds like a bell.'

'I hear it.'

Clang, clang, clang.

The wind whipped stinging dust into our eyes and the backs of our legs. I shone the torch to light the way for Carrie, but at the entrance I stopped.

'Go on in. I'll be there in a minute.'

'What are you doing?' she asked, breathing hard.

'I need to go, too.'

'I'll wait for you.' Her teeth chattered.

'I'll be fine.'

'I said I'll wait.'

'Oh, never mind.'

Inside, Arden was sitting up. 'Where have you two been?'

'There's a noise. Like a ship's bell. Do you hear it?' Carrie said. 'It's freaking me out.'

Arden stared up at one of the high, gaping windows. After a moment, she snapped out of her trance and slid from her swag. She picked up something glinting, metallic. Her flick knife. She held it loosely, paced sideways to the entrance of the church and stood there, head cocked. Listening.

Clang, clang, clang. Faint, but still there.

I watched her expression carefully. There was nothing. It was empty.

'It could be a loose roof sheet. Or a rattling pole. It's just the wind,' she said. 'It's okay. Go back to sleep.'

'I want to go and check,' I said.

She waved the knife. 'I've heard of people being sliced in half by flying corrugated iron,' she mused. 'Better stay inside. It's nothing. There's only us. It's just the wind,' she crooned. 'Everyone, go back to sleep.'

The tip of the knife followed me as I lay down and covered myself.

I waited.

An hour later, Arden was asleep. Hard asleep. Her long, matted hair fanned out over her pillow, snaking onto the floor. The knife had slipped out of her grasp.

I took it. I slipped outside and crept around to the side of the church. The hatch door had been opened. The weeds surrounding it were trodden flat, oily handprints marked the edge.

I used the point of Arden's knife to prise it up. It swung open easily.

I didn't know what I expected to find. Most of all, I prayed that Silence would appear out of the dark. But he didn't. There was nothing alive down there. The air was still and dead. It was sucking emptiness, a vacuum.

The torch beam moved over shadowy, twisted shapes covered with decades of dust and dirt. A steep flight of steps led down, down and the dark pressed closer. My heart raced. I started shaking and couldn't stop.

I took a deep breath. Footprints in the dust. I stepped into them. I followed them to a corner where they stopped near a dark, huddled mass on top of a mouldering crate.

Underneath a sheet of canvas that crackled and dissolved in my hands, I found Silence's things.

The knife was cold and certain in my fist. I leaned close enough to smell the sweetness of Arden's breath. Everything was wrong; her breath should be foul. She should be hideous. She should be dead.

I raised the knife and ran my fingertip along the blade. I left a bloody fingerprint on her pillow.

It was like cutting through an umbilical cord. I considered leaving her dreadlock lying next to my fingerprint—but that would have been too dangerous. It wasn't the time for petty gestures.

So I placed the knife back where I'd found it. I tucked the dreadlock into my pocket.

A talisman, to keep.

It was the longest night. An unbearably bright morning. I hadn't slept and I staggered outside, squinting.

I went through the motions. Packed my things, chattered about returning to the city to find Silence. I accepted heartfelt hugs and goodbyes from Bree, Carrie and Joe.

Arden relaxed. She was upbeat, full of energy. She couldn't wait to get out of there.

Finally, Arden and Malik started the car. The others stood by, ready to wave us off.

'Let's go. We'll drop you in town.'

I looked at Arden and tried to remember what it was that I'd found so charismatic in the beginning. The light slanted away from her, as if repelled. She was so beautiful, and always would be, but now I could see all her shades of crazy. How *off* she was. How nature made its most deadly creatures alluring precisely so they could lure their victims close.

Maybe that was the thing about beginnings—they always seemed better than middles or endings. And if I only ever had beginnings and my past was so perfect, then the future would never measure up. I didn't want to live like that.

'There's nothing here for you any more,' Arden said.

How many times had I told myself that?

I knew for sure in that instant—it was only ever what you did today that counted and I'd promised Silence I wouldn't leave without him.

I shook my head. 'I'm staying.'

'What?' She had a moment of confusion that morphed into fear. 'Get in the car.'

I smiled. 'I won't make it on my own. I want to stay.' I linked an arm through Bree's and kept my expression blank.

The effort was too much. My nose started to drip.

'We'll be ready to go when you get back,' Joe said.

With the others looking on, there wasn't much she could do. 'You're bleeding,' she said and wound up the window. The troop carrier sprayed us with dust.

Bree stared at me. 'I don't understand,' she said. 'What's going on?'

'I have proof,' I said, wiping my nose. The blood was pink and thin. 'Maybe now you'll believe me. We have to find him.'

Chapter Twenty-eight

AiAi went lookout. Carrie wandered off into the bush. Darcy and Joe took the outbuildings, haysheds and water tanks. Bree and I scrambled under the church.

Bree went down first. I hesitated at the opening. I took slow, calming breaths as she disappeared into the murk. Could I face it again, that crypt-like deadness, the ceiling pressing down like the lid on a coffin?

'What if we don't find him?' Bree called.

I thought of Silence's things, hidden in the crawlspace. His sleeping bag, shucked and loose as a discarded sock. Clothes, a rusted razor, his toothbrush—too many things left behind. I remembered his notebook, etched with all the things he wanted to say, but couldn't.

'What if we do?' I called back. I shook off my dizziness and followed her.

'You know that Darcy or AiAi will tell her we've been looking, don't you?'

'Yes. I don't care any more.'

We huddled close with a single torch, crept through the labyrinth of boxy storage spaces with a ceiling so low we had to squat in places. The bobbing disc of light caught on pieces of furniture entwined like new-age sculptures, broken pews and crates of gold-leafed Bibles stacked high.

The air under the church had been used up long ago. It reeked of mildew and old things turning to dust. We had wisps of webs in our hair, dust in our lashes and cold sweat on our skin. Bree caught her leg on a rusted nail. A trickle of blood travelled from her knee to her ankle.

Each dark corner led to another. My bones ached with cramp and cold. We breathed through our mouths, shuddering relief when the rush of old air from some hidden, closed-up space proved to be just that—old air.

The shout, when it came, made me jump. It sounded far away and I couldn't tell who it was, but the pitch was unmistakeable.

Bree grabbed my hand. I could feel the vibration of her fear. We shimmied out of the hatch door and ran blindly until we could hear voices.

Carrie and Darcy were waiting at the base of the old tank.

'What?' I gasped.

'Joe is in there,' Darcy said. She hooked her thumbs in her belt loops and rocked on her heels, looking down at the ground.

'What?' I said again, gagging on the word.

Carrie shook her head and bit down on her lip.

I scrambled up the ladder and shone my torch into the black hole.

Joe was standing with his back to the wall. His breaths came quick and shallow. A flickering torch was lying half sunk in wet leaves. I traced the direction of his stare.

'No,' I breathed.

Silence was curled up under a blanket of leaves, like a sleeping child. He looked peaceful, as if someone had covered him over and tucked him in tight. The pale moon of his cheek was blue, blue as a fragile egg, and his forelock fringe was neatly brushed aside. His bare foot poked through the leaves; his fist was in the air; and all around him the proof that he'd died as he'd lived—without hope.

Breath left my lungs in a whoosh. The sky tilted and I grabbed the edge of the ladder to keep myself from falling.

Joe watched in horror as I lowered myself into the tank. I had to touch Silence one last time.

I passed the back of my hand across his cold cheek. I kissed his cold lips and pulled his hood over his face. All essence of him was gone.

Joe snapped out of his trance. He lurched from the muck with a rude, sucking sound. Wordlessly, he passed me his torch and a handful of sharp, cold metal. He hoisted himself onto the roof of the tank and lay there, heaving.

Above me, a piece of sky, benign and blue.

Joe pulled me back up. Out on the roof, where Silence and I had claimed the stars, I opened my hand and stared at Joe's offering.

'They were screwed in,' he said. 'From the outside. He couldn't get out even if he . . .' his voice broke.

'Maybe he climbed in there. Maybe he was hiding,' Darcy said from below, her eyes bleak.

My hand flew up. I threw the four rusted metal screws at her.

'Did he tighten these up, Darce?' I yelled. 'Did he screw

them down so tight he couldn't get out once he was done hiding? How could he do that *from the inside?*'

These were the images in my mind that would play forever: Silence sleeping, his raised, defiant fist, muddy claw-marks on the walls of the tank, ten thousand dings and dents. He'd tried so hard to get out. And all the while he would have screamed in his useless old man's rasp as the knee-high muck he stood in sucked up precious oxygen.

When we'd all woken to the strange, rhythmic clanging, Arden had reassured us. She'd crooned like a den mother. Had never seemed more benevolent and *human. Nothing can hurt us here. Because there's only us. And we're family. It's just the wind.*

Or the strike of a rock on tin. Like the one Silence had clenched in his fist.

'They're back,' AiAi puffed, white-eyed, skittish as a foal. 'They're coming. What's going on? Did you find anything?'

Joe slid down the ladder, mindless of daggered splinters in the palings. He folded in half and collapsed onto the ground. His face was white and slack; his hands shook as he tried to light the nub of a burnt-out cigarette.

Carrie hugged herself and rocked, her jaw juddering.

Darcy, kneeling in the dirt, her hands over her face, her fingers interlinked like a church and steeple. Praying.

Bree moaning, *No, no, no.*

'Did you find him? Did you find Silence?' AiAi's eyes darted around to each of us, trying to piece together a picture from all those fragments of grief.

I slumped on the roof of the tank, visible for miles. I didn't care. My limbs felt leaden, like I was getting the flu.

My feet were stained dark. Everything was painfully acute: the cooling tin on the back of my legs, the slow slug of tears on my cheek, the stink of damp and death.

And something else, a quickening, white-hot in my veins.

'We can't let on that we've found him.' My voice was flat, dead. 'Not until we're away from here. I'll get us all out somehow, but she can't know. Darcy?'

She nodded, her chin tucked into her chest. 'I still don't believe she could do this.' Her fingers plucked at a matted strand of her hair. 'She loves Silence.'

'Loved,' said Bree. 'She loved him.' She took AiAi's hand and put a finger against his lips. 'You've gotta keep a secret, mate.'

Carrie said. 'It's six against two. We've got to take the car and go.'

'How do we do that?' Joe asked. 'None of us is a match for either of them.'

Darcy's face was set in a combination of despair and disbelief. She was torn, and AiAi didn't count. If Arden told him to do something, he would. His devotion ran that deep. It was four against four—the bases were evenly loaded.

I climbed down the ladder.

'How did you know?' I asked Joe. I'd been looking in all the wrong places. I should have sensed something—*I* should have known where to look.

Joe pointed at the tank. 'The other side,' he said. He hugged his knees and buried his face in the crook of his arms.

I followed his footprints in the dust and looked up. On the outside wall of the tank, Silence's name was etched in the rust and the dirt. Seven high, chalky-white letters. He'd written big, just like I told him to.

A few kilometres away, at the edge of the desert, a plume of dust rose and settled behind the troop carrier.

I watched them come.

There was nothing else to do but seal him up again, a pale comma curled on a bed of rotting leaves. Some things aren't meant for this world. They're too fragile, and life breaks them.

Chapter Twenty-nine

Fresh grief feels like this:

Your mind is a maze and every pathway leads to a bricked-up wall, the one where you can see the real world just on the other side, but you can't reach it. It's a feeling like someone's scooped out your insides with a spoon and all that's left is a shell that walks like you and talks like you, but your body and soul have parted ways for a time. Your senses don't fire and you can't connect with another human being because to string all that grief together like a strand of paper dolls would create something as powerful as an atom bomb—you'd implode. So you're all alone. And, for a short while, at least until it sinks in, you can fake anything.

I watched the others go about their business. They didn't look at each other. Their movements were jerky. They all seemed to have found something interesting at ground level. I knew from experience that this was normal: to divide and separate like oil droplets on water. It was instinctive, animal self-preservation.

Start packing, I told them. *The sooner we get out of here the sooner we can get help for Silence.*

That was stupid, of course. He was so far from saving. I meant justice. That's what I meant.

The troop carrier pulled up. Arden and Malik had returned too soon—a round trip took three hours and they had been gone for less than one. Which meant something had made them turn the car around.

I went into the church. I erased all signs that I'd been there. I put on my boots. They were heavy and uncomfortable. I rolled my swag as tightly as I could, using my body weight to squeeze all the spaces out. I pressed so hard that the rough canvas chafed the skin off my knuckles. While I was looking around for anything I'd missed, Arden stepped through the entrance.

We took each other in.

Her: tall, imposing in her combat boots, impossibly clean.

Me: small, filthy and scared.

My knees were knocking, my nose was blocked, my eyes ached from dust and tears—but I had hate. In that moment it was huge and whole, filling up the empty space that losing Silence and Vivienne had left inside.

'You're back early,' I said. My tone was blasé. Exactly how I wanted to sound.

'The road is flooded about twenty kilometres out,' she said. She fingered the stump of her dreadlock. 'We'll have to try another way.' She frowned at me. 'Are you okay?'

'I'm fine. Why wouldn't I be?'

She touched her fingertip to the raw skin under my eyes. 'You look like you've been crying.'

'It's the dust.' I backed away.

Arden turned and stood with her back to me. She hit her forehead with the flat of her palm. 'Think, Arden, think!' she hissed.

My dread rose another notch.

'We need to head for higher ground,' I offered. Even to me, my voice sounded paper-thin.

Arden shook her head. 'We just wasted half a tank of fuel. You don't get it, do you? I'm responsible for *lives*. They *depend* on me.'

'We're not as isolated as you think. We'll just get as far as we can. Someone will come . . .'

Play it out. Make her calm down. Keep her focused. We need to leave, or at least try to, before her wheels fall off altogether.

Arden grabbed my hand. She squeezed it twice, let it drop and touched her hair again.

I felt her fear and indecision and, for a split second, I pitied her.

She got me good with her sucker punch.

'You found him, didn't you?' She looked so sad.

I watched her finger that frayed end and I knew. It was my fault. I was the reason they'd turned back. I'd blown everything. Now we were all witnesses she needed to erase.

I coughed to kickstart my heart. 'I don't know what you're talking about,' I whispered.

For an instant she looked confused. But she must have seen something in my eyes, my expression. I'd given myself away.

'It was an accident,' she said. 'He must have had an asthma attack. He just stopped breathing.' Her breath caught and her eyes glazed over. 'I didn't want you all to be upset. It was easier to let you think . . .'

253

'He's been keeping his inhaler in his pocket since we've been here,' I said carefully. 'Because of the dust.'

'Look at you,' she said and stared down at my feet. 'You're filthy.'

There were muddy marks, halfway up my calf, from where my feet had sunk into the wet leaves inside the tank.

Arden shook her head again, touched the stump. 'And this . . .' she sighed. 'I suppose the others know, too?'

'Just me. I found him. Only me . . .' I lied.

Arden started to cry. 'Why would he get in there? I told him to hide, not commit *suicide*.'

'Did you check?'

'Did I what?' She looked away.

'Did you get in there and check? Did you touch him? Before you screwed down the . . .'

'He was dead.' She still wouldn't look at me.

'He was still *alive* last night. You heard him. You *knew*!' I screamed. I flew at her with my fists but she batted me away.

Malik came. He stood in the doorway, saying nothing, as always. Just there.

I sat down hard on the floor. 'You knew and you let him die,' I cried. 'You could have done something.'

'Shut up,' she hissed and put her hands over her ears. '*Shutupshutupshutup*.'

For a full minute there was nothing but the sound of our breathing. The dust I'd kicked up hovered in the air. Arden rocked herself. Malik put his hand on her shoulder and she jerked away.

She gave a tiny smile. 'He was my first,' she mused. 'I

found him in the station, sitting there. He'd been waiting for days, waiting for Amy to come back. He'd still be there if I hadn't saved him.'

'Where did you take him that night? Before you burned down the squat?' I asked her. I needed to know why Silence had been different after that, even more lost.

'He wanted to leave. With you.' She gave me a look loaded with disdain. 'So I took him to places we used to go. You know, we hung out. I reminded him of all the good things. I thought they meant something to him.' She sneered. 'And he said he was still leaving.'

'What did you do?' I had to know. Even if it was only her version of the truth.

She winked at me. 'Plan B. I reminded him of the bad things.'

'He was just a *kid*,' I sobbed. *How bad could they be?*

Arden seemed faraway. She was smiling to herself. 'He held up a service station. When he was fourteen. Got away with it, too,' she said. 'I just took him back to remind him, get a slushie, you know . . . I didn't think the same guy would be working there.' She snorted. 'Fucking *priceless*. Silence walks in, realises it's the same guy, and the guy recognises him. Then this guy launches over the counter and comes at us with a fucking *machete*, screaming that he was going to chop him off at the knees . . .'

I gasped and she remembered I was there.

'He's okay, I mean, obviously he didn't catch us, otherwise . . .' she ended on a sigh. 'He was okay.'

So that was it. Silence had decided he wanted to be somebody else, somebody *good*. He'd wanted to start over. He'd tried to ask her to let him go and Arden had rubbed his nose in his past. She'd destroyed what little hope he had left.

'Did you really think I'd let you take him?'

'What? I wasn't *taking* . . .'

'See it from my side. You wanted Silence. You tried it on with my brother, and with Malik.' Her eyes were deadly slits. 'I made you part of my family and you tried to take everyone away from me.'

Thoughts were grappling, but nothing made sense. *Her brother? Wish was her brother?* Shock started in my centre and spread. The skin on my arms broke out in blotchy welts as if I'd been smacked. Right then, I hated Wish, too. I couldn't separate them—any feelings I had for him became entwined with my hate for *her*—it felt like someone was burning holes in my brain.

'I took your money.' Arden smirked. 'I know you think it was Darce, but I took it.'

I hadn't asked, but she'd told me anyway.

'It was getting boring. I needed to change the dynamic— you were going to leave.' Her voice got low. 'I wish I had just let you.'

It was something we both agreed on. If I had left back then, would Silence be dead? Was it some kind of random butterfly effect, or Arden's orchestration? I thought of Vivienne's belief in magic, omens, luck, whatever. There was no magic. No cosmic balance of right and wrong. No signs. There was only death and ego and madness.

The insolence of Arden in confession mode left me feeling sick. I staggered upright and wrapped my arms around my waist.

'You're crazy,' I said. 'You can't own people. You can't make people love you.' I spat it out like a poisoned dart but she didn't flinch. 'You can't force them to respect you.'

'You sound like a fortune cookie,' Arden said, then as an afterthought, 'Wish came for you, you know.'

'What?'

'He came that afternoon.'

'It doesn't matter now,' I said.

'It does matter. He didn't come to see me, he came to get *you*.' She gave a catty smile. 'I told him you'd already gone. But *I* came back for you, didn't I?' She made it sound like a threat.

I had to have the last word, whatever happened next.

'You killed him,' I said and a fat tear rolled down to my chin. 'In a hundred different ways, you killed him, starting from the moment you took him from that train station. And you still think you saved him.'

Arden made a gagging noise.

Right then, Bree peered from behind Malik. 'We have to go now. The trailer's packed, and the car.' Her eyes were wide and fearful. 'The road's going under.' She looked at me, back at Arden. 'What's going on?'

'Tell everyone to get in the car, Bree.' Arden drilled Malik with a stare that was loaded with meaning.

Malik took a sidestep in my direction.

They were going to leave me behind.

Malik wrapped an arm around my waist and lifted me as if I weighed nothing. I kicked out at Arden with my boots as he dragged me past her, but she dodged, an expression of distaste on her face.

A quick flash of Bree, running after us. Carrie shouted something I couldn't understand. Malik's hand covered my mouth and nose. I sucked air through his fingers but I couldn't get enough.

My body hit the stairs that led beneath the church; pain registered in my head, my back, my elbows and knees. Everything blurred. And the weird thing was, even with my fear of enclosed spaces, it seemed like the safest place to be.

Chapter Thirty

Darkness. Darkness for an eternity.

Pain all over, liquid pain that had no centre. It was everywhere. Even my hair hurt. How long? Minutes. Hours. I opened and closed my eyes but nothing changed. I was stuck in an underworld, a cold, damp ever after.

I shifted one leg and it shuddered like an unoiled hinge. I tested each finger as if playing a scale on a piano. Unbroken, just stiff. My clothes were wet. The ground should have been hard, but it was doughy. Sludge. Sensation hit slowly.

One.

Thing.

At.

A.

Time.

Think.

I am Liliane Brown. There. The cortex for other thoughts. *I am alive. Under the church. I'm alive under the church.*

It was quiet, except for my own breathing and a musical tinkle like a wind chime in a breeze. But there was no breeze. Dead air, the air inside a tomb. Four walls of darkness, pressing down.

I felt my face: straight nose, puffy lips, eyes that had

cried. One tender cheekbone. Stickiness in the hair behind my left ear.

There were things at the edges of my mind, waiting to get in.

I twisted onto my back. Straightened my arms and legs. Stretched and flexed. *Vitruvian Man*, star jumps, snow angels in the dirt. I tried to remember things I'd seen, things I'd done. My memory was in small, scattered pieces.

I am Liliane Brown. I am alive.

Is that all there was? Was it enough? Shouldn't there have been more?

I reached out my hand and locked it onto something cold, cylindrical. Vertical. The leg of a chair. I squeezed tight, pulled, levered my body upright. The chair gave, objects toppled and fell. I rolled sideways and butted against the bottom of the steps. Crashes, thuds. The chairs settled and there was silence.

Silence. This was one of the thoughts waiting at the edges of my mind.

I had to get out.

Blood was flowing again. My feet tingled and burned. I felt for the steps: one, two, three, four. They were wet.

I walked up on my hands and knees, stopping on each step to feel the space in front of me. *Splat. Splat.* Sounds, like stomping in puddles of rain. How many steps? Five more. Nine steps. The last one, rotten and splintered. A piece stuck into my palm. I found it with my lips, pulled it out with my teeth. The pain made every other ache seem distant. It woke me up.

I pressed up with my uninjured hand. The hatch door.

Freezing drips ran along my palm, down my forearm to my elbow. My teeth tapped together. I bit down, clenched my jaw. I pushed harder but the door wouldn't budge. I put my shoulder into it, the side of my head and neck. Nothing.

As I pushed, the droplets fell faster. Rain? I pressed my ear to the door and listened. Muffled sound, like it was travelling through a tunnel. A symphony of drips—*bong, bong, bong, ting-ting, bong*. I thought I was delirious, dreaming.

Ting-ting. Bong.

My exhaustion was bone deep. My heart drummed a slow beat like an animal closing down for hibernation. Was this the start of hypothermia?

I shuffled back down to the bottom of the steps and stood up. I jogged on the spot and tried to rub some feeling back into my fingers. Then, arms stretched in front of me like a sleepwalker, I mapped out my surroundings, feeling around in the space, pacing out the steps. The stairs were behind me, a collapsed stack of chairs and pews in front. To my left, Silence's belongings under the rotten tarpaulin, and to my right, crumbling crates and a narrow path that led further under the church.

There should have been some light; the church had more leaks than a sieve. I thought maybe it was night outside—but that would mean I had been unconscious for hours. My sense of missing time was more disorienting than the endless dark and the cramped space. How long had I been there? Had they left without me?

Silence's things, suspended above the wet ground, were still dry. I unzipped his sleeping bag, wrapped it around my shoulders and climbed up onto a crate. The bag smelled like dust and emptiness—nothing of him. The wood flexed but held. Dampness seeped through the thin material, but so did warmth. Intoxicating warmth.

My whole body was numb. I'd heard or read somewhere that the ability to feel pain is the first thing to go.

That's not true. The ability to *care* goes first.

I wanted to rest, close my eyes, just for a moment. A few minutes, that was all.

I woke. Kept my eyes squeezed shut. Loosened the knots in my muscles. I said something out loud, involuntarily, but at least it proved I was still alive.

'Water.' It was a croak. Two parched syllables on a shallow breath. I cleared my throat, said it again. 'Water.'

My thirst was unbearable.

I opened my eyes.

Slivers of light sluiced through the floorboards above. There was water all around me. It was everywhere. The river, pouring in. I could hear it, running, trickling, sloshing, sucking, slurping—all the sounds that water makes. There was too much, not enough.

Water drags you under, weighs you down, makes you sink.

I slid off the crate, still wrapped in the sleeping bag. My boots filled up. The water was up to my knees. Outside, the river must have broken its banks. It was drowning the town. The bag soaked it up and I let it fall. It went under. My pulse was picking up pace, throbbing in my temples. Fear, like grasping fingers, squeezed my throat.

I scooped a handful of the river water and sniffed. It

was foul, muddy, strung with weed. The first salty mouthful I spat, the second I swallowed. The third I brought back up in a convulsive dribble. The next few slid down into my empty stomach and hit with the force of a jackhammer. Even though it tasted like sludge, I kept drinking slowly until I wasn't thirsty any more.

As I drank, one clear thought, a single technicolour image, surfaced: a tiny caterpillar thawed from ice crawls out onto a glacier and, driven by instinct, seeks the one thing it needs to sustain life. It doesn't know that the odds are against it. It doesn't think that it will probably die tomorrow. There is only the will to survive from this moment to the next because without the present, there is no future.

An uncertain future seemed like the one thing I wanted more than anything else. It wasn't fair for my mind to give up when my body clearly wasn't done.

I sat for a while, legs hanging over the edge of the crate, dangling in the water. My boots weighed me down like anchors. My pounding head calmed. My stomach settled. In that short period of waiting the tide rose another two inches. I watched it and gave in to the terror. Finally, my brain seemed capable of stringing ideas together.

The logistics were these: the floor of the church was built up, raised about a metre above ground level. So far, the water was only coming through the sides, which meant the water level outside was less than a metre deep. If it rose above the level of the floor it would pour through the floorboards, the cellar would flood—and I would drown.

But if I put the logistics aside and focused on what I knew—how I *felt*—it was hopeless. There was only resignation, and fear. Put the two together and you had a recipe for self-destruction.

The fluid in Vivienne's lungs, Alicia Brown lying face-down in a ditch, the cord wrapped around Belle Brown's neck—on one side, Vivienne's truth, the only truth I'd ever known, and a curse that wanted the end of me.

On the other side, free will. The chance to plot my own destiny. So much of what I believed was founded on what Vivienne had said; her stories were woven through my entire existence. But if Vivienne's stories weren't true, then this was not the curse. The water was not dogging me, the last of the Brown women, to carry out a predetermined fate. This was Mother Nature: indiscriminate, brutal and unstop-pable, but not vindictive. Not evil. Not like a human being could be evil.

I could choose not to believe.

The way I see it, you have two options. Run, run like hell, Vivienne had said. *Or dive in.*

Water can make you float, I thought. *And I can swim like a goddamn fish.*

I scrambled up the steps. Water poured out of my boots. There was only one way in or out—through the hatch door, which was probably pinned by the weight of the water outside. Above, the floorboards were held together by caked dirt and rusting nails. In places, they were rotting through. Could I punch a hole big enough for a person, or prise them apart? I tested the gaps with my fingers. The floor above my head was solid and far too thick, but beneath the pulpit, where Arden and Malik had slept, it was worn thin, ready to collapse.

264

I waded through the floating debris. Further in, the ceiling—or the floor—was lower and I had to half crouch, half swim. Near where the pulpit should have been there were too many things in my way. I pulled down boxes and chairs and set them adrift. In the far corner, above pieces of furniture so old and rotten they'd fused into one solid piece, was a square cut into the floor.

Another hatch.

I crawled to the top of the pile. My foot plunged through hollow wood and my calf was shredded. I could taste the tang of blood from my bitten lip; my eyes were gritty with falling dirt. I clawed at the square and pressed my fingers desperately into the gaps, but there was no give.

The ceiling started to rain.

I screamed. Out of sheer hopelessness and fear, I screamed. The sound forced its way up from my lungs, through my throat. It reached a pitch I'd only heard in horror films; it echoed around the cellar and burst home against my eardrums.

And when the scream died away, the ceiling above me shuddered. Dirt, shaken loose from the square opening, showered down. The roof was collapsing. I cowered and put my arm over my face.

A crack, a groan, and the hatch door lifted.

Shafts of brilliant light, a stairway to the afterlife. A hand.

When I backed away, it beckoned.

An empty hand.

I reached out. I took it.

Chapter Thirty-one

'I couldn't,' Darcy sobbed as she hauled me up and out. 'I couldn't.' She was wet through and shivering, her clothes streaked with red mud. 'I heard you screaming down there.'

'It's okay. I know,' I said, breathless. I found myself patting her shoulder, even though my legs were giving way under me. I collapsed onto the floor of the pulpit.

'They're not far behind,' she gasped and tried to pull me. 'Malik had to carry AiAi. The water's nearly up to here.' She flattened her hand mid-thigh. 'If Arden finds out I let you . . .'

'Why did you come back?' My voice was raspy, not my own. 'Why did you let me out?'

She let go of my hand and looked down at her feet.

'The car got bogged,' she said. 'We spent the night out there. There's no water and no food left.' She pulled my hand again. 'Come on, hurry! They'll be here soon.'

'Why did you let me out?' I demanded.

Darcy looked directly at me for the first time. I noticed her eyes were green, deep-set, intelligent. She'd never lied or pretended she was something she wasn't. There was nothing two-faced about her.

'I figured you'd know what to do,' she said and started crying again. 'Tell me what I have to do.'

That was the big question. What to do. 'I don't know.' I shrugged helplessly. 'I'll find the car. But she has to think I'm still down there.'

She nodded.

'I'm going,' I said and panic flickered across her face. 'But I'll be back.'

I unlaced my boots, slipped them off and dropped them into the hole. They tumbled down the stack of furniture and disappeared underwater.

'I'll think of something, don't worry.'

She nodded again and helped me up. The church floor was going under.

'You should try to get the others onto a roof. This one's too high, maybe one of the houses. Can you do that? Can you swim, Darce?'

'A bit. Enough. Can you?'

'I can swim.'

I wanted to tell her, *I've been running away from this my whole life.*

I left the church and dropped low into the floodwater. It was shallow enough to wade, but I would have been too visible. Only the top of my head and my nose cleared the surface. Floating branches and other debris made a soup, swirling with deadly missiles. The water was freezing but the sun blazed overhead.

I swam away from the church, heading for the track that ran behind it.

'There!' somebody yelled.

I ducked under with only half a breath. There was no way to navigate by sight. In seconds, I was lost. My body fought to float so I grabbed handfuls of grass and pulled myself under. I crawled along the bottom for as long as I could until my lungs were bursting.

I came up in plain sight, only metres from where I went under. A sea of brown water with a head sticking up—I couldn't have been more conspicuous if I'd been waving a flag.

Arden and Malik were behind the others, AiAi draped over Malik's shoulders. Bree and Carrie were at the front. Joe was pointing straight at me.

Carrie yelled, 'Shit. We thought you had drowned.'

I almost answered, but then I saw Darcy.

She was waving frantically from the top step, drawing attention away from me. They were looking at her. They hadn't seen me at all.

I dived under again. My leg was stinging where I'd scraped it but the cold soon left me numb. I stayed under until I was sure I was out of sight. I surfaced when my hand hit an obstacle and I couldn't swim any further without getting my bearings.

I was behind the church, near the stack of wood. Through the gaping window above, I could hear voices inside. Arden was shouting, Bree was crying.

'There's nothing we can do! Everything's gone under!' Arden screamed.

There was a slap, then quiet.

I pressed up against the church wall and tried to suck

breath without whooping. My throat was raw, my lungs ached.

I heard the sound of legs wading through the water, so I paddled away from the church and took cover in the trees.

'Come back inside. There's nothing we can do,' Arden called.

Joe and Bree were standing in the water at the side of the church, near the outside hatch.

Joe kneeled down and felt under the surface. 'It's here, somewhere.'

Bree's expression was bleak. 'I don't see how . . .'

'We have to try.'

'What if . . . ? Oh, God.'

'I know. Just help me. Get Carrie, too.'

They were trying to get me out.

I was about to show myself. I took two steps clear of the tree cover and waved. At that instant, Arden appeared.

She raised her hand—a mirror of mine—whipped her arm back, and released. Her knife flew true. It buried its blade in a beam, centimetres from Joe's head.

Joe lost his balance and fell back against Bree. They huddled together with the water lapping at their chins.

'What the fuck, Arden?' Joe yelled, his face dripping. 'Are you trying to kill all of us?'

Arden didn't waver. 'Just stop it,' she said. 'Stop trying to save her. Come inside now.'

'It's wet in there,' Bree said, shocked.

I lowered my arm and swam off, picking my way carefully through the trees. I kept the direction of the road within sight so I wouldn't lose my bearings.

That knife and the look in Arden's eyes made everything seem impossible.

I forged through thigh-deep water, stumbling into unseen holes, dunking under countless times, heading in the direction I figured they would have set out in the car. Every second, I expected to see Malik coming after me. I got lucky. Just when I thought I might have to turn back, the car appeared around a bend in the road like a mirage I'd summoned.

They'd only made it about a kilometre down the road before they'd got bogged. It was stuck in a rut, the keys still in the ignition. The front tyres were almost completely submerged. Mud spray covered the whole body, camouflaged it. If it wasn't for the glint of sun on metal, I'd have waded right past.

A troop carrier will take you anywhere—if you lock the hubs and ask it nicely. When I was fourteen, Vivienne got a job as a cook on a cattle station. She would let me take lunch out to the men in the paddocks, so I learned to drive anything that was handy—motorbikes, four-wheel drives, quad bikes and, once, a tractor.

I felt for the hubs beneath the water and turned them. No wonder they'd got bogged—two-wheel drive was useless in mud. If I could just drive the car out of the ruts, maybe I could get help.

Inside, the floor was muddy and strewn with crumbs and paper. They'd eaten everything. There were some dry clothes in the back but it seemed pointless to change. My stomach was so empty it felt like it was folding in on itself. In the glove box, right at the back, I found a half-empty water bottle. I gulped the water down. It tasted like liquid plastic, but at the same time, heavenly. Clean.

My hands were sweat-slick. I wiped them on my jeans and turned the key in the ignition. The engine started in gear, the car jolted forwards and stalled. I depressed the clutch and turned the key again. The sound of that engine was the most beautiful music, but it was loud. *Would the sound carry? Could Arden hear it from this far away?*

I was light-headed with panic and hunger. My hand fumbled with the gears; they crunched and ground and the engine stalled again. Even if she heard, it would take them fifteen minutes or more to reach me. I had time.

Slow down, Friday. Think.

I found four-wheel drive and eased off the clutch. The wheels spun and an arc of water and mud shot out behind. The engine was screaming, but the car was going nowhere.

I slumped back in the seat. It was useless. I'd have to swim out.

I got out of the car. Listened. The bend in the road made it impossible to see if anyone was coming. The bush was alive with birdcalls and insect wings.

I had nothing left—no energy, no will, no faith. Not even tears. My head ached. I found the source of it: a gash behind my left ear that had crusted over but was still tender.

I climbed the nearest tree—a big red gum with a trunk as wide as four of me—if only to get away from the water. Straddling a horizontal branch, safe up high, I could just see the church in the distance. There was no movement.

I wondered if they knew I'd gone.

Then it hit me. Darcy was waiting for me. Silence, in his own way, in death, was waiting for me, too.

Think. Do something. Start walking. Something.

I clambered back down and felt around underneath the back wheels of the car. Just mud and slop. I couldn't even have dug it out if I'd had a shovel. My arm came away caked in mud to the elbow.

Let the tyres down.

The thought came from nowhere—something I knew, without understanding how I knew it. I found a sharp stick, unscrewed one of the caps and let the air escape from a tyre until it was half flat. The car sagged to one side. The next one was harder. The valve was under the water and my fingers were slippery. Once I had a steady stream of air bubbles, I kept up the pressure until my shoulders burned with the strain.

Two down. Two to go.

The last tyre refused to go down. I was panting, worn out. My fingers were claws, rigid with cramp. My teeth were chattering. Three tyres would have to be enough.

I started the engine, shifted into first, and pressed the accelerator. The car lurched forwards, but the wheels still spun.

In desperation, I slammed the gearstick into reverse. For a second, the wheels turned on the spot, then the car launched itself backwards, out of the ruts. It rammed the base of a tree and stopped.

I smacked the steering wheel in celebration, then glanced over my shoulder. *Did they hear?*

I eased forwards, avoiding the section of road where the

car had got bogged. Slowly, I followed the line of trees, the gap between the river and the scrub, where the remains of the road would be.

Exhilaration gave me strength I didn't know I had. The steering was hard work, but the car was moving, pushing through the water, leaving a widening wake behind it. Doggedly it kept going, and I had to stop myself from putting my foot down and leaving that town far behind.

I knew if I hit bitumen, I wouldn't be able to go over forty. The tyres would blow. That meant it could take hours to reach the nearest police station.

It was about another two kilometres before the flood-water started to recede. An incline led up and out. Small hills rose above the drenched valley. There, on the side of the hill, a mob of kangaroos watched me curiously.

I parked the troop carrier on dry land under a she-oak tree. I left the keys in it and headed back the way I had come, soaked through, shivering, but triumphant.

I had a plan.

It was the most insane decision I'd ever made—to go back. I'd never had possessions. All things were disposable. Sometimes Vivienne and I would leave with nothing but pockets full of dust; there had never been anything I couldn't bear to leave behind.

But this time there was something I wanted more than escape.

Chapter Thirty-two

I had lost track of time. How long had it taken me to get back to Murungal Creek? More meaningless time passed as I sat, hidden in a tree near Silence's tomb, waiting. A chill breeze started as the sky turned pink, then orange, then purple. Being seen was not my biggest problem now. Falling asleep was. My head nodded, my chin hit my chest and, *snap*. Over and over.

While it was still daylight, I could see and hear almost everything. Carrie, AiAi, Joe and Bree were huddled together on the roof of one of the houses. Arden and Malik came and went from the church. Darcy was sitting on top of a rainwater tank, apart from the others.

In the late afternoon, Carrie stripped off her wet clothes and laid them out on the corrugated iron to dry. The others soon followed.

In my hiding place, I did the same, except I hung them over a branch.

An hour later, I dressed quietly, careful not to lose my balance. The clothes were more or less dry, apart from the insides of my pockets and the crotch of my jeans. Everything smelled like wet dog. They were going to get soaked again, so I appreciated the lingering warmth from the sun while it was there.

There wasn't much conversation. Silent despair seemed to be the mood. A couple of times I felt the burn of Bree's stare, but then I realised she was looking at the big tank. Where Silence was.

Twice, Joe begged Arden to check the cellar. Arden responded with a shake of her head and a tiny smile that made my blood run colder, my heart beat faster, my hate grow stronger.

I waited until the horizon turned black.

An eerie, yellow moon hung like a Chinese lantern in the sky. It draped a glow over the outback, threw long shadows onto the ground. Complete darkness would have been better—but there was no conversation, no torchlight, just sleeping bodies on roofs and enough breeze rustling through trees to cover any noise I might have made.

I dropped into the water with barely a splash, stifling a gasp as the cold hit my skin. I moved in slow steps through the floodwater, swinging my legs in smooth arcs to dull the splashing. I worked my way over to the tank where Darcy was sleeping on top.

'Darcy,' I called softly. 'Here.'

She rolled and peered over the edge. 'Shit! I thought you weren't coming back.'

'Listen, the car—it's parked up on a hill about two or three kilometres out that way.' I pointed. 'Take the others and stick to the road. Do you understand?'

She nodded.

'If I'm not there soon, go without me. The tyres are down but it'll go. Keep it in third gear and don't go over forty.'

'I can't drive.'

'Joe can do it, he has to. Wait for a sign.'

'What kind of sign?' she asked.

'You'll know.'

'Arden has lost it.'

'I know.'

'What are you going to do?'

'Give you time,' I promised.

Behind the church, I found the coil of barbed wire, the axe in the tree, a stone the size of two fists. One by one, I lugged them over to the tank. One by one I set them in place: I left the stone and the axe by the side of the tank; I unrolled the wire and strung a snare between the base of the tank and a tree, just beneath the surface of the water.

I went back again.

The boat, once the most foreign object in that barren landscape, was now the only thing that belonged. It was jammed between two trees, but afloat. A few centimetres of water pooled in the bottom, but it seemed to be a slow leak.

I used my whole body weight to push it free and set it adrift. I waded out, towing the boat behind me, until I was at the corner of the church. I got behind it, gave it a hard shove, and sent it sailing out into the open.

The hull glowed in the moonlight. The boat slowed, turned, and bobbed gently, like a ghostly apparition.

A boat—a *boat*—in the desert.

I felt Vivienne's magic all around me. All the pieces of my life, aligned, all the roads that led me there, signposted. The stars were my witness, and the trees, the moon, the drowning town. *Throw stones, make waves,* she always said. *Rage, rage against the dying of the light*, she would sing, out of tune. Her beads would rattle and her bells would jangle and she'd look a little crazy and wild. But now I knew, although her words may have belonged to others first that didn't make them untrue, just as her stories didn't make me less than who I am. I am me because of them, *because* I believed.

I watched the boat for a while. It was surreal, the stillness of it, when all around, the trees swayed and the water rippled.

I thought of the statue in the park, the newspaper clippings stuck to the walls of the squat, the night we torched Vivienne's car. Grandfather's lamp. How we remember, how we keep living.

I wanted to live, to take the open road before me.

I thought of Wish. Whatever we'd had together, however brief and wrong, it had made me believe that it was possible to connect with another human being.

And I thought of Silence. New memories were no less precious than old ones, and I vowed that I would tell his story one day. It was unfinished, even though he was gone. Vivienne wasn't the only person I'd ever love.

Someone was awake. I heard a gasp, then low voices. Silhouettes, standing on the roof. Arden pointed at the boat and said something in a quavering voice.

I worked my way back from the church and climbed up

the ladder onto the top of the tank. I stretched out flat and raised the rock in my fist.

Sorry, Silence. I'm so sorry.

I bashed the roof of the tank with the rock. Pieces of it broke away and ricocheted into my face, but the sound rang clear and true.

Clang, clang, clang.

Clang, clang, clang.

Like a ship's bell.

On cue, torchlight swung in my direction. A babble of hysteria rose.

I kept hitting the tank.

Clang, clang, clang.

The sound was mournful in the night and my chest was tight with emotion. I realised the rock had split in two and I was crying. I threw the pieces of rock into the water and waited.

The torch flicked off.

As I'd suspected, Arden sent Malik.

His hulking body moved towards the tank. A dark shadow with a bullet-shaped head. Twice he stumbled and fell, landing face-first in the water. I watched him go under, surface, then continue in his silent, relentless way.

Come on, come on. That's it.

As if sudden instinct kicked in, he veered the long way around the tank.

Shit! I didn't know if I'd said it aloud, or just thought it, but Malik looked up. Our eyes met. His shock passed quickly and his eyelids flickered in a slow, crocodile blink before he disappeared from sight. The ladder creaked and a torch came on again. The beam played over the top of the tank and hit me full in the face.

I wriggled to the opposite side, levered myself over the edge and dangled from my fingertips. I couldn't find the platform with my feet. I was just hanging there, above a stack of wood jutting out of the water, deadly as a reef.

I heard Malik walking over the top of the tank towards me and, when I looked up, my knucklebones were bloodless and gleaming like they had no skin.

Malik reached down, gripped my forearm and tried to haul me up.

It would have seemed the act of a saviour, but my skin crawled. I would rather have fallen. I grabbed his arm with my free hand, yanked myself up towards him, and bit down on the base of his thumb.

Malik yelped and let go.

I planted my feet against the side of the tank, pushed off, and back-dived over the stack of wood.

The water hit hard. I went under, felt my nose burn, the soft ground against my back. It was enough to break my fall but the impact stole my breath. I came up with a whooping gasp, arms flailing. I stood, dripping.

After the blackness underwater, the moon was unbearably bright. Malik was frozen in a diver's stance, poised on the edge of the tank. At Arden's shout, he jumped.

His body took my legs out from under me. His arm was a garrotte around my throat, dragging me back under.

This time, my lungs were full to bursting.

I struggled weakly. After about thirty seconds, I let some air go, made my body go limp. Concentrated on counting to the steady *whump* of my own heartbeat. *Thirty-five, thirty-six, thirty-seven.*

Malik's arm still pressed down, his other hand on top of my head. I imagined his hand was Vivienne's, that she was singing a whimsical song. It was just a drill. At any time I could tap her hand and she would let me up, but I wanted her to be proud. *One-forty-six, one-forty-seven* . . .

I was twelve years old, in the deep end of the public pool in Warrnambool and all around me there were other children, splashing, playing, diving. I was quiet and still, sitting cross-legged on the bottom. *One-sixty-six* . . . I had gills and a pattern of blue-green scales where there should have been skin . . . *One-seventy-two* . . . the pressure on my head was gone and I floated up, up, but I wasn't ready, I could have stayed longer. When I broke the surface, a man had hold of Vivienne's arm and he was shouting at her about *drowning* and *child abuse* and she was yelling back at him, *you don't understand, she needs to do this*, and he was shaking his head and calling her crazy . . . *one-seventy-nine.*

I could have stayed down there forever. The water was getting warmer. Down there, Vivienne was so close. I opened my eyes. The murk shimmered and shifted until the water was dimpled and blue. There were symmetrical patterns of tiles all around me. Kids' flailing legs and plunging bodies that swooped down in a plume of bubbles. *One-eighty-six.* Vivienne was so close I could see her. Her hair curled like octopus tentacles and her skirts were the billowing body of a jellyfish. She was mouthing words I couldn't hear. No bubbles escaped her lips.

One-ninety-four. Best time ever. Are you proud of me, Vivienne? I can't hear you! Please . . .

She drifted away.

I caught the corner of her skirt and reeled her in.

She kicked out and I screamed, *Stop! Stop running away from me!*

The water rushed in.

Vivienne looked at me sadly and shook her head. She gave me a little push then drifted close.

I grabbed her hand and pulled her.

My lungs collapsed. The corners of my mind started to fade out.

Vivienne's lips touched mine and I heard her voice. It was garbled and strange, full of dirt.

Drowning is easy. Breathing is hard.

I coughed and let go.

I was floating, somewhere in-between. I had breath, but I was numb. My body butted up against something unyielding. The base of the tank. A trickle of muddy water leaked from the side of my mouth.

I sat up.

The water was so cold. How could I ever have thought it was warm? How long was I under? Everything was too clear and too painful not to be real.

Teeth chattering, I looked around. Nobody. Malik had gone.

I waded unsteadily out into the open. Overhead, the moon was past its highest point and starting to fall.

'God, don't you ever die?'

At first, I didn't see her.

She was so still, lying in the water underneath the tank, hidden by the stack of wood. Her profile was half in shadow, half illuminated, her chin tilted at an awkward angle. Her black box was held in the crook of her arm like a baby.

I waited for fear, but it didn't come.

Arden tried to turn her head. Her knife hung loosely from her other hand. She lifted her arm and I flinched.

'Come closer,' she said dully, waving the knife around.

'Where's Malik?' I looked over my shoulder.

'Gone after them.' She laughed. 'I'm at a slight disadvantage here.' The movement sent a wave of water into her open mouth and she sputtered. She raised her chin. 'I'm st . . . uck.'

She was caught up in my trap, snagged on the maze of barbed wire strung underneath.

I paddled closer and watched her, still wary. 'Did you think it was Silence? Did you come to save him this time?' I asked.

She looked confused.

'No. You came to see if I was dead,' I said flatly. 'Curiosity killed the rat.'

'Help me,' she said.

'I won't.'

'Malik will help me.'

I picked up the axe I'd hidden earlier and whacked it onto my open palm. 'No.'

She kicked one leg in anger and sent a spray of water into my face.

I stepped closer, darted forwards and yanked the box out of her grasp.

She swiped with her knife but her efforts were sluggish, like she was drunk. She was caught by her hair. The more she struggled, the more the barbs worked their way into the dreadlocks to pull her under. She tried to hack at her hair with the blade but the angle was too acute. Her nostrils were flared, her lips pressed tight to keep the water out.

'It's no use,' I told her. 'The water's still rising. Now, where's the key?'

'Come and get it,' she dared.

'Give it to me and I'll cut you free,' I lied. I raised the axe and rested it on my shoulder.

'I don't believe you.'

'That's probably wise. Doesn't matter anyway.' I tucked the box under my arm and waded off, swinging the axe.

'Wait!'

I stopped.

'It's in my back pocket.'

I shrugged and kept walking.

Arden screamed. She sobbed. She called for help until her voice cracked. In between, she gasped for breath.

Her fear was like a drug to me. I walked slowly; I wanted more.

Arden screamed for Malik. For her mother. Her sobs were desperate when she finally called for me. 'Please!'

I let her cry for an eternity before I turned around and went back.

When I was close, she called, 'Catch!' and threw something at me.

I lunged, but my hands were full. I watched the object land and dance on the rippled surface—but it wasn't the key. It was a small, blue canister.

Silence's inhaler.

I waded back, set the box safe up high on the corner of the tank base and embedded the axe into the wood. I reached down, prised the knife from her stiff fingers and placed it on top of the box.

Arden waited, as if she'd asked me a question. The tip of her nose was pink, peeling, and a tic pulled at the corner of her mouth.

I focused hard on that imperfection and the balance of power shifted irrevocably. We weren't so different, she and I.

I pushed her under. I put my hands around her throat, and I squeezed.

She had no chance to take a breath. Her hands clawed at my face, clutched at my hair, fluttered and fell. She ran out of fight quickly.

Two minutes. Two minutes was long enough for an ordinary person. I held her under, felt her struggles weaken and watched her last gasp leave her in a series of burst bubbles on the surface.

I didn't bother to count. I waited until the rage was fed, then let her go.

There was quiet. Stillness. The shape of her underneath. Sighing wind and the *plink-plink* of droplets leaving my chin, marking circles on her grave.

Oh, God.

The rage was gone but there was deadness in its place. Wherever she was now, she'd taken a piece of me with her. This was my drowning. This was how the water would take me.

I used her knife. I cut through the rope of her hair, hacking, sawing, until her body drifted free. I cupped the back of her head in my hand and gave her my breath. The water took the weight of her. With my knee in her back, I punched her chest.

It took so long.

Breathe.

'Breathe!'

When Arden came to, her lips were blue. The river inside her came up and out. She gagged and flailed as I pulled her clear of the barbed wire, then she clung to me. I prised her arms from my neck and wrapped them around the trunk of a tree.

'What happened?' she stammered.

She was shaking. In death, her eyes had changed colour— the irises were muddy, blurred around the edges. She sat up and rubbed her chest where I'd hit her, touched the raw patch where I'd scalped her skin.

'I saved you,' I said.

She blinked. 'Why would you do that?'

To save myself.

'How did it feel?' I asked. 'How did it feel when you screamed and begged and no one came?' I picked up the box and slogged through floodwater in the direction of the road.

Arden didn't try to stop me.

I didn't look back.

Just outside the edge of the town, I passed Malik, floundering and bellowing, making his way back to Arden. He was alone. He hadn't found the others.

I melted into shadow and waited.

Malik froze. A shudder ran through him, as if someone had walked over his grave.

I slipped past him, unseen, concealed by trees.

Chapter Thirty-three

I wish I could say that everything that happened after was a blur—but it wasn't. I remember every detail. The painful progress, rolling along doing forty for so many hours—it felt like we were passing through the same patch of landscape, over and over. The quiet. Nobody spoke for so long it was as if we were all mute. Like Silence. I watched Arden's necklace swing hypnotically from the rear-view mirror until I couldn't stand it any more. I ripped it away, wound down the window and tossed it out.

Joe drove, if you could call it that. He sat rigid in the driver's seat and looked at the speedometer more often than he watched the road ahead.

We slept and woke and slept again. I felt like I could sleep for a hundred years.

The first country police station we came to was unmanned. It was morning by then. I had decided only one of us would walk into that station, and that it would be me.

'Hey, Joe,' I said, as he went to pull away. 'You need to pump up those tyres.'

He nodded.

Carrie pushed AiAi aside and stuck her head through

the window. 'You'll find us when you get back to the city, won't you?'

'Sure,' I lied.

'Promise,' she said.

Darcy turned away.

'Hey, Joe,' I called out again, dragging out the leaving. I didn't want to be alone. 'What day is it?'

He took his foot off the accelerator. 'It's . . .' He stopped to think.

'Never mind,' I cut him off. 'I don't need to know.'

They drove away with Bree looking through the rear window, tears rolling down her face.

I very nearly ran after them.

In the hour before an officer arrived, I sat on the front steps with Arden's box on my lap. A dark stain formed on my jeans: the river water I'd brought with me, leaking from a corner of the box. I watched the stain spread slowly, like a pool of blood.

I tipped the box sideways and the leak became a gush. A trail of water trickled down the steps. I smelled that rank, muddy odour that would never really leave me.

The padlock was small and flimsy, the kind you'd find on a cheap diary, and when I twisted it the catch broke off in my hand. I rummaged through the contents. Near the bottom, I found what I was looking for.

Arden had taken Silence's pages—did they hold some proof of her guilt?

The paper was soaking wet, the pages fused together. My hands shook as I peeled them apart and laid them flat on the warm concrete.

The ink was blurred and illegible in places, some sentences only fragments, but the format was unmistakeable. It began with his full name and place of birth and ended with a quote about God only taking the best. In between, he'd listed a short lifetime of imaginary achievements.

My stomach twisted. Arden hadn't taken his pages because they were incriminating—she'd taken them as *insurance*. I let out a shriek of frustration.

A man setting up a butcher's sandwich board across the street looked up, alarmed.

I knew why Silence had written his own obituary—it was meant for his wall. But anyone who hadn't known him would have seen it as a suicide note. But *I* knew. He was forgotten, left waiting in a train station for his sister who never came, and he believed that remembrance was love.

I tore up the pages, ripped the paper into tiny pieces, rolled them into balls, and flicked them into the gutter. I closed the box and hid it behind a bush.

If I couldn't protect Silence, I would protect his memory.

I wish I could say that I told the absolute truth—but I didn't.

In my version, I named only Arden and Malik. I described them as accurately as I could, as they were, beautiful, bold and brave, before they became nothing. I told the officer they were alive, out there somewhere, and that Silence was dead. In my story, the others were ghosts. No, I didn't know their real names. No, I didn't think I would ever see them again. No, I didn't know where to find them.

I wish I could say that I bore the ordeal alone and that I did it with grace and dignity, but I cried. I cried during the hours-long interview until I was hoarse and the police officer gave me a break. He let me use the station's shower and I cleaned up my face as best I could. I hardly recognised myself. With my short hair and big eyes, my skin raw from sun and exposure, I looked old. The cut behind my ear was healing badly, set in a patch of bald skin.

I thought of Darcy. Her empty hand that pulled me up into the light. How I still didn't believe in magic. Not omens or premonitions or that a future could be foretold. But something inexplicable had happened out there.

I fell asleep on a couch. When I woke, Grandfather was there. I wasn't surprised, because I was the one who had called him.

He spoke using his hands and long, legal jargon and a booming voice. I saw flashbacks of Vivienne when he pushed his tongue between the gap in his teeth and thought hard about what he was going to say next.

I felt weightless, relieved that someone else was dealing with it all.

He signed forms, fielded questions, took notes. In comparison, the police officer seemed small behind his desk. He shrank further when Grandfather pointed out that much of the interview had taken place without an adult or guardian present.

'You can go,' the officer said, finally.

'I don't have to go back there?' I squeaked.

'A patrol will head out. Until we can ascertain whether there has been a crime, you're free to go.'

Grandfather fished around in his pocket for his keys. He put his heavy hand on my injured head, ran it down my cheek and cupped my chin. Then, as if he realised that touch could unravel us both, he let it drop to his side.

He held the door open for me.

Outside, I stood on the kerb, squinting in the sun. I had nothing. Even less than I had before.

I looked up the road and saw the familiar grid-style streets. The red dust I craved. Ancient trees that would have a heartbeat if I pressed my ear to them. I looked down the road and saw barefoot children and wandering dogs.

I took a step off the kerb, held a wet finger to the breeze, read all the signs. It was the same sleepy town I'd lived in or passed through a hundred times before. It was as good a place to start as any.

But I felt nothing. Not a beat of nostalgia or wishful thinking. Nothing.

I picked up Arden's box.

Grandfather watched me without expression as I climbed into the back seat of his ancient, dusty Mercedes.

I tucked the box under the passenger seat and helped myself to a mint from the console. Our eyes met in the rear-view mirror and I gave him a tired smile.

Grandfather cranked up the volume on his radio and I heard a familiar country song. He pulled away from the kerb, kicking up dust, and we left the town behind.

I stretched out on the back seat and closed my eyes . . . Troy Cassar-Daley. 'Everything's gonna be alright.'

I smiled again. You could find relevance in anything if you looked hard enough.

Grandfather passed his jacket over the seat for me to rest my head on, and drove.

He said nothing.

The stop-start motion of the car and the smell of exhaust told me we were nearing the city. I saw landmarks and buildings that didn't seem alien any more, just different from what I was used to.

'You're awake. Where do you want me to take you?'

I had assumed he would take me back to his house. I figured he'd lock the door and hide the key and spend the next ten years lecturing me about how irresponsible I'd been. I wasn't sure how to feel about the fact that he was letting me go again.

'The train station,' I said quietly. I added, 'Thank you.'

'You need to be available for questioning. I gave my word.'

'I'll be around.'

He sighed like he didn't believe me. 'Did you find him?'

'Who?'

'Your father.'

'What makes you think I was looking for him?'

'It's human nature. To want to know where you came from.'

'It doesn't matter that much to me any more.'

It didn't. If I couldn't find all the pieces of me within myself, I sure as hell wouldn't find them in a stranger.

My life would always be full of unanswered questions. I would always wonder if, had I taken another direction, Silence would have lived. I'd always regret my fascination with Arden and my desire to be like her. I would question my past, whether Vivienne was somebody I ever knew at all. Did the stories come first? Or did I? Did I survive because of everything that Vivienne taught me, or is there something at work that I'll never be able to explain? Growing up is made up of a million small moments in time, and one of the most painful is the moment you're severed from the whole, when you realise that your parent is complicated and fallible and human.

'You know, where you've been isn't as important as where you're headed.'

'Vivienne used to say that,' I said.

'Hmm.'

He parked the Mercedes illegally with the end sticking out into traffic. He opened the car door like a chauffeur.

'There are some things I need to do . . .' I said. I picked up the box and got out.

'Then you have to do them.' He sighed. 'I tried, you know. I cut Vivienne off without a cent. Then I tried to bring her back. You, I offered you money and I let you leave. It seems there was no right way to keep either of you.'

I wanted to say something—but I couldn't find the right words.

He opened his wallet and pulled out a handful of fifty-dollar notes. 'Don't argue. And here.' A mobile phone. 'I never did figure out how to work the bloody thing. Use it, if you need to.' He handed me the money and the phone, closed the rear door and stooped to climb in. He stopped and looked over his shoulder. 'You look just like her.'

He left me blinking on the footpath.

Chapter Thirty-four

It was atonement, I suppose. Or a pilgrimage, depending on how you look at it. I had this niggling need to put things right. Or as right as I could make them, given the circumstances.

One dead, two missing, six lost—and me. I was none of those things. It was up to me.

I sat on Silence's bench in the train station for a long time. I watched passengers come and go. A few looked curiously at Arden's box, like it was possibly a bomb, and to me it was. Tick-ticking away.

I checked the cameras overhead, my figure mirrored in their black, plastic bubbles. I counted them: one, two, three, four. Four different angles. The one nearest to me that must have captured the image in the paper, and the one I wanted— the one I'd hoped for—across the tracks on the side without pedestrian access.

I couldn't even remember the exact date I had left Grandfather's house; it seemed so long ago.

The security guard remembered.

'I shouldn't have you in here.' He frowned and showed me into his office. 'Come on, then. Just a minute or two.'

He played the recording for that day, that hour, that

blink-and-miss-it minute. He replayed it from all four angles, each time whistling a long, low note.

'I thought you were on drugs,' he said shaking his head. 'Nobody thought to rewind further back. We didn't check the far camera. The police and the papers only have the footage of you. Would you look at that?'

But I couldn't look. I turned away. It was enough for me to know that Silence wasn't invisible, that others would see him too.

I bought some new clothes—a T-shirt, underwear, jeans—all a size smaller than I usually wore. I used most of the rest of Grandfather's money to book a room in an inner-city hotel.

The bored girl at the desk didn't ask for ID. She didn't pay any attention to my hacked hair and puffy face. As I handed over the cash I saw that my fingernails were ingrained with red dirt and the palms of my hands were cut and peeling.

The girl gave me a key. She tucked the notes away in a cash drawer. The whole transaction was completed using about fifteen words.

My room was on the ninth floor. It was basic, not quite clean, but the shower was hot and the soap smelled nice. The cut above my ear stung and throbbed. I avoided washing it but the water still ran pink. In the glare of fluorescent light my legs were covered with purpling bruises, the skin stretched thinly over my bones.

I thought about loneliness. How it's not something you catch and mostly we choose it. How a trouble shared is a trouble halved but things like love and joy are multiplied when you have someone to share them with. I looked out of the window. On the street below there were hundreds of people—thousands, maybe—going about their business without touching, speaking, or acknowledging each other's existence.

I sat on the edge of the bed, wrapped in a towel, and picked up the bedside phone.

The girl answered.

I asked her what number I should call for directories and she replied in an bored, automatic tone. When I thanked her and told her to have a good day, the line went silent for a few seconds.

The girl sounded surprised. 'Sure. I hope you have everything you need.'

'Yes. Thank you.'

I called the number and got put through.

'Can I speak to Alison Dunne, please?'

I waited. The on-hold music was interrupted by a woman saying the call was being diverted. Please hold.

I held.

Then she answered.

I told her who I was.

Alison Dunne, intern, asked what she could do for me.

And I said, 'I want to tell you a story.'

Now, the box. Part of me wanted to throw it off a bridge and see it sink below the surface so that any reminder of Arden would be gone forever. I wanted it to fill up with water and mud and drift to the bottom. That would have been a fitting end. I'd been carrying the damned thing around for two days and it was heavy.

After I finished speaking with Alison Dunne, I closed the curtains and sank into the mattress and just lay there, staring at the neon numbers on the clock, thinking I'd never sleep.

I woke up swearing. Morning had come and gone. The blinds were closed and when I whipped them open the sun was high and blazing.

I dressed and took the stairs. I came out in the lobby and the girl behind the desk looked up with a smile. It faltered when she saw my face.

'Are you okay? Did something happen to you?'

'I'm fine. Thanks for asking,' I said. 'I'll be back later.' I felt stupid for saying that—it's not like I had a curfew.

'Yes, well, you've paid for the week. I figured you would,' she said. 'Are you on holiday? I could give you some brochures.' She grabbed a handful from the display behind her and shuffled them into order.

'Thanks, but I think I'll be here for a funeral.'

'You think . . . ? Oh.' She tucked the stack away and clasped her hands in front of her.

'Actually, it's more a celebration of a life.'

'That's a nice way of looking at it.'

'I'm Friday,' I said with my hand on the door.

'Rebecca. Bec,' she answered and pointed to her name badge. 'I'm here if you need anything.'

I thanked her again and stepped out into the sunshine.

It was that easy to get to know a stranger.

* * *

The patch of green in the middle of the city was yellowing. The sun had burned the crisp edges of the grass; walkways were littered with bottles and cans. The rearing statue was unchanged except for a few new tagged initials on its rump. I touched a hoof and thought about how we leave our mark on the world—that one man could inspire a monument in the middle of a city but others could only leave their initials behind.

'Bree,' I called when I got close.

She was sitting with her back to a tree, headphones in, her eyes closed.

'I'm back,' I said.

She opened her eyes. 'I didn't think you'd come.'

'Here I am.'

'Is it . . . over? Did they find . . . ?' She didn't finish.

'I'm still waiting to hear. Have you seen the others?'

She wound her headphones around a finger. 'Yeah, they're around. Joe's got his old job back at the markets. AiAi's with Carrie and Darce most of the time. They're looking after him.' She groaned and put her hands over her face. 'It seems wrong, doesn't it? To keep on living?'

That was how I'd felt the night I left Grandfather's house, after Vivienne died. But now I disagreed. 'Here,' I said and thrust Arden's box into her hands.

'What's in there?'

'Open it.'

Bree jiggled the catch. She ran her fingertip over the padlock's torn edge.

'I've gotta go,' I said and stood up. 'Things to do.'

'Like what?' She cocked one eyebrow. 'Stay.'

I shrugged. 'Get busy living.'

'Wait . . .' She opened the box. 'What's all this?' She let out a low whistle. 'That's a lot of money. How . . .'

'Think about it. She had to be putting a thousand bucks a week in that tin.'

Bree fished around inside and pulled out her mobile phone. She held up a fistful of wet notes. 'What am I going to do with all this?'

'Share it with the others. You'll find a use for it.'

'Here. Take some,' she said. 'You could start over.'

I shook my head. 'It belongs to you guys. Anyway, new beginnings aren't all they're cracked up to be.'

'Where will you go? Will you be okay by yourself?'

I nodded. 'Yeah.' I stuck my chest out. 'I am descended from kings,' I joked.

'Really?' she said.

'No. Not really.'

Bree closed the box. She shoved it towards me. 'When they bring him back . . . I mean . . . here. You know what to do with it.'

'You're sure?' I took the box.

'I'm sure,' she said.

'I'll come back soon,' I promised.

'I'll be gone for a while, but give me your number. I'll call you.'

'Where are you going?'

'Cooktown,' she said. 'To stay with my auntie. They live the old way.' She looked away, embarrassed. 'Everything was so big out there, Friday. You know?'

'I know,' I said.

*   *   *

The following day, I walked barefoot through familiar streets, a newspaper jammed under my arm. I cut through an underground car park and came up in a quiet lane where seedpods burst under my feet. I worked my way through winding streets and alleys to the rows of old terraced houses, strung along like a paper chain. And where the chain was broken by a patch of blackened earth, I stopped.

I ducked under the sagging tape fence and stepped around the debris. The section of interior wall was still intact, lying flat, but the newspaper clippings were bleached by sun and rain. In the backyard, where the pond used to be, there was a dry well and a snake-shaped skeleton, its bones picked clean.

I opened the newspaper and slid out the pages. I spread the sheets out over the old clippings and pinned down each corner with pieces of wood.

There was a montage of pictures of Silence and me. If you clipped them into squares and flipped them front to back, they would have played like a miniature movie scene.

The pram rolled away.

Silence ran to the edge of the platform.

He jumped onto the tracks.

I dashed after him, I peered over the edge.

The pram came back up as if plucked by the hand of God.

While we fussed over the baby, Silence's figure blurred like an apparition and disappeared between the stationary train and the far wall.

The headline said simply: THE BOY NOBODY SAW. The

last frame was in colour, zoomed in and blown up. You could see the blue of his eyes, his silver fringe that hung above them, his teeth that didn't quite fit. The caption underneath read: *Lucas Emerson (Silence), our tragic hero.*

In the photo, he was waving.

Two days after the newspaper story, four days before his funeral, Alison Dunne called to tell me that my friend had come home.

Silence's body went unclaimed by his family. His sister Amy never showed.

I thought of his spirit, trapped in that train station forever, and it nearly broke me. I wanted him to have his memorial, something solid and glorious to say he'd been here, but when I turned up at the crematorium carrying a box full of money that stank like riverweed, I was too late.

A city of strangers had already claimed him.

On my last night in the city, a still, clear night just before dark, I went to the cemetery. Crickets went quiet where I stepped and started up again when I'd passed. A layer of mist hovered above the ground. Trees huddled and whispered.

I found Silence's grave by heading towards the glow of scattered candles and the scent of citronella and hot wax. I'd missed the service—I didn't think I could stand to hear the detached, pre-packaged spiel I'd sat through for Vivienne—and waited until well after, when everybody would be gone.

But they weren't.

I sat alone, far away from the crowd on a grassy mound. Hidden by darkness, I watched.

Every funeral should be like his. Nobody was quiet or reverent—instead, the sound of laughter and tears mingled together. People kept coming in a steady stream to place flowers on Silence's grave. When it was covered, they put them on other graves. There were messages from children written in crayon, clippings from the newspaper, notes on pastel paper.

Silence's funeral and headstone were paid for by donations from people who never knew him but who wished they had. He wasn't forgotten. He would have loved that.

I saw Bree and her family sitting in a circle, I heard them singing a low, joyful song.

AiAi had new sneakers that glowed white in the dark.

Joe was playing He-Loves-Me-Not, sprinkling petals over Carrie's head.

Darcy wore a hoodie and most of her face was in shadow. Carrie whipped the hood away and tousled her head—shaven to the bone—and they started a slap-fight that ended in a hug.

And Wish. He was watching, like me. Standing apart. He was so like her he made my chest ache and I had to turn away.

I took the note I'd written for Silence and, instead of sticking it to his headstone with the others, I let the breeze carry it where it would.

The piece of paper flew. It soared—up, beyond the trees and into the clouds—and took with it the last few lines of Vivienne's poem, perfectly remembered:

There in the silence of the hills,
I shall find peace that soothes and stills
the throbbing of the weary brain,
for I am going home again.
I love you.
Friday.

Chapter Thirty-five

Grandfather's cat was waiting by the front gates. It stalked me along the driveway, tail twitching, moving between a regal saunter and a mad dash to catch up. Every few steps it stopped to shake dew from its paws. I reached the end of the driveway and the cat disappeared through a gap in a hedge.

There was something different about the house, or maybe I just missed it before. It wasn't the imposing mansion I remembered; it was sad and empty and old.

I crept around to the back of the house. The hexagonal verandah of Vivienne's fable popped and creaked. Beyond it, a rectangle of weed-choked grass the exact shape of a swimming pool.

The windows were dark, apart from the dining room and the dying room—Vivienne's lamp was on to guide me home. I dropped my bag onto the porch and raised a fist to knock on the back door—but something made me stop.

Music. Tinny and distant, like an old gramophone playing. I heard the chink of crystal, the sound of pieces smashing to the floor, scattering into corners.

I moved to the window, pressed my face against the glass and peered into the dining room.

Grandfather selected a whisky glass from the tray next to him. He rolled it in his palm. I remembered there being six; now there were two. He swigged from the glass in his other hand until it was empty, then wound back both arms. Both glasses hit the chandelier and exploded into pieces.

I gasped and took a step back.

He sat there, showered in fragments of glass and crystal. This was his grief now, uncivilised and raw. He looked up and saw me through the window. He stared as if what I did next would give him some measure of me.

I felt closer to him. I'd lived it. Grief leaves a space that has to be filled. I wanted him to know that I knew. An emotion too big to contain swelled in my chest.

I prised a hefty rock from the dry wall surrounding the garden bed. It was as smooth and chilled as an ice sculpture and I needed both hands to lift it. I paced back seven steps, raised the rock above my head, and heaved it at the glass between us.

It exploded. The noise was louder than I expected, less than I'd hoped. Startled pigeons fluttered out of a tree. Shards hovered, then plummeted like falling stalactites onto the sill.

When the tinkling stopped, the music played on, a woman with a whiny voice singing about regret.

Grandfather was still, his palms pressed flat against the table.

The curtains billowed like beckoning hands.

Grandfather's lips twitched. He laughed and smacked his hand down like a gavel. 'We've made a mess of things, haven't we?' he said.

I nodded.

He levered himself out of his chair and came around to open the door.

I followed him into the entrance hall. I waited exactly one minute before I asked the question.

'Tell me why she left.'

Grandfather picked up my bag, slung it onto the bottom step of the stairs and went into Vivienne's sitting room. He switched on a light, turned off the lamp and unplugged it.

'No need for this any more.' He sat on the edge of Vivienne's hospital bed. The side dipped under his weight. He touched the pillow lightly, like he was scared to erase her.

'Her bed's still here,' I said.

He sighed. 'Sometimes we keep the physical objects until memory is enough.' He covered his face with his big hands. 'I have some of her things to give you. She said I should wait until you were ready.'

'Things?' *Was I ready?*

'Things that belonged to her, that she left behind. The rest she said you must find for yourself.'

I glanced around the room. The white noise inside my head was finally quiet. I saw the signs, now that I was looking.

There was a low bookcase next to the bed, loaded with thick-spined, dust-coated classics I'd never read. I saw by the marks on the carpet that Grandfather had pulled it close, so that Vivienne could reach. I saw fingerprints in the dust, a book of stories by Henry Lawson. And I saw a patch of unlikely symmetry: a wide red spine nestled between six blue ones.

Owain Glyndwr, The Story of the Last Prince of Wales.

I slid out the book. There was an envelope pressed between its pages.

Grandfather stayed my hand before I opened it. 'I was hiding them for her as she wrote them. She said you would have questions and there was still so much she wanted to tell you. There are more, take your time.'

'Tell me why she left.'

'It's complicated . . .' he started.

'That's what she said.'

'I forced her to make a choice. Between you or me.'

'But I wasn't even . . .'

'She was pregnant.' He smoothed the creases on the envelope. 'The last thing she said before she left was she couldn't make a good choice, so she . . .'

'. . . made one she could live with,' I finished.

We were alike in ways that couldn't be accounted for by eye colour, features, or a gesture, a word. Some kinds of crazy you make for yourself, others you inherit.

I went up to my room. There were still traces of me, undisturbed: my long hair on the pillow, the pile of stuff I left beside the bed, the cracked bar of soap in the bathroom.

I unpacked my clothes and placed the rolls of money on the bedside table. I'd see them when I woke and they would remind me that there was more I had to do. Silence deserved a monument more lasting than memory—a statue of him on a bench in the train station maybe, or a bronze figure of a hooded boy leaning to kiss the fish—because memories change depending on who's doing the remembering. And you had to honour your dead.

The mobile phone rang. Wish sounded far away.

'You left,' he said. 'I saw you. We're still at the cemetery. There was a reporter here, asking for you. You should see all the stuff people left—pieces of paper, notes everywhere. Candles. A woman sang "Amazing Grace".'

I picked up Vivienne's pearls and let them pour through my fingers.

'Are you there?'

'How did you get this number?' I asked.

'Bree.'

I heard Grandfather's heavy tread on the stairs. His footsteps stopped at my door and then moved on. I swung my legs onto the bed and curled up there, fully clothed in the dark in a room that felt like clouds.

'They still haven't found her. Or Malik.' Wish said it too casually, like he was trying to spare me his pain.

Arden. Someday I hoped she'd find peace. Power, like love, is given. It isn't something you can take.

'I will kiss you again,' Wish said.

I pressed the phone hard against my ear until it started to burn.

'I need to know you're okay. Say something.'

Moonlight spilled into the room and the pearls were warming against my skin. I felt for Vivienne's T-shirt under my pillow. The fabric was soft and I could smell her now that the memory of her dying had faded.

One day, I thought, if I let time pass in one place, only the good things—the things I wanted to remember—would be left. There would be this day, then the next, then the one after that. I could do one day at a time. And if home wasn't a place, maybe it was a connection. Something woven from loose ends and mismatched threads that took time to knit together, like fractured bone.

Maybe family were the people who came looking for you when you were lost.

'I don't need saving,' I said.

He laughed. It was short, humourless. 'I know.'

The lump in my throat eased. It shifted, it shrank.

'You will kiss me again,' I promised.

Just before morning I woke shaking, haunted by the ghost of a dream.

It wasn't a bad dream. I knew the script. The faceless mannequins had mouths and they were smiling. I grasped the empty hand and felt bulldust puff between my toes. I took the knife, cut through the vines and, at the far end of the corridor, the door swung open.

There was nothing on the other side, but I wasn't scared.

I sat on the window seat with my chin in my hands, stared out at the rectangle of lawn, and waited for first light.

The sun was a pink stain on the horizon when I slipped downstairs. My furry escort met me at the back door and led the way along a path to a garden shed. Inside, I found a shovel leaning up against a wall.

It takes time to believe again.

I broke ground where the middle of the pool would have been.

About half a metre down, beneath black earth, the shovel grated and stopped.

Acknowledgments

My thanks to the team at Text who make everything seamless; to my editor, Penny Hueston, for her faith, energy and for seeing the things I didn't; to Steph Stepan for being fabulous.

Thanks to my agent, Sheila Drummond, for being in my corner.

To my literary ladies, Allayne Webster and Rebecca Burton, thank you for reading the bare bones of this book and for saying all the right things. I'll porch-sit and prattle with you guys any time.

Thanks to my fellow authors—anyone who ever smiled at me in a crowd, took me under their wing and made me feel a little less lost.

And last but never least, thanks to My People. You know who you are.

Vikki Wakefield

Vikki Wakefield is an award-winning Australian author of contemporary YA fiction. After high school, Vikki worked in banking, journalism, communications and graphic design and, after an extended writing drought of fifteen years, she enrolled in a professional writing course. During her study she rediscovered young adult books and found her voice.

Vikki's writing has been described as 'original, real, startling and beautiful' and she also writes short stories, articles and film scripts. In her spare time she tries to paint, draw and play basketball. She was born in Adelaide and still lives and writes there. *Friday Brown* is Vikki's debut UK novel.

Find out more about Vikki Wakefield:

Twitter: @VikkiWakefield
www.vikkiwakefield.com
www.facebook.com/VikkiWakefieldAuthor